THE**DEVIL**THEY **MADE**ME

SHEA**SWAIN**

ISBN: 978-1-7357267-1-7
Cover: Mario Patterson Covers
Editor: Pam Howard
Format: SSW Publications

Other Books Written By:

Shea Swain
The Pulse of Provocative Romance

What Lilly Wants
previously known as Lascivious
An Erotic Novella

INVIDIOUS Betrayal
A Full-Length Paranormal-Sci Romance

ABSOLVE
A Short Romantic New Adult Drama

The Changing of the Seasons
Winter's Icy Heart
A Taste of Spring
Contemporary Romance

Chained to the Devil's Son
A Full-Length Dark Romance

The Binding of the Halo Series
Four Full-Length Paranormal Romance Series
The Binding of the Halo Book I
The Awakening of the Halo Book II
The Descent of the Halo III
The Battle for the Halo IIII
&
The Coesen-Origins

Heaven on Hell Universe
A Contemporary Romance with Sci-fi undertones
Heaven on Hell Island I
Proposal from Hell II

Dark Bright: Claiming his Angel
A Paranormal Sci-Fi Romance

Love and Infection
A Paranormal Romance

IF YOU LIKE A BOOK CONSIDER LEAVING A REVIEW
THANK YOU

THE DEVIL THEY MADE ME

PLAYLIST on Spotify

Track 1: White Lines by Grand Master Flash and The Furious Five

Track 2: Cream by Wu Tang Clan

Track 3: All I Do Is Think of You by Troop

Track 4: The Love We Had Stays on My Mind by Dru Hill

Track 5: Hit 'Em Up Style by Blu Cantrell

Track 6: It Takes Two by Rob Bas and DJ Easy Rock

Track 7: Tell Me by Groove Theory

Track 8: Before I let you Go by Backstreet

Track 9: You Got me by The Roots

Track 10: I'm Still Waiting by Jodeci

Track 11: Hurt You by The Weekend

Track 12: Planet Rock by Afrika Bambaadaa

Track 13: 90's melody by The String Queens

No matter how much dirt you throw over the past, some things won't stay buried.

DEMIGOD

ONE

PRELUDEOFAGOD

Then**1983**

DEMI

When he heard voices downstairs, Demetrius kicked his sheet away. He rolled over then slowly pushed off the bed and stared at the flickering black and white static image that came on the television after the station shut down for the night. The cassette tape his homeboy J-boy made was playing on low. Afrika Bambaataa's *Planet Rock* just ended then dead air before *White Lines* by Grandmaster Flash and the Furious Five started up five seconds into the song.

Shaking his head at his friend's shit effort at making a mixtape, Demi swung his legs off the bed and rubbed his head as he glanced at the big black flip clock on his dresser. It read just after three in the morning, but that couldn't be right. His mom had to work in few hours and she never stayed up late or woke this early.

Except, the voices rising from downstairs told him that she was up.

Demi placed his bare feet on the wood floor but quickly raised them and hissed. *That's damn cold.* Fully awake now, he used his toes to lift his socks from the floor and pulled them on one by one. He pulled on his sweatpants, the shirt that he took off and tossed across the bottom of his bed last night, before walking over to the window and pushing the curtain aside.

Remnants from the snowfall a few weeks ago was still piled up at the bases of the street lights. The glow from one of the lights bounced off a shiny black Maxima, grabbing his attention. Demi narrowed his eyes. He saw the same car pulling off from in front of his house last week. He couldn't make out who was driving it and when he asked his mother, who was standing in the doorway watching it ride away, she wouldn't tell him.

Demi looked over his shoulder. The voices from downstairs were growing louder. He let the curtain slide free of his fingers as he stepped away from the window and moved toward his bedroom door. The floorboards creaked with every step he took.

When Demi turned the knob and pulled his bedroom door open, he took a step back. Narrowing his eyes, he asked, "Who the fuck is you?"

The man standing on the other side of his doorway raised a brow. "Grab your shit, you going to live with your father." The man rushed past him to his closet and started filling one of Demi's duffle bags with clothes.

Demi took another step back but kept hold of the doorknob as he followed the stranger with his eyes. "I don't have a father," he said. He turned-up his lip to show his clear disgust for the word father. "Get the hell out of my house."

He'd seen the man who his mother said was his father maybe twice. He was told by his momma that his father wasn't worth the soul the lord gave him, but she had fallen for him anyway. That was all he heard about the guy. His mother didn't speak of any of her family, and Demi never met his father's family, so there was no one to talk about his donor either.

10

The man inside his bedroom stepped closer, grabbed Demi's upper arm as he was turning and stepping out of the room, and pulled him back. Demi stumbled back and twisted, falling to his knees. He growled in anger as he crawled over to his bed and grabbed the revolver he kept under the mattress. He swung his body around so that he was sitting on his butt with his back against the side of his bed and the gun aimed at the man's chest. Several nickel bags of weed hit the floor, but Demi kept his eyes on his target as he listened to his mother arguing with someone downstairs. The voices were much clearer with the door open.

"Lil nigga…" the man started to say but stopped when a gun shot rang out. He grabbed the duffle bag and ran out of the room.

Demi's entire body shook as he jumped to his feet and ran out of his room. He was right behind the man, both pounding down the stairs. Jumping over the last few steps, Demi turned the corner and tried to push past the man to see into the kitchen.

Blood…

"Ma!" he yelled. The gun Demi still held fell from his limp hand to the floor with a thud. "Ma," he called out again as he tried pushing past the man. All he saw was his mother's hand and a lot of blood leaking around it. "Mama!" he screamed as the man took hold of him. Demi fought to get free, to see around the men who stood in the way.

"Bring him," the man who stood over his mother said.

Demi fought harder as he kept screaming for his mother.

"Grab his gun," the man who'd busted into his room said as he lifted Demi over his shoulder and rushed to the front door.

"Mama," Demi moaned.

What just happened? It wasn't real. It can't be real, he told himself as the frigid night air stung his entire body.

"Damn," someone said from behind them as Demi was tossed into the backseat of the Maxima. "You couldn't get him some fucking shoes and a coat marfucker? I should shoot yo ass too."

"Man," the man beside Demi said, "you kinda made packing hard to do."

Demi sat with his mouth open and tears running down his face as he peered at the man who slid into the driver's seat and was looking over his shoulder at him. Demi frowned as he stared into a familiar face. His face, only older looking.

"I'm gonna kill you," Demi swore, as he stared back at the man.

"Get in line," the man next to him said with a chuckle.

Demi's father stared at him for a few seconds then reached over the front seat and punched him in the face. Demi's head was rocked back from the force and his lip felt like it exploded; he soon felt the blood running down his chin, but he just grunted as he balled his fists up and prepared to attack.

"You just lost your mother, so I'm gonna let that shit that just came out of your mouth slide." The man turned and started the car. "I'm your father and you will respect me, or I will beat that shit into you."

"Carlos, stop fucking around. You acting like nobody heard that loud shit," the man beside Demi said as he looked around and beat at the driver's seat.

"Shut the fuck up, Ciro," was all his father said as he sped off.

Demi licked his bleeding lip, sealing his oath with his blood.

Now**2001**

DEMI

Standing in front of the tinted floor to ceiling wall of windows, Demi peered out over the landscape from the Keystone's penthouse but saw none of the amazing scenery that convinced Krysta to choose the building. Instead, he focused on the reflections in the dark glass. Three of the most important people in his inner circle sat in his living room.

Two were focused on the television. It seemed that just about every news station reporting the evening news was focused on the explosion that rocked the area this morning, killing Sasha Fuchs.

"Everything's been handled, Demetrius," Arthur said as he lowered the cellphone from his ear. "I'll outline the details for you tomorrow."

Demi turned around and acknowledged Arthur with a nod. He knew his friend would take care of the everything including contacting Sasha's next of kin and offering Demi's assistance with funeral arrangements. That was what Cohen's Law firm did, they took care of the details.

"I have to head out but if there's anything else I can do…" Arthur said, standing. He walked around the chair he vacated and approached Demi. As he got closer, Arthur extended both arms as if moving in to hug Demi. Then, he seemed to think better of it and extended a hand for shaking. "I'm really sorry about Sasha."

Demi shook Arthur's hand, allowing the connection a moment longer than usual. Even when they were teens, Arthur Cohen was always too touchy feely. Today had gone to shit for all of them so the least Demi could offer his old friend was a brief connection.

"Sasha was your friend too, Brains," Demi said.

Arthur gave Demi a sad partial grin at the mention of his old nickname. It was a name Demi hadn't used since they graduated high school.

He and Arthur met Sasha together years ago. She worked at the courthouse in the licensing department. During their meeting, Demi admired how detailed and knowledgeable she was, so he offered her a job. She didn't accept right away but Arthur seemed to have convinced the beauty during a follow up meeting. Demi had a feeling Arthur never did completely get over his crush on her, even after he married.

"I'll check on you tomorrow," Arthur assured him.

Carver got up from the sofa and walked with Arthur to the door. He returned a few minutes later to the same spot on the sofa. Demi silently regarded Carver. He and Arthur must have had a few words for each other. Those two talking was odd, but this was an odd day.

Demi glanced at Krysta. She was apparently too wrapped up in the news to notice, or didn't care how close Carver sat beside her. Demi strolled over to the bar, made him and Carver a drink, then stepped down the three stairs from his library and bar to join his friends in the living room. He handed Carver the drink before sitting in an adjacent chair.

"Thoughts?" Demi asked, after taking a swig.

Krysta looked over at him, raising her head from her knees she had pulled up to her chest. Her eyes were wet with unshed tears, her beautiful face strained with emotion.

"Could be a power grab," Carver answered, though Krysta usually took point when discussing business.

"New faction?" Demi asked. "Or an old one?"

Carver grimaced. "It will take time to shake loose a lead on the streets. Are you going to call a meeting with your—"

"No," Demi interrupted. "I'll contact them separately."

"Your partners may know—"

"Not yet." Demi said, cutting Carver off again. He had a bad feeling. It was like an itch at the base of his neck, under the skin. A new faction or even an old faction who heard of his street days might want to prove themselves or have a score to settle was a possibility, but the more he thought about it the less Demi felt that it was feasible. One of his business partners being involved didn't quite fit either, but until Demi obtained more information, he wanted to protect those he cared about.

"Krysta, I want you with me tonight."

She nodded.

Demi finished his drink then stood. He had to place some fresh linens in the spare room for Krysta. "Carver," he placed his glass on the table in front of him, "get some rest."

"I'm going to stick around too," Carver said. His friend relaxed back on the sofa.

Demi nodded, knowing Carver would want to stay beside him until the current threat was resolved. The thing was, they were no longer teens, and Demi didn't want another friend caught in the crossfire.

Climbing his staircase, Demi tried to clear his mind, but by the time he made it to his bedroom, he realized it was useless. Who knew who the hell wanted him dead? Demi sat down on the side of his bed and opened his nightstand drawer. There were only two things inside.

He reached over the small rainbow notepad and lifted the cell phone out. The notification icons at the top of the screen told him he had several messages and double that in missed calls. No doubt they were from his associates, ones he rarely saw or dealt with unless there was a reason. Demi ignored the waiting messages and dialed a number he rarely called.

"What do you need me to do?" the person on the other end asked.

There was no greeting. Just business from the Mayor.

"I want you to conduct business as usual, Brand," Demi said. "There's no need for you to get involved."

"Let me know if you need anything," Brand said.

Demi disconnected the call. He fell back on his bed and exhaled. If he had been driving his car this morning like he usually was, he'd be dead. A series of random events led to the horrific outcome.

Sasha contacted him the night before about a proposal. She drove over and because they worked through the night to fine-tune the proposal, she spent the night. When she went to Demi's garage to retrieve her car the next morning, she discovered her rear left tire was low, almost flat. It seemed she was periodically filling the tire with air instead of getting the tire plugged or replaced. Since she stayed at Demi's, she didn't put air in the tire the previous night. Once she told him, Demi planned to drive her to the office, but he was sidetracked so he let her use his car.

Damn.

Demi pulled the envelope he folded and placed in his pocket earlier today and took out the letter. *If it wasn't for this letter, I would've died in that bomb blast today with Sasha.* He held it above his face and read it again.

Demetrius Carrion,

I must speak with you. Can you meet me at the library on Franklin and 43rd at noon?

An old friend

The sealed envelope was delivered not by mail but by hand to his building the day before, but Demi didn't check his mail until this morning. At the time, he thought it odd that there was no postage, so he called Sasha and told her to take one of his cars and go to the office instead of waiting for him to take her.

Demi wanted to talk to the doorman who was on duty when the letter was delivered. By the time he was able to reach the doorman at home, the bomb under the driver's seat in his car was triggered and exploded just a few blocks from his home.

Security footage of his building's garage showed nothing out of the ordinary. As for the letter, all Demi got from the doorman was that a woman he'd never seen before left the envelope at the front desk.

Who was the woman?

Demi sat back up and reached into the opened nightstand drawer and took out a rainbow embellished notepad. He opened the pad and flipped it to a random page. All the pages had basically the same content. Demi compared the writing on one of the pages with the writing on the letter.

To him, the writing was similar but maybe that was because he wanted it to be. Demi closed the pad and put it back inside the drawer, then he folded the letter back up, slipped it into the envelope, and slid it under his pillow.

If the letter was from her…

Demi needed to find her.

She inadvertently saved my life.

My life, he thought again as he rolled over and focused on the clock on his side table. He watched the second-hand tick around the face. *Tick…tick…tick…tick.*

"My life," Demi said out loud then laughed dryly. His life and the lives of everyone around him were cursed. Just like…

"Demetrius, you are the love of my life, son. You know that, right?"

"…and I cost my mother hers," Demi said. He groaned as the memory of her scent hit him in the gut.

Then**1983**

DEMI

Demi inhaled deeply, enjoying the fragrant scent of cocoa butter coming from his mother. It wasn't the runny thin lotion containing a smidgen of cocoa butter that some people used, but was instead the all-natural pure cocoa butter tube that she kept in the refrigerator on the top shelf of the door. He turned his head and looked at his mother, Maddie Gaines, as she sat down beside him on their well-used but comfortable sofa.

He sniffed the air around him again, inhaling more of his favorite smell. His mother was lifting a cheesesteak sub to her mouth, but she paused and looked over at him.

"I don't mind if you use it, ya know," she said with a knowing grin.

"Use what?" Demi asked as he rolled his eyes. He reached forward and grabbed a few fries. Demi smashed them in the ketchup he squirted on the sub paper wrapper he was using as a plate, then stuffed them into his mouth.

"My stick of cocoa butter. I know you like it." His mother shrugged then bit into her sub.

"I don't like it," Demi said, looking at her.

His mother didn't respond until after she chewed the food in her mouth and swallowed. She licked one of her fingers then said, "Nothing wrong with admitting you like it. I like just about everything about you."

Demi's mouth fell open. His mother yelled at him so much he thought she would go hoarse. Hell, she yelled at him way more than Tony's and Robert's mothers did with them. Demi was always in trouble. He was forever doing something his moms didn't like.

"Not everything," he said low and under his breath as he looked away and down.

"I like…" she began. "No," she said as she reached down and touched his leg, "I love everything about you Demi. You are a good boy, and if you want you can be a good man. I don't like some of the things you *do*, but I absolutely love you and I know your potential."

Demi looked back at his mom, feeling as if he *was* a good boy even if it wasn't true. He wanted to be good. For her, he might try to be better.

"One day you are going to hate my cocoa butter smell," she said, placing her sub down. "Better get all you can now." She jumped on him, tickling his sides with her greasy hands.

Demi fought to push his mother's hands away as he laughed. He knew he would love the smell of cocoa butter forever.

"Stop! You want me to throw up," he threatened.

Maddie laughed. "Fine," she said, letting him pull away and right himself. "Eat."

Demi fixed his t-shirt then scooted to the edge of the sofa and pulled the bag he flattened and was using as a plate for his sub and fries closer. He glanced at the television as he picked up a fry and tossed it into his mouth. *Fame* was on. Demi hated the sappy ass show but his mom loved it, so he endured.

He should have endured more…for her.

TW

Now/**one week after car bombing**

DEMI

Demi pushed the chair back and stood. He straightened his tie, pulled down his cuffs, then walked around the conference table toward the door. A few eyes followed him but Marlin, the project leader, continued to address the attendees, feeding them figures and images to support the changes that were soon to be in effect.

Demi didn't need to be in the meeting, but since he lost Sasha so brutally and suddenly, he forced himself to attend in an effort to keep his mind occupied. It didn't take long for Demi to realize that his efforts were pointless. Every word spoken around the conference table ran into the next. Her loss was too great to mute.

Demi made it out of the conference room without anyone stopping him. A week had passed since the explosion, and no one at the office seemed to be taking the loss any better than he was. Their expressions…well, their expressions spoke of grief and loss. And when they looked at him…

His employees had questions that he couldn't answer.

He needed to get some air. But Demi didn't make it to the elevator before he heard his name called out. He glanced to his left to see his secretary jogging toward him.

"Mr. Carrion," Rachal said as she caught up to him. "I don't mean to bother you but," she continued in a tone that was considerably lower than before, "detective Monahan phoned again. I told him you were in a meeting and would return his call at your earliest convenience." The look on Rachal's face was one of sympathy and apprehension as she patiently waited for his response.

Demi stood in the middle of the hall. He flipped the hem of his jacket up with his hand then placed his hands on his hips as he looked down at the tips of his shoes and the floor. He felt his temple thrum with every beat of his heart, and he had to squeeze his eyes closed to block out the light coming through the windows to his right that irritated his eyes.

"Rachal, I'll handle Det. Monahan from now on."

The sound of Krysta's voice was like a lifeline; Demi exhaled in relief. When he opened his eyes, he saw Krysta leading Rachal away from him.

"Are you sure?" Rachal asked, sounding unsure. "He specifically asked for Mr. Carrion."

"I'm sure," Krysta said confidently as they turned down the hall where Rachal's desk and Demi's office were located.

Demi avoided looking at anyone else as he made his way to the elevator. He didn't know the look on his face, but he suspected it must have been lethal. It wasn't until he was stepping out into the lobby of Celestial Towers, that he realized that on each floor the elevator stopped, those who seemed to be waiting to get in waved him on. Usually it mattered to Demi how he was perceived. Today, he didn't give two shits.

Celestial Towers was grand, and each time Demi stepped foot inside the building he marveled at its design and beauty. Building the two-building 300,000 square foot office complex, with an underground mini-mall connecting the two towers, and a ground level courtyard between them, was one of Demi's greatest accomplishments to date. The hoops he had to jump through, the connections he had to cultivate, the debts he called in, and the pockets he had lined... Yet, whenever he looked at this magnificent building, he felt all his efforts were worth it.

For the most part, the lobbies in each building were identical, but Demi had a water wall feature placed in building one where his office was located. Running water was always a sound that soothed him. Whenever he felt like blowing shit up, he sat down on one of the benches in front of the wall.

Demi nodded to the people who greeted him, but his eyes stayed glued to the ocean blue wall. The water flowing down was barely visible, but the calming sound of the steady stream of water hitting the pool below was audible and appreciated.

Sitting on the bench alone, Demi did something he rarely did in public. He closed his eyes and leaned forward, placing his elbows on his knees. He breathed in slowly and exhaled with the purpose of relaxing.

"You good?"

Demi recognized the voice. He nodded in affirmation, but was he? The security footage from the parking garage in his building showed nothing unusual. Many people came and went from the garage. Problem was, there was no clear footage of his vehicle, because Demi often parked out of view of cameras.

Demi sat upright then opened his eyes. He reached for his tie and loosened what felt like a noose from around his neck. "I'm alive," he said as he looked up at Carver, who stood in front of him.

Carver nodded at Demi then turned his head to his right.

Demi followed Carver's gaze. He focused on the two smiling women who seemed to be appraising his friend then him. Demi chuckled to himself. Even with him and Carver being dressed to the nines, looking like typical wealthy businessmen, women should be leery. Women should sense the darkness emanating from them. But he knew it was mostly likely the darkness that attracted the women.

"Let's walk," Carver said, barely giving the attractive pair more than a glance.

Demi interpreted that to mean Carver wanted to talk.

Neither man spoke as they walked toward the courtyard. When they stepped outside, they began to walk slowly, following the paved stone path that circled the courtyard.

"Why didn't you tell me about the letter?"

Demi kept his gaze forward even though he felt Carver's eyes on him. "You don't work for me anymore. We are partners but—"

"We are brothers," Carver interrupted, accentuating the word brothers.

"...and *brothers*," Demi conceded, "but I want you to leave this alone."

"We look after one another. You ride, I ride. That is the way it's been since high school. It's the way it will always be," Carver said, moving his hand to tap Demi on the chest. "This new you... I don't understand this person you're becoming. Secretive, distant. What's your deal, God?"

Sighing, Demi looked down then over at his friend as they continued to walk. "We *are* brothers," Demi said, "and that's why you have to stay clear of whatever this is. I just have a lot on my mind."

"We stick together—"

"We do," Demi said patiently, yet still cutting Carver off. "But I want you safe. You are about to step up to another level, Jackson. We've managed to stay out of prison and basically clean, working under the radar. It's one of the few things I can thank my father for. UGod's plan to come up in the corporate world by using me at the forefront gave me something to focus on and a way out from under him. I've worked hard to get what I needed, making certain the shit I did became just whispers and hearsay, just so I could succeed and make my life what it is now. I'm not about to risk it all by reverting back to who I was. And I damn sure won't risk your climb or your life. If keeping the rest of my family and what I've built safe means playing the game…"

Demi realized Carver was no longer by his side. Looking back, he noticed that Carver slowed then stopped, so he stopped a few paces ahead.

"You really trying to go at this blatant act of war like this?" Carver asked as he shook his head.

Demi didn't respond as he stared back at Carver.

Carver chuckled. The laugh was dry and lacked humor. He tapped his finger against the side of his leg. It was a tell, one that told Demi Carver was concerned, annoyed or both. Right now, Demi didn't know which, but he continued to stare at his friend, trying to read deeper.

In response to the way Demi was regarding him, Carver shook his head again then said, "Whatever, God," he sucked his teeth. "You want the blue-mafia on this and not your man… Fine with me. And just so you know, when Sasha died," Carver said as he turned back and walked away, "I lost a member of my family too."

Demi watched Carver pass the door they exited and disappear around the corner, using the pathway between the two towers. He knew he made the right decision, keeping Carver and Krysta out of this, but he wondered if he should have been clearer.

In the past week, no one on his payroll was able to shake loose any information about the bombing, except the components used in the bomb were unremarkable and could be purchased just about anywhere.

Demi fared no better in his search for the person who wrote the letter. He watched the security footage from the day the letter was dropped off. Demi wasn't familiar with the old gray-haired woman who dropped the letter off with his doorman. He placed a man at the meeting place–a library–each day to scope out anyone who seemed to be looking for someone or even anyone shady. That was a bust too.

With no leads, Demi handed the letter off to his connections at the police department, hoping they could find something he didn't see. Maybe they could pull prints or otherwise connect it to someone.

Demi stared at a man walking toward him. He stiffened as the man passed, prepared for an attack, but the man nodded then continued toward the building. Demi rubbed his head as he started walking around the path.

Being suspicious like this wasn't his style. He was tired, angry…hurt. He felt as though everything he'd ever done was coming back to haunt him; like every shit decision he ever made was a hundred-pound weight holding him down in an ocean of murky water. He felt like life was smothering him.

Demi knew something was coming, and there was no way he could explain this feeling to Carver that would make sense. His goal was to keep Krysta, Carver, and Cohen safe. He'd done some fucked up shit under UGod and as a member of his crew, the Congregation, as well as on his own. That someone wanted payback was to be expected. But it was unlikely that he, Demetrius Carrion, left anyone alive who was or would now be in a position to get revenge.

In any case no one else needed to pay his dues—whatever Demetrius owed for his past actions—with their lives. Hell…he wasn't worth it and hadn't been since the year his life changed for the worse.

Then1983

DEMIGOD

Demi watched as the man who called himself UGod strolled inside the apartment building in front of him. The lobby of the building was built with no doors in the front or in the back and each landing on each floor was open and visible from Demi's vantage on the sidewalk. He watched the man climb up the first set of stairs to reach the second floor.

Demi's attention was pulled back to the lobby. The wind ruffled discarded coupon booklets on the floor under the mailboxes caught his attention.

"Welcome home, lil nigga."

Turning his head, Demi glared at Ciro, following with his eyes as the asshole passed him and proceeded along the sidewalk toward the building. Ciro and UGod, the man claiming to be his father, were apparently brothers. Neither one said that to Demi, but he gleaned that info from their conversation during the four-hour drive from his house. UGod was the younger of the two, but he also somehow seemed to be in charge.

"Punk ass," Demi said as he looked around. He shivered as the wind picked up and a strong breeze blew around him. It was dark out and cold. With no apparent options, Demi walked toward the building and over the chilled grass then paved sidewalk in only his socks. He thought back to the scene at his house, his mother lying on the floor bleeding, unable to help her or to even help himself. As sadness threatened to overwhelm him, he forced it down, allowing his anger and hate to surface.

"This ain't my home," Demi said as his long strides pulled him almost side by side with Ciro.

Demi felt a hand on the back of his shoulder right before he was shoved forward. He stumbled through the main entryway and into the building, stubbing his toe.

Fuck.

Demi braced himself on the steps that led to the second floor. He kept quiet the entire drive, thinking about what happened, his options to get away, while not letting the pain of his loss overwhelm him. He didn't know these fuckers; except he knew they were killers without a conscience; and now. he was on their turf. That meant he had to be in survival mode. That also meant he had to bite his tongue because what he wanted to say might get him shot.

The taste of his blood pooling in his mouth from biting his tongue grounded him as he silently counted to calm himself.

"If you say so," Ciro said, his lip curled in a smirk. "Get upstairs before your dumb ass get sick and he blames me." Ciro grabbed him by the arm and dragged him up the stairs.

Demi stumbled up two sets of stairs, with the asshole holding onto him until they were on the third floor at which point Ciro threw him forward, toward an open doorway. This time Demi managed to stay on his feet. He narrowed his eyes and tightened his jaw as he watched Ciro walk into the apartment. He didn't have a lot of options right now.

Reluctantly, Demi followed Ciro inside, but he had to jump aside when the asshole launched the door at him. The door slammed closed. Rolling his eyes, Demi moved his gaze around the apartment. He frowned.

The place was basically bare but messy. How it could be both, Demi didn't even understand. The living room contained one large puffy black leather sofa, a huge floor model television, a gaming system sprawled on the floor, and a small side table that sat in front of the sofa. Another small table with a boom box on it, four chairs, and a workout bench with weights stacked against the wall was in the area Demi assumed was a dining room. A few full black trash bags lined one of the walls. The kitchen was small based on what Demi could see from where he stood.

There was nothing homey about the place. There were no plants or pictures like Demi had at his house. No curtains covered the window blinds, and the window ledge in the living room was being used as a storage space for VHS tapes and cassettes. He didn't see a tablecloth or placemats on the glass table, or any cookie jars on the counter.

Demi started thinking about home and then his mom, but he blocked that shit before something else encroached on his senses. The smell...

Demi wrinkled his nose as he tried to figure out what the funky odor was.

It smelled like a dirty weed spot and unwashed ass like these assholes smoked nonstop. It definitely wasn't his home. Before he fell asleep in the car, Demi read the highway signs and paid attention to the exits they took, so he basically had an idea of how to get back home. He just needed to steal some money from these fools and hitch a ride.

"Where's his shit?" UGod asked as he walked into the room toward Demi.

"I'll bring it up later," Ciro said. He walked over to the sofa, bent and picked up what looked like the tv remote, then flopped down on the sofa.

"You hungry boy?" UGod strolled past Demi and headed for the kitchen.

If they thought he was eating in this motherfucker...

"Fuck you," Demi said. His plan for survival probably took an instant nosedive with the words that just escaped his mouth. He couldn't see UGod from where he stood but he knew the guy was no punk like his brother.

Ciro laughed as he glanced over at Demi. "You're gonna learn," he said, then he continued to laugh as he hit buttons on the game controller he now had in his hands.

Demi was still standing by the door when UGod walked back into sight. He carried two paper plates, each with a loaded sandwich and a pile of chips on them. Demi had to admit the food looked good and he was hungry, but he wasn't going to admit that to them.

He kept his eyes on UGod as he placed the plates on the table. When Demi saw UGod turn around and walk his way, he put up his fists. *Fuck this.* He ignored Ciro's laughter as he rushed UGod. Demi glanced up at UGod just as he wrapped his arms around the man's waist to take him down. By the smile he saw on UGod's face, Demi knew he'd made a mistake.

UGod braced himself by taking a step back then Demi felt the man hook his arm around his neck, keeping Demi pinned to his side. The first blow to his side rocked Demi up off his feet but he didn't fall because his head was secured to UGod's side. The several blows that followed were to his stomach. The pain was unlike any he'd felt before.

By the time UGod released his neck and he dropped to his hands and knees, Demi thought he was choking up a lung. Nausea hit hard as he cried and coughed. Through his watery eyes he could barely make out UGod's shoes backing away as Demi threw up all over the linoleum floor.

"Told you your ass was gonna learn," Ciro said in a nonchalant tone. He didn't even look away from the television.

Demi coughed a few more times before spitting out the remaining vomit in his mouth. He tried to stop crying, but his stomach hurt too much.

He wanted to go home. He wanted to kill them both, and he would do it right now if he could find a way. Why was this happening to him?

"Yo, clean that shit up. It stinks," Ciro said.

Demi refused to look at the asshole. He just sobbed as he sat back on his ass.

"Yo," Ciro said again, "tell lil nigga to clean that sour smelling shit up."

"Shut the fuck up 'fore you clean it up. And, go get his shit out of the car," UGod said. "Demi?"

Ciro mumbled something under his breath, but Demi heard him get up and start moving around.

Demi soon heard the front door open then close, but kept his eyes closed and his mouth shut. He wasn't a complete fool. Even though another "Fuck you" was on the tip of his tongue he swallowed it. He knew this man was nothing like his mother. UGod wasn't gonna let him get away with saying slick shit.

"There is a bucket, pine cleaner, and scrub rag under the bathroom sink in the hall. Get it," UGod ordered, "and get that shit up. Then shower, change, and come back here to eat. We need to get some shit straight. You need to know how it's going to be from now on."

Demi pushed past the pain and slowly climbed to his feet. He shuffled to the bathroom and found the things he needed. He knew how to prepare the cleaning mixture because he used to help his mother scrub the floors when he was younger. So, he mixed the disinfectant with warm water inside the bucket. When he stepped back into the living room, his bag was on the floor by the front door, but Ciro was nowhere to be seen. UGod sat at the table eating.

It didn't take long for him to clean up the mess, but he almost hurled a few times from smelling it. When he was done, Demi grabbed the bucket handle and his bag then stomped back to the bathroom. He began to cry again as he cleaned the bucket and the rag. When he finally got inside the dingy shower, Demi cried as the hot water rained down on him. He cried because he knew his mother was gone and he felt guilty because he couldn't help her. He cried because he had nowhere to go. He cried because the same blood in that asshole sitting in the other room ran in his veins, and that asshole shot his mother like she was no more than a dog on a street.

He just…cried.

UGod was still at the table when Demi entered the living room again. Demi was starving at this point; he wanted that sandwich. He looked around the room as he walked to the table. Still no Ciro. UGod pulled the blunt from his lips, then after a few seconds he let out the smoke.

"Rule one, don't ever fucking disrespect me. What I say goes. Don't follow and we have a problem. I usually solve my problems with a couple bullets." UGod pointed to Demi's head then heart. "I am your father and you will do what I say when I say it. That's rule two." UGod put the blunt to his lips and sucked. He blew a stream of smoke out. "Your home is where I am. You are my seed, my legacy. A DemiGod, you get me?"

Was that a question? Demi frowned.

When UGod got up out of the chair and walked to the back of the apartment without waiting for an acknowledgement, Demi figured it wasn't. Demi sat down at the table, feeling numb. He'd never cried as much as he did in the last few hours. And the more he thought of everything that happened, the more he wanted to cry. He couldn't stop the tears that fell from his eyes. They were like huge raindrops that didn't slide down his face but just dropped from his eyes to his lap as he hung his head.

"Just think," Ciro said.

Demi wiped at his face as he looked over at Ciro. He wasn't sure when Ciro arrived, but he narrowed his eyes at the piece of shit.

"If he didn't get shot last year, you wouldn't even fucking be here." Ciro chuckled as he gripped the game controller. "Fucking Asian tells him some fortune cookie bullshit, that a man can only live forever through his offspring. And this marfucker starts driving hours just to watch you. Talking 'bout how smart and tough his seed is. Your weak ass ain't shit. Then he goes and snatch your dumb ass up and wants you to be his legacy and shit. Why? Who the fuck knows? We got

Krysta. She the truth," Ciro sneered as he flipped his hands in the air. "You ain't shit."

Demi rolled his eyes at Ciro then turned his back on him. He didn't give two shits about a fortune or what UGod thought of him. The fact that asshole watched him without him knowing was creepy as hell though. And fuck Ciro and whoever the hell Krysta was.

Demi looked down, seeing the sandwich. He moved his finger over the bread which was a little hard from being left out. His mother would have wrapped his food up until he was ready to eat it.

She can't wrap anything anymore.

The truth of that burned more than anything. New tears fell as Demi picked up the sandwich and bit into it.

THREE

Now

DEMI

As usual, Carver's nightclub which was named after its owner, was off the hook. The DJ was playing a hot mix of hits by female artists. *Hit 'Em Up* by Bleu Cantrell had the dancefloor lit. Demi sat in the VIP section, a high raised area with a clear view of most of the dance floor and bar through a guard rail in front of him.

Relaxed back on the white leather booth with his legs spread out lazily in front of him, one straight the other bent, Demi lifted a glass to his lips. He enjoyed the hint of vanilla and caramel as the aged whisky slid down the back of his throat with a slight burn.

Demi worked his tongue around his mouth then ran it over his teeth as Evan, one of his security guards, approached. Usually, his security detail consisted of two men positioned at either of the two staircases on the ground level leading up to the VIP section, and one at the top with him. Tonight, Demi only brought Evan, who stood on the top level with him.

Carver, being Carver, sent two of his guys over to guard the staircase. Two others were standing on floor level just a few feet away from the stairs.

Demi didn't want this kind of coverage. If he did, he would have brought his own men. He sighed as he kept his unfocused gaze on the crowd below, but he gave Evan a nod.

"Grace is requesting entry at the east staircase. Brenda and Brandy at the west, Mr. Carrion," Evan said as he held a 2-way radio poised by his mouth.

Demi shook his head. The foxes were scrambling now that Sasha was gone and Krysta wasn't around. He chuckled but his laugh lacked humor.

"No entry," Evan said into the 2-way radio, then he returned to his post at the center of the balcony that overlooked the club.

Demi finished off his drink. The remaining ice jostled as he placed the glass on the oval table to the side of him. As he lifted one of four remaining whiskey-filled glasses, he glanced over to the east staircase just as Carver stepped onto the landing and made his way over. Demi kept his eye on Carver as he walked up, only looking away when his friend took a seat beside him.

Carver leaned forward, lifting one of the glasses of whiskey. He gave it a sip then he gave Demi a sideways questioning look. "You drinking in public now?" Carver asked after several seconds of being ignored.

Normally, Demi lived by certain rules to protect his safety in the streets. In order to be on point and aware, he never drank or got high in public, even at Carver's spot, which was like his haven. It wasn't that he was much of a drinker, and he'd long stopped sparking up, but if he did want to let loose, he did that shit at home.

"I can't get loose in your spot?" Demi asked with a raised brow.

"You know what I mean, Demi." Carver placed the barely-touched whiskey back beside the other glasses.

"What I want to ask you is…why are you stretching that tight ass shirt to its limits," Demi said then cracked a sly smile. He took another gulp of whiskey. Demi watched Carver look around the empty VIP area then to Evan. He knew what was coming next.

"Where's the rest of your security, and why are you sitting here alone?"

Demi smirked knowingly. He knew Carver well enough to know that Carver already knew the answers to his questions. That was why, when Carver saw him enter the club and VIP area alone, he sent his guys over to hold him down. Demi was alone because Sasha was dead. He didn't have security with him because…Sasha was dead.

No one else needs to get hurt.

"How long have we been tight?" Carver asked.

Demi looked at Carver and smiled as he recalled the day they met.

Then1987

DEMIGOD

Demi slung his backpack over his shoulder and closed his locker. Feeling as if he was being watched, he looked over his shoulder. Directly across from him on the other side of the hallway was a brawny motherfucker leaning on a row of lockers peering at him.

Raising his brows, Demi stared back. The guy was light skinned with hazel eyes, a bit taller than him, and well-muscled with a scar that sliced down his left brow. When the kid wouldn't look away, Demi narrowed his eyes and asked, "What the fuck do you want, man?"

The kid just shrugged but kept staring.

I don't need this shit.

Demi turned around and closed his eyes. He thought the administrators letting *him* into this prestigious school was a reach, but that kid looked dangerous as fuck. *Wow.* "Shit," he said under his breath. He would like to find out just how dangerous this fucker might be; but if Demi got into any more trouble, they would kick him out, and it was just the third month of his freshman year.

Rolling his shoulders, Demi started down the hall. He was deciding his plan of action as he walked toward the exit doors. The guy was trailing him. If he led the fucker off campus, maybe...

Demi sighed as his eyes landed on Barret Hensley, who stepped out in front of him with a shit-eating grin on his pasty ass face.

"I heard your black ass is out of here boy, if you—"

That was all Barret got out before a shadow moved past Demi. The next thing he saw was Hensley's racist ass lying on his back and the light-skin giant standing over him. Students swarmed around them, laughing and pointing.

"Carrion!" Dean Weasley yelled as he pushed through the building crowd and stopped in front of them.

"What?" Demi asked as he met the judgmental gaze of the Dean.

"He tripped," the giant said as he reached down and grabbed Hensley up like the dude was a ragdoll.

"Jackson Carver?" Dean Weasley said with awe.

"Yup, I saw it. Barrett should get glasses," a guy in the crowd said.

"I saw him trip too," another kid agreed.

Frowning, Demi watched as everyone agreed with the blatant bullshit lie. No one at this white bread damn K-12 private school ever gave him a damn thing, let alone an excuse. He had to fight these assholes for respect and even though they knew he gave out ass whoopings like candy on Halloween, every year one of these preppy dumbasses still tried him. Even with his high GPA, the teachers still looked at him with suspicion and never defended him. But this motherfucker, a guy who Demi never even met, gets love from get-go.

"Un-fucking-believable," Demi said under his breath as he perused the sea of pale smiling faces.

Barrett blinked several times as he looked at the giant, then he said, "Sorry for bumping into you, Carver. It won't happen again."

"Come on, Barrett," the Dean said, taking Barrett from Carver. "Let's get you to medical."

The crowd started to break up. Some of the kids patted the Carver kid on the back as if they were touching a movie star. Still confused, Demi decided to just walk away. He made it a few feet before he realized the giant was still following him.

He spun around to ask the guy what the hell was his problem, but Krysta came skipping up and wrapped her hands around the giant's neck.

"Carver," she sang then kissed him on the cheek, "I see you've introduced yourself to DemiGod."

"Don't call me that shit," Demi hissed. He took note of the way the Carver kid's eyes lowered and how uncomfortable he looked with Krysta hanging onto him.

"Fine," Krysta said, letting go of the giant and bowing in front of Demi. "Shall I call you Prince of the Underworld then?"

Demi sighed as he spun on his heels and set off for the freshman exit doors again.

"Wait for us," she called out.

"If you weren't my cousin," Demi said when she and Carver caught up to him, "I'd probably beat the shit out of you."

"Awww," she said mockingly, "I love that you don't let my being a girl dissuade you."

"Who's the giant?" Demi pushed open one of the double doors and they walked outside of the main building. He turned toward the car loop and headed for his ride.

"He's our new defensive tackle who is going to lead Laure Prep to victory. That's what everyone is saying anyway," she said, taking Carver's hand in hers. "We've known each other for forever. He and our dads were homeboys back in the day, but Carver's mom moved him away. He's back now. I asked him to keep an eye on you because you can't get in any more trouble."

"Does he talk?" Demi asked, looking at Carver.

"He talks," Carver said.

Demi nodded to his driver who held the back door open as they walked up. He waited until Krysta slid over the back seat before getting into the car. "You coming?" he asked, looking at Carver, who stayed on the curb.

Shrugging, Carver moved forward. Demi slid over to give him space.

Once Carver was seated beside him, Demi said, "Good looking out, but you don't have to fight my battles man." He meant it too; Demi fought just fine.

"It's what brothers do," Carver said, looking at Demi as if confused.

Demi frowned at Carver and the giant smiled. Demi smiled back. *Brothers, huh.* The only person he considered family was Krysta and she was true fam, being Ciro's daughter. She was the only one who shared UGod's blood and was a member of his father's gang, the Congregation, that he didn't hate.

But maybe…

Demi looked thoughtfully at Carver.

Now/**Club Carver**

"Demi," Carver said, touching Demi on the shoulder. "You straight?"

Demi focused on Carver; whose brows were pinched together in consternation. Carver motioned his thumb over at Evan. Sighing, Demi blinked a few times before slowly turning his head and looking at Evan.

"Yeah?" Demi asked his bodyguard. His thoughts were a bit fuzzy.

"Mr. Houston would like entry," Evan informed him.

Demi shook his head no, then wiped his hand over his face. *Shit.* "I'm good," he said as he turned his attention back to Carver.

"You think that's wise? His uncle probably sent him here to offer his condolences," Carver reasoned, "since you are ignoring his calls."

Demi shrugged then said, "You can talk to him then, if you're so concerned."

"Maybe you need to go home and get some rest."

"Nothing home but an empty penthouse and shitty memories," Demi said as he swallowed the last of the whisky in the glass he held. He leaned forward and placed it on the table next to the empty ones, but he didn't pick up another. "You believe in karma, Carver? That all the grimy shit I did," he said then chuckled dryly, "is coming for me?"

"We all did grimy shit to get here," Carver said as he spread his arms out, referencing his club. "We did what we had to do. We buried those who would have buried us." Carver frowned as he and Demi held each other's gaze. "Fuck man, this is the time we bask in our fucking rewards. The time we live shit up. Not rolling the fuck over on some guilt shit."

"Some of our hands are stained with blood." Demi held up his hands and said, "And then there are mine. They are soaked in blood."

"And you didn't have to handle shit like you did. You have this stupid ass idea that you have to do everything on your own. That's bullshit man. Back then, I was ready to run into hell with you just like now, but you on some ole solo, up and up shit." Carver stood.

Demi knew his friend was upset.

Carver ground his jaw as his right eye ticked like a clock. It was a clear sign he was holding in his frustration.

"Family cover family, DemiGod," Carver said as he looked down at him.

"Why do you keep calling me that?" Demi reached forward and picked up another whisky. "You know I've always hated that name."

"I'm thinking you need reminding who you are," Carver said, picking up the empty glasses, "so WE can hunt this fucker out here hunting you, as a crew."

Demi placed the glass to his lips and threw his head back, swallowing it all in one gulp. "Can't hunt ghosts." He watched as Carver fumbled with the glasses, trying to get them all.

"Fuck ghosts," Carver said as he slammed the glasses back down on the table. "I'll send Golden up to clean. I'm going to talk to Houston." He stomped off and down the west flight of stairs.

Demi offered his friend a half-assed salute then reached for another shot glass. He frowned when he realized he had no whiskey left.

GISELLE

Giselle's heart drummed as soon as her gaze landed on him. From where she stood, across the narrow street by a lamppost, she had a clear view of the nightclub's entrance. She waited for over two hours for the club to close and for him to come out. And now, there he was walking toward a waiting vehicle that was parked at the curve.

"Demetrius," she whispered.

Darting into the street right when the light changed to green, Giselle barely made it out of the way of an accelerating car. She heard and ignored the angry shouts of the driver and the blare of his horn as she raced across the street.

"Play your music and keep your eyes on me, alright?"

Those were the last words Demetrius Carrion ever spoke to her. That day was the last time she saw him. Until now. Demetrius was mere steps from her. Within reach.

Finally.

With a clear view of him now, Giselle noted a lot about him had changed. He was just eighteen when they last saw each other. He'd gotten taller and his shoulders were wider; he looked physically slim yet with a well-muscled chest and arms. Demetrius was still gorgeous with his toffee-toned skin, deep set eyes, and full lips. She wondered how a man could be that perfect. He embodied such raw sex appeal, was intelligent, and always so confident. No man should have so many weapons at their disposal.

"Demetrius," she called out as she raised her arm and waved. Giselle tried to push through the people crowding the sidewalk. "Demetrius," she called again.

He must have heard her, because she saw him raise his head and search above the crowd of people who were exiting the club. When their eyes met, she saw that same haunted gaze she saw that day.

"Demetrius," she said again, overcome with emotion, but this time his name came out like a whispered prayer. As the last syllable of his name left her lips the gunfire started.

DEMI

He had to be hallucinating. He heard his name but that wasn't the odd part. Demi heard his full name, but no one used his full name outside of the office; and he thought he heard it being spoken by a familiar voice. But that couldn't be.

Demi touched Evan's arm to brace himself as he looked around and out over the crowd. He drank a lot, but he had something to eat and even burned away some of the alcohol he ingested by playing pool and darts in Carver's private game room. Yet, he heard…

"Demetrius."

And saw…

Could it be her? See…this is why you have rules, he told himself as he peered over the crowded sidewalk at the woman. He shouldn't have drunk so much outside of his home.

Demi smiled at the woman he thought resembled *her* so much. He took a step forward, toward her. It was as if he was being pulled. All sounds, traffic, voices, music, disappeared as their eyes locked. He focused on her lips as they moved. He heard her call his name a third time, but as he tried to get closer a look of worry crossed her beautiful face right before fear replaced it.

"Wake the fuck up, Demi! Get down!" Carver yelled from somewhere nearby.

Demi felt his shoulder being pulled but shrugged away. "I have to get to her," he said as he moved forward, pushing through screaming and scrambling people. The distinct sound of bullets whizzing by his head caused Demi to lift his arm in defense, but he couldn't tell where the shots were coming from.

Seeing an opening in the crowd, Demi reached who he thought was his Angel, managing to cover her with his body just when a familiar burn exploded through his side. The sound of gunfire coming from behind him, from his allies, was somewhat of a comfort.

"Mr. Carrion," Evan said, touching Demi's shoulder. "We need to move inside now. We got you covered."

Pain had a way of clearing the mind of a whiskey buzz. Demi raised himself from squatting over the woman. As he did, he peered down to see if he was really holding on to who he thought he was. He held his breath as he used his hand to smooth her long thick hair away from her face.

Giselle! It's Giselle!

His pulse went into overdrive when she opened her eyes and looked into his. He only held her gaze for a moment before the chaos around him prompted him into action.

"Where's Carver?" Demi demanded.

"I don't know sir but we have to move…" Evan started to rise but looked down and stopped. "Fuck, Mr. Carrion, is that your blood or hers?"

Demi moved his attention from Evan to look at the woman. She looked down at herself as well. Sure enough, there was blood on her blouse. The woman looked up at Demi then her eyes fluttered before closing.

"Giselle," he said softly, as she relaxed into his body. Lifting her limp body, Demi was reminded of what happened to Sasha, and he swallowed a wave of fear and worry that rose into his now-clear mind. He carried her past several armed bodyguards who were now at the entrance and made his way into the club. Frightened people who were hiding inside made it hard to navigate, but he managed to get Giselle to a booth and lay her on the table.

"Where's she hit?"

Demi saw a pair of hands appear over Giselle, pulling and tugging at her shirt then lifting her arm and shoulder before he was able to register Krysta's voice. He'd never been so thankful to see anyone in his life. He didn't even know she was here tonight.

"Found it," she said, grabbing his hand and pressing a white cloth into it. Krysta then pressed Demi's hand over Giselle's left shoulder. "Keep pressure on the wound." Krysta raised one of Giselle's eyelids and flashed her tiny keychain light over her eye a few times in different motions then did the same to the other. "Did she hit her head?" Krysta asked.

"I…maybe," Demi said as he thought about what happened.

Did I take her to the ground to cover her too hard?

"We need you over here," Carver said as he came rushing up, waving the EMT's to the table.

"Excuse us," one of the emergency workers said firmly as he pushed Demi out of the way.

Krysta raised her hand to put a barrier between Demi and the emergency workers as she addressed them. "Upper shoulder bullet wound…"

Her words faded as Demi stood up straight and backed away several paces while he watched them work on Giselle. He raised his hands to touch his head but stopped when he noticed the blood on them. With each passing moment he stared at his bloody hands, he found it harder to breathe.

"Yo, you alright?" Carver asked as he came to stand beside Demi.

Demi looked over at Carver, absent-mindedly noting the sweat covering Carver's face and drenching his t-shirt.

"Hey," Carver said as his concerned gaze bore into Demi's eyes then over his body. He jolted to attention when he peered down at Demi's left side. "Shit, man." Carver inspected the rest of Demi's body before he focused back on Demi's left side. He called out, "He's been shot too."

One of the EMT's came rushing over to them. Demi barely felt her lifting his shirt where there was a concentrated spot of blood collecting. All he could do was focus his thoughts on Giselle. She'd come back to him and he couldn't lose her now. He couldn't lose her again.

My Angel…

FOUR

DEMIGOD

Their laughter rose above the rest of the noise as they huddled close together at a table in the food court. Each of the girls looked over at him one by one then they all lowered their heads and laughed louder. All except one. She hadn't looked over at him yet.

"Why the hell do they keep laughing like that? Shit's annoying," Carver said, pushing to his feet. "Imma go see if Krys is done with her nails."

Demi nodded but didn't take his eyes off the girls sitting in the food court, one in particular.

"You gonna be here?"

Demi turned away from the girls and looked up at Carver. "I might roll out. Beep me."

"Come with me or just wait for us here."

Demi shook his head. Carver took that bodyguard shit too seriously sometimes. "I'm straight. Just beep me."

"Whatever," Carver said as he waved his hand dismissively. "Just don't hook up with that scandalous bitch Shannon."

Demi smiled then shrugged.

"I'm out." Carver spun around and walked away from Demi.

When Demi turned his attention back to the gaggle of girls, they weren't sitting at the table anymore. He stood up and peered around the mall for them. He was sure he could have the blonde in a dark corner on her knees within ten minutes of starting a conversation.

An image of her friend, the pretty black girl with the killer body, popped into his head. She was the only sister in the group. She was also the only one of them who wasn't checking him out.

Jasmine… Gabriella… No…Giselle is her name.

Their fathers were business associates and they maybe shared a class or two, but Demi didn't know her, per se. In all honesty, he didn't like girls like her. That made it even odder that she popped into his mind when all he wanted to think about was the blonde sucking his dick.

Demi shook his head then turned and looked down another section of the mall. A flash of pink denim jacket caught his eye. Grinning, he walked toward the path of the pink jean jacket.

If he had to guess, he would say that the girls assumed he would follow them, because the blonde looked back at him with a seductive smile as she continued to walk. Like at the food court, her friends looked over their shoulders too, laughing and urging her on.

Yea, pump her up, Demi thought. He moved around a few people to keep the girls in sight as they walked toward the exit. A dark corner in the parking garage would be the perfect spot for what he had in mind.

Demi followed the girls through an exit door into a long well-lit corridor that led to the parking garage. Aside from them, Demi noted a couple in front of the girls moving in the same direction and a guy with a ballcap walking slowly toward them, heading for the mall. He didn't give the couple a second thought, but he kept his eyes on the guy who kept his head down as the girls passed him.

He don't want no static.

Demi looked ahead after the guy passed him. The blonde was at the end of the corridor, holding the door open. When she blew him a kiss, Demi threw his hand up and acted as if he caught it. Just as he was placing his hand to his mouth, he was slammed against the wall from behind.

"Give me your shit," a husky voice said close to his ear. Demi felt something sharp being pushed against his side.

Demi's face hit the rough gray stone-like wall hard enough to bust his lip. He cursed as he braced his hands flat on the wall. He heard the blonde scream, and when he turned his head toward her, he presumed she had run off, because he only saw the door swinging closed.

"You are going to have to kill me motherfucker because I ain't giving you shit," Demi hissed. He used his hands on the wall to push back a bit to gauge the fucker's strength, but the guy forced him forward again, harder this time.

Demi grunted but pushed off the wall with force this time. He turned and pushed the guy back. Demi saw the light shine off the knife the guy carried, and he dodged to get out of the way. But he felt the cold metal catch him as he fumbled to unzip his jacket and get his gun.

A flash of color caught Demi's attention, and the next thing he knew the guy was covering his head. Demi looked up just as the girl swung her purse again. It hit the guy on the side of his head as he fell to the ground trying to dodge out of the way.

"I've called the cops you creep!"

Demi pulled out his gun and pointed it at the guy, but the girl jumped between them, blocking his view. She held up her hands, making it impossible for him to shoot the asshole as he ran away toward the mall entrance.

"Did you hear me?" she asked, looking him in the eyes. "I said, I've called the police."

"Are you crazy?" Demi asked.

She frowned and a confused look crossed her beautiful face.

"No. Why?"

Demi stared at her for a few minutes then burst with laughter. He immediately flinched, because laughing made the stab wound he forgot about ache. Pulling his jacket off slowly, he dropped it to the ground.

"Giselle, come on. Let the police handle it."

Demi eased out of his holster as he looked over his shoulder at her friends standing outside of the corridor with the door open. The blonde looked antsy.

"We should get out of here!" another one of her friends yelled.

Demi knew the mall cops would arrive before the real ones did. He balled up his holster and pushed it and the gun at Giselle. "Take this. I'll get it later," he said.

Giselle looked down at his extended hand. Without a word, she took the items and held them to her chest.

"Go," he said, motioning to her friends with his head as he covered his wound with his hand.

She tucked the gun and holster inside her jacket, gave him a nod, then rushed off toward her friends.

As Demi watched her disappear through the doorway and into the garage, he heard the sirens. He fell back against the textured wall then slid to the floor. He looked to the mall door at the end of the hall, and as he did, he saw the bloody knife. He also saw a small rainbow cover notepad, a pen cap, and a tube of lip balm near his foot.

Demi reached for the pad.

Now

Demi pushed to his feet when he saw the doctor entering the room. He glanced over at Giselle, who lay unmoving on the hospital bed, then back to the doctor. "We met briefly last night, I'm Dr. O'Brian, Ms. Johnson's surgeon."

"You're her frie—"

"Fiancé," Demi said as he extended his hand. The doctor gave him a skeptical look but extended his hand and shook Demi's. "So, basically, the projectile was limited to the left breast. The entrance wound was in the inner quadrant of the left breast, beginning at about four centimeters away from the areola. Its path tracked horizontally and erupted under the armpit. We removed the foreign object and patched her up. Ms. Johnson seems to show signs of a concussion as well. If there are no complications she can go home in a few days."

"Thanks, doctor," Demi said. He noticed Carver by the door but focused back on the doctor.

"I was told you were shot too," the doctor said, moving his gaze to Demi's side.

Demi pulled up the fresh shirt Carver bought him and exposed the bandage on his side. "Just a flesh wound, through and through," Demi said as he lowered the shirt back down.

"I pulled your medical records, Mr. Carrion. Seems you've had approximately eight bullet wounds and two stabbings. I don't know what happened tonight, but I hope whatever *it* is doesn't show up here."

"In my youth, I lived a different life. Those days are behind me. I am a businessman now. Tonight, I happened to be in the wrong place at the wrong time."

"Good," the doctor said. "We will move Ms.," he looked down at his clipboard, "Johnson to a room soon."

"Thank you," Demi said. He watched the doctor's look of surprise when he turned to leave the room and saw Carver. The man avoided even looking at Carver as he rushed off.

"You didn't have to scare the man," Demi said as he sat back down in the chair and looked up at Carver.

"Fuck that clown," Carver said. He looked over at Giselle. "How she doing?"

Demi noticed the frown on his friend's face but didn't address it. "She's alive," Demi said, looking at Carver. "She's here." He heard the awe in his tone but didn't care. Demi stood when he realized Carver wasn't going to get the other chair beside the gurney. "What do you have?"

Carver led the way out of the room. They walked through a set of double security doors, but before they turned the corner, Carver eased Demi into a small hollow.

"Before we go into the lobby, there's something you should know."

Demi frowned, wondering what it could be. When they arrived, the hospital techs gave him Giselle's things. In her purse there was a motel key and a receipt for the room. "What is it?" he asked.

Carver rubbed his head as he looked down then up again at Demi. "The room wasn't empty."

Demi tilted his head back as he tried to process the possibility of Giselle having someone important in her life. "She has a man?"

"Sort of," Carver said. "We brought him here."

"Why would she come looking for me if she has someone?" Demi frowned. He opened his mouth to ask Carver why the fuck he would bring…but he checked his shit. Of course, Giselle's man should be here with her. Sighing, Demi moved past Carver and walked toward the seating section of the lobby.

"Wait," Carver said, rushing behind him. "You don't understand."

Demi glanced back at Carver as he turned the corner. What the hell could be wrong with the guy that Carver felt he needed to be warned? But as Demi faced forward and his eyes moved from Krysta, who sat in one of the chairs, to the object of Krysta's attention, he stopped in his tracks.

Raising his brows in confusion, Demi looked to Krysta, who offered him a grimaced smile, then to Carver who moved to stand in front of a kid who sat in a chair beside Krysta.

"He says his name is Cassiel Demetrius Carrion," Carver said.

Demi raised a brow as the kid looked up at Carver then over at him. Cassiel pushed off the chair and stood. His expression was blank as he walked over to Demi.

"Can I see my mom now?"

A couple hours later

Demi leaned back beyond the wall he stood beside and looked inside the hospital room. Cassiel was sitting on the edge of the bed beside Giselle. She was moving her hand over his thick curls, smoothing his hair down as they talked. When she noticed Demi watching, she immediately looked away.

He saw the fear in her eyes. She wasn't even masking it.

She's afraid of me.

...and she should be. With all of what he'd put her through, he didn't blame her.

Demi straightened up and looked at Carver. "Do you think he's mine?"

Carver raised a brow. "Are we looking at the same kid?" Carver asked, clearly being sarcastic.

Demi leaned back again and studied Cassiel's features, again. The kid was smiling at something Krysta was handing to him. Before, when they were in the lobby, Demi couldn't think straight, let alone note any similarities he and Cassiel may share. But now, he saw some of the physical traits. Aside from being light-skinned, Cassiel looked a good deal like him when he was about that age.

"Hell, have you seen how Krysta's been doting over him? She can see it just like I do." Carver grimaced then added, "Plus, he's what, about nine years old? That shit adds up."

Demi rubbed his head, trying to make sense of the past few hours...weeks. It was as if his past was coming for him. Before Demi had a chance to respond, he felt a presence beside him. He looked down.

Cassiel was there.

At Cassiel's age, Demi remembered laughing and having fun even though he was a hellion and bad as fuck. But Cassiel seemed cautious, reserved, and quiet—somewhat like Demi remembered becoming after UGod got his hands on him.

"Mom says I need your permission to go with Aunt Krysta," Cassiel said, looking up at him then quickly looking down.

Demi felt his heart pulse, so he rubbed his hand over his chest.

Aunt Krysta? The kid was... The kid is...

Demi's thoughts were jumbled. All this—Giselle coming back into his life after nine years, with a son who looked like him... Suddenly, Demi felt...lost.

What do I say?

He looked to Carver for help.

Carver stepped forward and said, "Sure kid, you can go with your Aunt Krysta. After you get some rest, she'll bring you back tomorrow to see your mom, alright?"

Cassiel nodded. He put his hand out as if he wanted to shake hands.

But Carver held his hand up.

Cassiel bubbled with laughter as he jumped up and slapped Carver five, then he turned and regarded Demi. "You'll be here tomorrow too, right?"

Demi glanced at Carver, who nodded. Demi placed his hand gently on Cassiel's head and said, "I'm not going anywhere."

The boy offered him a half smile then followed Krysta as she passed by. Demi noticed Krysta was smiling hard, and she was even glossy-eyed as they walked away.

What the hell? Krysta?

Demi couldn't help frowning. The woman would hang a person with their own intestines formed into a noose without batting an eye, but Cassiel had her all teary-eyed.

"Look," Carver said, touching his shoulder. "There are things you need to know. The motel they were staying at is a shithole. The room was clean, but as we packed her and the kid's things… Let's just say that Giselle doesn't seem to be doing well financially. Their clothes are old and worn. The kid had some books but them shits are old and nothing else. The woman next door to them, who is probably living at that dump long-term, seemed to be checking in on the kid while Giselle was gone, but he was in the room alone. She heard us when we entered the room. She didn't want to let Cass go with us, but he somehow recognized us. Told the woman that I was his uncle Carver and Krysta was his aunt."

He knows them…us.

"There is something else you need to consider, Demi," Carver said. "Her showing up now is a huge fucking coincidence with everything else happening." He reached out and squeezed Demi's shoulder. "I'm not saying she's involved in this shit or working with someone trying to get at you but-"

"I know Carver. I'm focused."

"Good. Now, I gotta dip. I got a partial tag number when I ran after that fuck last night. Going to see what I can dig up."

"I appreciate it, but I want you to stay out of—"

"We're brothers, man. We need to handle this within the Family," Carver told him.

Demi sighed. How could he make Carver understand that he wasn't for that life anymore? He'd been skating the rim of both worlds, but he was tired of it. Demi knew decades ago that he was going to transition to a more socially acceptable lifestyle, and he started working toward it the day he met UGod.

"I want the police to handle this."

Carver narrowed his eyes as he threw his hands up in the air then started to back away. "I'm out," he said before turning away.

Demi watched as Carver walked away. He remembered the sweat covering his friend the previous night. Wondered what caused it. Now he knew—Carver ran after the guy who shot him, Giselle, and three others at the club last night.

The love he had for his friend, for the Family...

Demi shook his head. That love was why he needed to keep them out of this.

When Carver disappeared around the corner, Demi turned and walked inside the room. Giselle was propped up on a pillow, but her eyes were closed and her head hung to the side. He moved toward the window and pulled the string to close out the midday sun's rays.

"I know you have a lot of questions."

Demi closed his eyes as her voice caressed him. It was a voice he thought he'd never hear again. He didn't turn around until he allowed the sudden pleasure of hearing it to pass. She was watching him. He knew the fear he'd seen on her face earlier was just beneath the surface.

Goddamn, she hadn't changed much. Her brown sugar skin tone was flawless and still carried the glow of youth. Her big beautiful brown eyes were just as easy to read now as they were then. Because of her high bun hairstyle, he couldn't tell if her dark hair was still as long as it used to be, but he saw she still wore it naturally curly.

"You shouldn't have come to the club. You could have been killed tonight," Demi told her.

Her emotions played out on her stunning face. She looked worried, then fearful, then determined. "You never came to the library…and I was worried that you wouldn't," she said, looking down.

It *was* her, she's the one who wrote the letter. She saved his life twice now.

When Giselle looked up, Demi looked into her eyes. Memories of their past shuffled through his mind.

"I looked for you," Demi told her, "after." Just a vague reference to that day set blue flames to his nerves. "I didn't want…" he started to say, but instead of continuing he looked through the door and out into the hallway. He never thought they would have this conversation, that he would have to explain his actions that day.

His escape was just a few feet away. All Demi had to do was start walking. But he closed his eyes and took a deep breath before looking back at Giselle. "I didn't mean for things to happen the way they did. I thought staying away from you would keep you off UGod's radar. But your father—"

"Was that why you were always so distant?" Giselle asked.

FIVE

Then/**Three months before the Incident**

GISELLE

Giselle felt the hairs on the back of her neck prickle again. The sensation caused her to look up from the class assignment handout she was working on and survey the room. Most of the class was busy writing with their heads down or looking off into space as if thinking of what to write next.

Looking over her shoulder, Giselle met Demetrius' gaze. *Everyone except him appears to be working.*

His unflinching brown eyes appeared dark at this distance, but she knew that close-up one could see they had specks of light amber in them. She knew because the few times she was close enough to see them, she committed the hue to memory.

After the mall incident, they hadn't said one word to each other for about a month, a week of which he was absent. He didn't even attempt to get his gun and gun holster back. She had to hide it in the back of her closet. If her parents found it... Giselle didn't want to think about that.

But, to be honest, she kind of liked having something of his.

They didn't talk again until about a month ago when she was at his house for some party. She wasn't sure the reason for the party, but Demetrius' father liked to throw them often. This particular party was during the day on a Saturday, and tame enough to allow the children of his friends and business associates to attend.

According to Giselle's mother, Mr. Carrion's parties could be wild.

For the party, Giselle wore her new bikini for the heated indoor pool, a one-shoulder design with a cut-out bodice and accented with a high-side polished chain. It was revealing in all the right places, but it covered her up enough for her parents to allow it.

That day, Demetrius watched her and it wasn't just for a few seconds here and there. Every time she looked at him, he was looking at her. That was her goal anyway—it was the reason she searched for weeks for the perfect swimsuit. When she came out of the bathroom, Demetrius was waiting in the hallway. At first, Giselle thought he was waiting for the bathroom. She didn't see any reason for him to want to talk to her. He hadn't since the mall incident. But…

"Royal blue is my favorite color," he told her.

Giselle was so nervous at the time that it was hard to swallow. "I know," she whispered.

At her admission, Demetrius closed the space between them, stepping so close Giselle was able to see the light amber flecks in his eyes.

"Angel," he said, so close to her that his breath caressed her lips, "you don't want my attention."

Her heart literally stopped beating. She was stunned silent, and though her brain was screaming for her to say something, she struggled to form any words. Giselle remembered she wanted to bang the back of her head against a door as she watched Demetrius smirk then turn to walk away.

At the time, she watched him as he slowly moved away with her mouth open and no idea what to do next. It didn't take long, but when she did recover her composure, she pushed her shoulders back and managed to force out of her mouth, "Maybe…"

She muttered the word so low and lost her nerve she didn't think he heard her, but he pivoted and looked back at her. *It's now or never, Giselle,* she thought at the time as she pushed her shoulders back and her chest out. "I said," Giselle spoke louder, "maybe I do."

Demetrius just smiled at her as he shook his head and walked away. For the rest of the party, she didn't see him. Maybe he left or went to his bedroom. Whatever the case, she thought she totally blew it.

Now, glancing over her shoulder again, Giselle met Demetrius' gaze head on. If she was bold, she would wink or pucker her lips and kiss at him. But she wasn't. So, she turned back around and tried to focus on the work Mrs. Howard handout.

Besides, flirting with him was a waste of time. Giselle saw all kinds of girls flirt with Demetrius at Laure Preparatory. Yet, it didn't seem he was interested in any of them. Except for Marcy Keen. When Marcy flirted with Demetrius, he flirted back. Up until Marcy, it seemed to Giselle that the only girl he bothered with was his cousin, Krysta Carrion. But for all she knew, he could be screwing all those girls who flirted with him.

Demetrius seemed focused on his studies which she thought was odd, because he was rough through and through. At least at school, he didn't appear too concerned about the girls who wanted his attention, and they wanted him despite all the rumors swirling around him.

Giselle knew the truth of those rumors. She'd seen his darkness, and it was scary. Yet, it wasn't a turn-off for her. But she knew if the people at school knew what she did, their interest in Demetrius would quickly turn to fear. Those girls were attracted to the idea of danger more than the reality of it.

She looked over her shoulder again. He wasn't looking at her this time.

"Alright," Mrs. Howard said, causing Giselle to face forward and pay attention. "Hand in the worksheet before you leave." Mrs. Howard raised her head and paused when the bell rang, signaling the end of class. "Read chapters ten through fifteen for homework."

"Giselle," Tessa called from her seat located three desks forward, "I have to get to gym early and talk with Ms. Warren."

"Okay." Giselle waved to her friend as she stood and packed up her stuff. As she made her way to Mrs. Howard's desk to place her worksheet in the classwork bin, Giselle looked over her shoulder. Demetrius was already gone, and a classmate was collecting his worksheet off his desk to hand in for him.

Giselle felt an odd sense of disappointment as she stepped into the hallway. She walked through the hallway leading to the gym, half-focused on what was going on around her while thinking about how Demetrius blatantly stared at her in class. She thought for sure that this time she'd seen something different in his eyes. Something other than him inspecting her like she was a poisonous plant.

Giselle entered the girl's locker room and changed into her gym uniform on autopilot as her classmates chatted around her. She closed her gym locker and walked over to the mirror on the wall. Her hair looked fine, which was always a concern.

Someone passing looked at Giselle and said something, but her mind was still on Demetrius. She wondered what he thought of her. So, she was a bit surprised when she moved away from the mirror and realized she was in the locker room alone.

Giselle jogged out of the locker room and headed to the field. The class was running track again today. Track wasn't her favorite sport but she welcomed it today, knowing her focus was shot. Being late getting onto the field a few times meant detention laps. She didn't want to be late even once if she could avoid it, so Giselle picked up her pace.

She was rushing past the bleachers when Demetrius stepped out from under them. Giselle stumbled to a stop before she ran into him. Confused, she just looked at him. It wasn't until she started moving again that she realized he'd taken her by the hand and was pulling her under the bleachers.

"You have my attention," Demetrius said as he stopped then spun her to face him. "Now, what're you going to do with it?"

Giselle glanced down at their connected hands then raised her head and looked around them, seeing the light between the stairs of the bleachers in the shade that surrounded them. Her pulse was racing. She was pretty sure her hand was sweating. The warmth on the back of her neck and back had nothing to do with the perfect spring weather.

What am I going to do with it?

Giselle moved her eyes over his face.

Demetrius' skin appeared smooth with a toffee tone that was flawless; and his pronounced brow shadowed his ever-aware deep-set eyes, giving him a dangerous edgy appearance. His nose was broad, and his lips...*those lips*. He had full wide lips that seemed to be in a constant cocky smirk.

Giselle looked down at their hands again. He was rubbing small circles on the back of her hand with his thumb. Was he trying to relax her? She looked back up and watched as his tongue peeked out and moved over his upper lip. That was all it took for her to do the boldest thing she'd ever done. Giselle stepped forward as she pulled her hand from his and snaked it up his hard chest, around his neck, and into his short dark tight curls that shimmered under the sun's rays.

When her lips grazed over his, she suddenly lost her nerve and was pulling back, but Demetrius placed his hands on her hips and pulled her to him. Her first thought when their lips touched was his lips were soft.

It seemed like he was letting her lead, but she knew it was a ruse. Giselle knew that Demetrius was in total control and he confirmed that when he took over the kiss, snaking his tongue over her lips and pressing against them for entry until she opened her mouth. She set her palm against his chest and moaned when he slipped his tongue into her mouth, but she sighed and gripped his shoulder when he placed his hands under her arms and pulled her closer.

The kiss was awkward at first. Giselle kissed a few times before, but they were just the pressing lips together kind of kissing. Never had she tasted another person's mouth, felt another's teeth graze over her tongue, or...

Oh!

Her entire body went stiff when she felt his penis harden against her leg.

Demetrius leaned back from the kiss and looked at her with a frown.

Giselle wanted to ask him what was wrong. She wondered what she did. But when he smiled, she felt the tension ease out of her a bit.

"You don't kiss much, do you?"

Giselle shook her head. "No, but I can practice," then she added with a whisper as she looked down, "...and get better."

Giselle felt a finger touch her chin and raise her head as he applied pressure.

"I can teach you. But only me," he said, lowering his head to meet her eyes.

YES! What, wait?

"If I'm only kissing you, then you can't kiss anyone else either," Giselle said.

"Deal," Demetrius said without pause. He chuckled then leaned in and kissed her lips again in a series of sweet pecks, but they were not like the ones she was used to. Each time their lips touched; the press of his lips grew longer and felt more sensual, as if he was telling her some sort of secret.

He was the one who made lower body contact first by raising her gym uniform shirt and placing his warm hand on her back. That first touch sent a jolt through her, causing Giselle to jump.

"Can I touch your body?" Demetrius whispered against her lips.

"Mmm huh," was her hazy answer.

Giselle missed her entire gym period as Demetrius gave her, her first make out lesson. They didn't talk much, it was just a few words of encouragement from him here and there, a lot of moaning, and a heap of touching. Only, she mostly kept her hands above his clothes and waist.

It wasn't until they heard voices that Demetrius stopped the lesson and pulled her close, wrapping her in his arms. The closeness felt so different from kissing, it felt more intimate. Feeling somewhat comfortable with him, Giselle rested her head on his shoulder as her gym class passed the bleachers. They were so far inside that no one would see them unless they came under.

After it seemed as if everyone had passed, Giselle awkwardly stepped back. "I guess I should go," she said as she looked down at the ground.

"Remember," Demetrius said, smiling as he tugged on the hem of her gym shirt. "No kissing any other guys. Just me."

"And no girls…just me." Giselle didn't mean it to come out as a question. She wanted to sound sure and unwavering, but to her ears she ended up sounding weak and pathetically jealous.

"Only you, Angel." He stepped up to her and placed his lips on the tip of her nose and kissed it before stepping back and smirking.

Giselle smiled as she touched her fingers to her nose. Then she turned and jogged away.

Now

Giselle moved her cottony tongue around her mouth, feeling little to no saliva. She reached out her hand, slowly. The pain she felt was minimal, but she was scared she'd rip the staples or stitches…she wasn't sure which the doctor said he used. Her fingertips grazed the condensation dripping from the small purple cup.

She glanced over at Demetrius. He was standing in front of the window with his back to her. From where she lay in the hospital bed, Giselle could see from the tall building there was a city landscape outside. Maybe there was a park below or a road. Whatever the case, Demetrius didn't see her trying to get a drink. Sighing, Giselle looked back to the cup.

"Let me help you."

Giselle looked up to see Demetrius striding over. Her heart pounded in her chest as she watched him approach. It did every time he set his gaze on her. Then and now.

She felt a bit taxed from moving around. "Thank you," she said as she relaxed back on the bed and dropped her hand. When Demetrius held the cup in front of her, she watched him as she took the straw into her mouth and took a few sips.

"How are you feeling?"

He must have asked her that same question a dozen times now. She knew she should be freaked about getting shot, but she was more freaked out by being in Demetrius' presence again. So many thoughts swirled around in her mind. She was finally here with him. It took so much for her to get her son here. So many things they'd gone without. So many things they'd endured.

Giselle swallowed the last sip she took then tried to move her legs to adjust herself. She discovered pretty quickly they were stiff. The movement caused Demetrius to looked down at her legs then up into her eyes.

"Should I call the nurse?" he asked, seemingly very concerned.

"No. I'm fine," she told him…again for the dozenth time today.

He nodded then said nothing more. That was all he did—ask if she was alright then shut down when he received her response. He hadn't spoken a word about their fractured relationship or her condition after he told her he'd searched for her after the incident and mentioning their fathers. That was more than an hour ago. Maybe he didn't think she knew what exactly spawned the INCIDENT.

Actually, Giselle knew the story well. Her mother often discussed the offense whenever life was hard for them. She spoke of her husband's mistake of dealing with UGod in the first place when the man's past was so vividly connected to the illegal dealings, even though he portrayed himself differently. Her mother spoke of how Giselle's father thought to steal from the man she equated with a wild animal. Her mother also bragged about how she left her husband and that Giselle would never see that bum again.

If Giselle recalled correctly, her mother loved the life her husband provided, spent his money, and plastered her fake smile at Mr. Carrion, the animal, whenever he was around. It was her mother who encouraged her father to get closer to Demetrius' father, to become invaluable. But none of that mattered now, really.

"I'm sorry to spring this on you so suddenly. We're not here to interrupt your life. I just wanted you to know you have a son. He's a great kid, Demetrius." Giselle wiped at the tears that ran from her eyes. "You deserve to know him."

"I deserve nothing. You owe me nothing," Demetrius said.

"We were both victims that day. He made—"

"I'm no saint, Giselle," Demetrius said. "You know this better than anyone."

He sat on a chair beside her bed with his head down. Giselle wanted to reach out and touch him. She wanted to run her hand over his head and down the back of his neck. She wanted to taste him again.

"I know but—"

Demetrius looked up at her. His eyes took on a lost faraway look. It was a look she'd seen before, and she wasn't ashamed to admit she was afraid of it.

"No, you don't know," he said then licked his lips.

Her gaze flickered to the movement but returned to his eyes, hoping he didn't see the desperation she suddenly felt to also lick his lips.

"Listen," he said in a low tone as he leaned closer. "I was heading down the wrong path even before UGod came for me. I'm not some innocent guy who had to do evil because of his evil father. The guy you thought you knew—,"

"I know you weren't a saint but that day—"

The chair made a screeching sound as Demetrius stood. He kept his head hung low. "Stop," he said. His tone was low and scary. "Don't." He scrubbed his hand over his face then glanced at her. "I'm going to get some coffee."

Giselle watched as Demetrius left her hospital room. As she stared at the empty doorway, she thought of the last night they had together. She thought of how helpless she felt.

SIX

Then 1991 / A week before the Incident...

The past few days at school had been hell. *What does he want from me?* Giselle sighed as she watched the second hand slowly move around the face of her Swatch. Demetrius said nothing to her for an entire week. It was as if all the time they spent together the last couple of months didn't even happen.

They didn't talk much in school. It was as if he didn't want others to know they were a thing. But he usually pulled her into some dark corner or an empty utility room, or under the bleachers to talk or kiss. And when they weren't in school, they hung out and dated like couples do. But four days ago, a man who knew Demetrius' father knew saw them out eating together. Since then, Demetrius had been ignoring her.

Giselle was excited to tell her friends she would be attending Cohen's party when she got the invite a few days ago. Demetrius and Arthur Cohen were friends and she knew he would be here. Maybe they could clear up whatever was wrong. But since she arrived, not only did Demetrius continue to ignore her, he wouldn't even make eye contact. Each time she saw him, she waited with bated breath for him to acknowledge her.

Tonight, his snubbing was unbearable.

Giselle knew now that she was wrong about Demetrius. He was just like all the other guys she'd been warned to stay away from. Her only saving grace was that she never told anyone about them. Not a soul. If Giselle was being honest with herself, she got the sense she was his dirty little secret from the start. If she had told her friends about her and Demetrius, she would have been humiliated tonight.

Giselle rolled her eyes as she looked down into the red cup she held. She couldn't wait for the party to end. The music was loud, she turned down several guys, one of whom kept following her around, and it was hot. Parties weren't her scene, and if she'd known she would be ignored she never would have come.

Giselle frowned as she raised the cup to her lips. She straightened herself up on the wall she was holding up, while watching her rhythm challenged peers dance to Rob Base and E-Z Rock's *It Takes Two*. The song was two years old. She managed another eye roll…

Since she was black, her peers assumed she liked everything urban in regards to culture; but she was raised in the same upper-class suburban world they were raised, and she hated most rap music. She'd known most of these kids for years, attending the same schools and socializing with them, following her father's instructions to blend in with "their" world. But lately she felt as if she stepped into the twilight zone. Over the past year she was befuddled to see how they found "blackness" cool all of a sudden; many of them switched from wearing clothing from Colors of Benneton to wearing Nike shoes and Russell sweat suits.

Well, it wasn't "all of a sudden". She could literally trace the beginning of their flip to "cool blackness"—it started when Demetrius arrived at their school. Then when Carver arrived, the coolness of black culture rose.

"There's some guys here from Inverness High," a guy called from the doorway, his chest heaving. "They're facing off with Carver and Cohen!" The guy then rushed off.

Giselle watched as just about everyone in the billiard room made their way toward the French doors leading to the back patio. Party attendees throughout the house were rushing out of all available exits.

Rolling her eyes again, Giselle decided it was time for her to go. She slowly walked the same path some of her peers did, making her way out of the French doors to the patio and around the house to get to where her Volkswagen was parked on the lawn. As she got closer to the front of the house, she heard raised voices. One that sounded like…

That guy didn't say Demetrius was involved, but she knew his voice. It was him.

Before she knew it, Giselle turned and started pushing through the crowd. When she reached the perimeter the crowd made, she gasped at what she saw. There was an all-out brawl between the two groups, and in the center was Demetrius standing over a guy. He had a wad of the guy's hair fisted in his hand, holding the guy's head up as he beat him in the face. Even though he was on his knees, Giselle could tell the guy was huge, bigger than Carver. But Demetrius, who was muscled but slim, was demolishing this guy's face.

A flash of light flickered off Demetrius' fist when he raised it then brought it down hard on the guy's face one last time before he released his grip and let the guy fall to the concrete. The look on Demetrius' face was one she'd seen before. It was the one she feared.

"Look out," Giselle called out.

Demetrius turned just in time to see a guy rush him, knocking them both to the ground. Giselle saw the streetlight glimmer off something metal that clanged to the ground and slid toward her. She hurried forward to pick it up but was knocked back and off her feet. She barely got a glimpsed the red headed guy with an Inverness hat who pushed her.

"Giselle," someone called out.

She fell back so hard she bit her tongue when her ass hit the ground. Stunned, she blinked several times. She focused on the metal thing again then reached for it and pulled it closer just as someone grabbed her under her arms from the back and pulled her to her feet.

Her gaze fell on Demetrius again. The guy who rushed him was lying flat on his face and Demetrius and Carver were stomping the red headed guy who knocked her down, with their big heavy brown boots.

That must hurt, she thought as she caught sight of the tree emblem that was burned onto the side of his boots. The blood on them was going to be hard to get out. Why she would think of the cleanliness of his boots right now was odd, but she reasoned that this might be her way of calming herself.

"Five-O!"

Several people started yelling that the cops were coming, then Giselle heard the sirens.

"Come on, girl."

Turning in the direction she was being pulled, Giselle looked at the person who had hold of her. "Krysta?" she said in amazement.

"Demi told me you were crazy, but I thought that mall shit was a fluke," Krysta said. She pushed panicked teens who were scurrying on the lawn to their cars out of their way.

"He told you about that?" Giselle asked, surprised.

Krysta looked over her shoulder at Giselle and rolled her eyes.

"My cousin tells me everything. Never ever get in the middle of a fight Demi is in again. You could distract him. And if you got hurt…" Krysta sighed. She faced forward and pushed through the people until they came to Demetrius' black Cherokee. Krysta opened the passenger door and ushered Giselle inside.

"I wasn't trying to get in the middle," Giselle said, holding up the heavy metal object. It was kind of oval shaped with five openings. If she stretched her fingers, they'd fit through the five holes and her palm fit over the oval circle.

Krysta stared at her for several seconds before snatching the metal object out of her hands. "He can't be with you, Giselle. He—"

A loud whistle caught the attention of them both, and effectively cut Krysta's words short. Krysta sighed then closed the passenger side door.

Giselle looked through the windshield and saw Demetrius jogging up to Krysta. The two talked. He glanced at Giselle then looked at the metal object Krysta held up between them. He took the metal thing, did some handshake thing with Krysta, then jogged to driver's side and pulled the door open.

Demetrius didn't even speak to Giselle when he got inside and started the truck. He just drove forward, kicking up grass and dirt on Arthur's lawn. Demetrius turned the steering wheel to the left, then right before speeding off down the long driveway. All the while he pressed his horn and barely avoided hitting other escaping teens in their cars with his truck.

Demetrius drove his truck over the curb and onto the street, heading in the opposite direction of the police cars with their lights flashing and sirens blaring.

"Wait, my car is back there, park on Arthur's lawn."

Demetrius chuckled. "You mean Cohen's lawn?"

"They didn't start calling Arthur by his last name until you did," she said, rolling her eyes.

Demetrius turned onto a main road and took the on-ramp that would put them on the highway.

"Where are you taking me?" she asked, looking at him.

"To my place."

Giselle frowned. The excitement of being with Demetrius was overshadowed by her independent streak. "You can't just take me somewhere without asking, Demetrius."

70

Demetrius glanced over at her then put on his turn signal and slowed a bit. He eased the truck onto the emergency lane and put it in park. "Will you go to my place with me?" *Wow.* He was so confusing.

"Why?" she asked him.

"Why?" he asked, sounding confused.

"Why do you want me to go to your place?"

"Please," Demetrius said.

Giselle sighed. She was a fool. A pathetic fool. "Whatever," she said, flipping her hand at him then crossing her arms over her chest.

Giselle slowly walked inside the apartment, ahead of Demetrius who held the door open for her. It wasn't big or even all that nice. If she were being honest, it was far from the lavish lifestyle they both were accustomed.

She stood in what was apparently the foyer, dining room, and sitting room all at once. There was a small counter that separated the tiny kitchen from the rest of the apartment. A small table with four chairs was straight ahead, and to her left was a living room set that looked to be leather. The sofa set looked pricey.

There were no pictures on the bare white walls, but blinds covered a small kitchen window and what she thought was a sliding patio door in the sitting room area. A gaming console sat on a coffee table and the wires for the controllers were sitting out for someone to trip over. Also, on the table were what looked like cigars and a lighter.

Does Demetrius smoke?

The sound of the door closing behind her caused Giselle to jump and whip her head around. Demetrius chuckled as he walked up to her and took her hand.

"You're still scared of me," he said with amusement as he led her toward the narrow hallway.

Giselle wouldn't deny it. He was right. She was scared of him, but not in the way he thought. She nibbled her lip as

Demetrius led her past a closed door and a bathroom. He stopped in front of another closed door. Turning the knob, he pushed open the door but Giselle peered over her shoulder at the one they passed. Unlike the door he just opened with a turn of the knob, that door had a bolt lock securing it.

"What's in there?" she asked, pointing to the door behind them. Giselle turned her head to look at him.

Demetrius starred at her for a moment. Then he let go of her hand and dug into his jeans pocket. He pulled out a key ring with only a few keys on it. He walked back down the hall and unlocked the door, turned the knob, and pushed it open. Demetrius held his hand out, presenting the room to her.

Giselle walked toward him. When she was in front of the room, she inched inside just past the doorway. Her eyes widened as she took in the contents of the room, a mini arsenal of weapons. There were guns of different sizes, knives, swords, and boxes that she read the caliber of bullets they contained. Then there were the numerous storage bins lined up along the walls.

"What's in the tubs?" she heard herself ask. Only she wasn't sure she wanted to know.

"Weed," he told her.

Giselle looked over her shoulder at him. He said it was weed so nonchalantly. "You say it as if having a war room and bins full of marijuana in an apartment is normal."

"It is normal…for me." He took her hand again and eased her back and out of the room. He then dropped her hand to relock the door. "So, what do you want to do Angel? Stay with the devil or…" he said turning to face her, "or I can take you to your car. But you leave me, you can never look back."

Giselle peered into his eyes. She felt in her soul that he meant what he just said, but the question was, *did she want to walk away from him*. Could she? In the short time they'd been together, even with him ignoring her, she didn't want to lose it. She wanted whatever he wanted to give.

It was pathetic. She was pathetic.

With her mind made, she linked her fingers through his. Demetrius led her inside the other room. It was big, almost the size of the spare room in her house, and this room was decorated, unlike the rest of the apartment. The furniture was dark wood, there was a bed with gorgeous coverings, and the curtains looked heavy. He even had a loveseat and floor model television in a little alcove area. There were two closed doors. If she had to guess, one was a closet and the other an ensuite bathroom.

Giselle heard a low vibrating sound. On the drive here, she heard the same sound repeatedly. She watched Demetrius pull out the same kind of black pager she saw doctors use and look at it before pushing it back into his pocket.

"Can I grab you something to drink?"

Giselle shook her head, no. She let go of Demetrius' hand then walked over and sat on the edge of the bed. She watched as he stepped out of his boots, thinking how convenient it must be to step out of them so easily. But she also wondered how he managed to keep them on without losing one throughout the day.

"Come here," he said as he walked to the loveseat. He pulled some things out of his pockets and placed them on the coffee table in front of it then sat back and patted the cushion beside him. The pager went off again, but he glanced at it then dismissively looked away and back at her.

Confused as to why he didn't want to be on the bed, Giselle stood, walked over to the loveseat, and sat beside him. She turned to Demetrius. When she realized he was watching her she leaned forward, reached out to the items on the coffee table, and picked up the metal object she had earlier.

"What's this?"

"Brass knuckles," Demetrius said. He plucked them from her grasp then pulled the weapon over his fingers and made a fist. "If you really want to hurt someone in a fight, you use these."

"And you wanted to really hurt that guy?"

"I did."

"Why? What did he do that was worth beating his face in like you did?"

Demetrius took off the brass knuckles and tossed them on the table. "He tried to take something I've worked hard to gain."

When the pager went off again, he picked it up and pressed a button on the side. He placed it back on the table then looked at her.

"Like your turf?"

Demetrius smirked then chuckled. "No, Angel. Respect."

Giselle felt something brush over her fingers. Looking down, she saw and felt Demetrius lay his palm over the back of her hand then link his fingers through hers. She watched as he lazily played with her hand and fingers, tracing patterns she was too mesmerized to decrypt. For a long while she was lost in the rhythm of his touch. Until he lightly trailed his fingers up her arm. That tickled. She giggled, yanking her arm away.

"Ah," he said, smiling. "I've found one of your spots."

Giselle smiled too. She rubbed her inner arm where she was sensitive. "One of my spots?"

"One day I'm going to study every inch of you until I find all of your spots, Angel. Then I'm going to start over and over again until I know every inch of you like I know myself."

Giselle felt even more pathetic because she wanted everything he just promised. All of what she was, all of what she had, could be his with little convincing from him, even when she knew he didn't even really like her.

…and knowing what she'd sacrifice for him for nothing in return…it kinda hurt.

She sat back and sighed. "How can you say those things to me now but wouldn't even look my way tonight? You've been totally ignoring me."

"There are things you don't understand."

"Then explain them?"

"It's complicated."

Giselle felt a familiar sting behind her eyes but fought it. She didn't want him to see any more of her weaknesses. But she had to know. "Is that your girlfriend paging you like that?" When he pulled his hand away, Giselle pushed off the sofa. She stared down at him. Her head was pounding. "I was completely lost the day you stepped foot inside Laure. I'm ashamed to admit that I wouldn't have said no tonight if you wanted me…all of me. But it seems you're nothing but a two-timer."

She was ashamed to admit she would have given him her virginity without a promise of forever. But what she hated most was a cheater. Giselle stormed off but didn't make it to the door before being pulled back. Demetrius wrapped his arms around her, holding her tight to him. He rubbed the side of his face over the side of hers.

"You leave me, Angel, you can never look back," he said close to her ear.

Giselle heard his voice crack. Felt the way he held onto her. The way his body trembled. In that moment, she knew that for all his strength and his blasé hard attitude, Demetrius was broken.

"On my life, I want only you," he said. "I want you so damn bad, Giselle. When I look at you sometimes, my chest hurts because I can't have you in all ways I dream of because I'm that grimy nigga you hear about on the news. And I can't be any other way if I want to rise."

"I have to go," she whispered.

"Just one night. Stay. We talk and that's it. Nothing else."

Giselle stepped forward but he held on, stepping with her as if they were glued together.

"I just want normal," he whispered in her ear, "with you...for just one night. Then I will let you go."

SEVEN

Now/**Hospital**

GISELLE

Giselle thought of that night all those years ago many times. How they talked until she fell asleep in his arms. He didn't so much as kiss her that night. They just talked about silly stuff. Stuff she didn't think an eighteen-year-old guy like him would be interested in. Stuff like her morning routine, the foods she liked, and girl gossip.

She woke up in his arms the next morning and he drove her back to her car. After that day, she saw little of Demetrius, and when she did see him, he didn't speak to her. That is, not until she saw him, his father, and his friends at her house the day of the incident.

Giselle relaxed back on the hospital bed and closed her eyes. For some reason she thought Demetrius would have slain his demons, like she had. But he didn't. He still seemed to be that gorgeous broken eighteen-year-old boy she fell hopelessly in love with at first sight without knowing him at all. She'd fallen so hard. And in the short time they shared together, Demetrius branded a lasting impression on her soul that no man could burn away.

Two days later

The sound of footsteps just outside the door to her hospital room alerted Giselle that Demi might be back. She didn't want to upset him again, so she kept her eyes closed and pretended to be asleep.

"Mr. Carrion, we need to talk."

Giselle heard the voice clearly just outside her room because the door was wide open.

"I'm kind of busy detective—"

Detective? He must be here investigating the shooting.

"Tell me," the detective asked, "who is Giselle Johnson? We've found little to nothing on her and she isn't too forthcoming."

When the detective tried to question her, she turned him away with little to no information.

"I'm busy," Demetrius repeated.

"We have her statement, but I can either talk to you or I can go inside that room and talk to her again," the detective said.

"What can I do for you, detective?" Demetrius asked, sounding reluctant.

"Who shot you? And I don't want that 'I don't know' bullshit."

"I truly don't."

"And you don't have any enemies," the detective said but quickly added, "Wait…I forgot; you've killed all your enemies."

Sighing, Demetrius said, "We've been through this before, Monahan. If you can't prove your allegations it's slander. Do I need to call Captain Bishop again?"

"I wonder if that pretty lady in there knows how dangerous you really are. That I suspect you in five unsolved murder cases, one of which you carried out when you were just fifteen years old. Does she know about your father?"

"What you need to be reminded of is that I graduated from Laure Prep with exemplary grades. That I was accepted into one of the most coveted universities in our great country and graduated with honors with a business degree. That a black man from meager means was able to apply himself and build a very profitable company of which I am the CEO," Demetrius said.

"Does she know that one of your lovers was just blown to bits a couple weeks back because of you?"

One of his lovers died?

"You…should leave," Demetrius said, his voice low.

She knew that was a threat. Demetrius' words sounded calm, too calm. A person who didn't know him would think nothing of them, but Giselle knew him.

"This isn't over," the detective said, then added, "DemiGod."

"You say you know me detective. If you truly know me," Demetrius said, his tone even more low and very measured, "then you should want *this* to be over."

Giselle didn't hear any closure to the conversation, but a few seconds passed before she heard what she assumed were Demetrius' footsteps as he entered the room. Giselle kept her eyes closed but relaxed, feigning sleep.

The bed sank some right before she felt a hand caress her right brow then down the side of her face. It was hard to keep her eyes closed and her face relaxed, but she managed. Soon, his touch was gone. Giselle opened her eyes, seeing that Demetrius had left.

If he knew what I had to overcome to get back to him.

Five days after the shooting...

DEMI

Shifting to his side in the chair, Demi rubbed his bent leg then stretched it out in front of him. The tingle running up his foot had him sitting up and wiggling his toes in his boots. He was getting to his feet when he heard a light tap before the door was pushed open and the doctor came inside.

"How are you faring, Mr. Carrion?"

"I'm healing up just fine." Demi shook the hand the doctor offered. "How is she doing?"

The doctor looked around him to Giselle. "She's doing good enough to be released today but you have to keep an eye on her. If the site of the stitches starts to show redness or pus, if she experiences extreme pain, or the site seems to darken, she needs to return. I'm prescribing her something for pain, but if she prefers, she can use over the counter pain meds. Keep her wound clean and dry and she should be fine. The nurse will be in with the discharge papers, some after-care instructions, and the prescription."

"Thank you," Demi said, shaking the man's hand again.

Just as the doctor stepped out of the room, Cassiel came running inside with his head down. He stopped inches away from Demi and looked up. The kid's eyes were full of hope and he had the biggest smile on his face as he raised his head. With a blink of his eyes, all of that faded and he looked down.

"Hello," Cassiel said as he backed up a step.

Krysta came walking in at that moment. Cassiel had been staying with her for the past five days while Demi virtually lived between the hospital's lobby and Giselle's room. Demi and Krysta looked at each other for a moment before she tilted her head. He knew she wanted him to respond to Cassiel in a fatherly way. He and his cousin had a few conversations on the subject, and he knew exactly how she thought he should regard the boy.

Demi patted Cassiel on the head like he'd seen Giselle do. His movements were stiff and a little slow. "You have fun with Krysta today?"

Cassiel took another step back and nodded. "She let me watch action movies and gave me popcorn and soda last night," Cassiel said with a smile. He walked around Demi and over to the bed then turned back and looked at Krysta. "Mom's still sleep. Can I go to that store?"

"He's talking about the gift shop downstairs," Krysta said, holding her hand out. "We'll be back."

"Bye, dad," Cassiel said to Demi as he moved around him and took Krysta's hand.

Demi raised his hand and waved. He slipped his hand inside his sweatpants and stood there, staring at the empty doorway for several seconds. When he turned around, Giselle was sitting up and watching him.

"I can tell him not to call you that."

So far, Demi managed to keep their conversations about personal stuff limited. She mostly slept during these past five days, and he made a concerted effort to keep his distance from Giselle even though he rarely left the hospital. This definitely wasn't the place for this discussion, but he did need some answers.

"How is it that he knows us? Carver said that Cassiel recognized him and Krysta."

"I wanted him to know about you so, I constantly talked about you and showed him the few pictures of you that I have. I kept the Polaroids from the carnival you took me to, and I had my yearbooks. As he got older, he asked more questions about you and about your life. I told him what I knew."

Demi shifted from one foot to the other as a hint of doubt scratched at the back of his mind. "And you're sure I'm his father?"

Giselle nodded. "I swear to you that I've never been with anyone before—"

"And after?" Demi asked, cutting her off.

"For years after," she admitted, looking down. For a few seconds, she watched her hands that rested on her lap then looked up at him. "It's alright if you want a paternity test."

To her credit, Giselle didn't seem upset about his questions. Her dark eyes showed nothing but what he thought was understanding.

"Look, you're being released," Demi told her, changing the subject. "I don't want you going back to that motel. I'd like you to consider coming home with me." He watched Giselle's eyes widen. "At least until I can put you up in someplace more permanent. I mean," he rubbed his head, "we do have a lot to discuss."

"The motel is fine, really. Plus, I have to settle up with them. I don't want to uproot your life, Demetrius."

"I've taken care of the bill and had your things moved," he told her.

"I almost got you killed. If you would have got into the car instead of trying to save me, you wouldn't have been shot. I just...I just wanted to give you the opportunity to know Cass."

"You need to know that the shooting is just one of two recent attempts on my life in the past couple of weeks. It is probably safer for the two of you to be as far away from me as possible, but I don't want you both out in this city without my protection."

"I don't want to make things uncomfortable for you and your girlfriend if we stay with you?"

Did she hear me?

Demi shook his head. "Giselle," he said, "the shooting wasn't random."

"Demetrius," Giselle said as she pushed aside the sheets that covered her legs, "I've accepted who you are a long time ago." She rolled her IV pole past him and over to the wardrobe chest. "I believe you will keep us safe. Now, I have to get dressed."

"Ms. Johnson," a nurse said with enthusiasm as she walked into the room and placed some papers and a medical packet on the bedside table, "I'm here to remove your IV!"

Demi watched as Giselle sat back on the bed and held out her arm and smiled. He was still reeling over her response to him asking her to stay at his home. That she seemed to not blame him and was willing to trust him with her and Cassiel's safety.

This woman…

She had a habit of trusting him even though he seemed to be the orchestrator of her ruin. Even though he was the one who clipped her wings…

The Incident

Then1991

Demi squeezed his eyes closed and hissed a curse under his breath when he heard the front doorknob rattle. He knew who was coming through the door before he saw the door slowly being pushed open and her stepping over the threshold. Aside from Mrs. Johnson, who sat on the sofa crying, no one made a sound as Hines, one of UGod's henchman, pulled Giselle inside the house and slammed the door shut.

Giselle gasped as she stumbled forward. Her gaze found Demi's and her bright eyes widened as if she was shocked that he was inside her home.

Demi fisted his hands and forced himself to stay still, but he relaxed them on either side of his legs when she righted herself and didn't fall on her face. He watched while Giselle looked around her living room. Her questioning gaze fell on her parents, but when they said nothing, she looked to Demi again. He got the sense she wasn't scared at all, but she should be terrified because everyone else in the room knew UGod was a stone-cold killer.

A glance around told Demi that no one but Krysta and Carver, his two-man crew, who were nearby, were paying attention to him. So, he felt comfortable openly watching Giselle from across the room. Her long thick dark hair was pulled into a tight single side ponytail. The beige pleated skirt she wore appeared crisp and clean, her long gray socks were pulled up over her knees, and the gray vest she wore over her white shirt was still buttoned up. After a long day at school in her uniform, she was still put together as if her day was just starting.

Giselle's physical beauty was apparent, but her innocence was also obvious to Demi; just as it was as soon as he laid eyes on her on his first day at Laure Prep. She was a nice girl. Too nice to be in this situation, but it seemed her father was a thief.

"Go to your room, Giselle," Mr. Johnson said, finally speaking up.

Demi knew it was too late for that, and by the look of interest on UGod's face…

"Stay where you are, sweetheart," UGod said to Giselle then he looked at Mr. Johnson. "You know what I think, Alex? I think your girl will do so much better than your wife."

"Please, don't do this," Mrs. Maria, Giselle's mom, begged.

Demi looked over at the woman from where he sat on the countertop in the kitchen. He met with the Johnsons a few times because Mr. Johnson was his father's accountant. Demi also sat in on meetings between the two men occasionally. He saw Mrs. Johnson more sporadically, and it was usually when UGod threw a party.

The fucked-up part about this situation was the Johnsons wouldn't even be in this mess today if UGod didn't ask Demi to go over the numbers a few days ago. When he did, Demi found some discrepancies. He checked the numbers three times and they just weren't adding up.

"Carlos, uh…Mr. Carrion, I'm sorry. I just… I had something come up. I didn't think you would miss the money before I had time to put it back. I can have the money for you tomorrow. I promise. Please."

What a fucking idiot. Demi stared at Mr. Johnson. *Why didn't UGod just kill the sleaze outside the man's office or somewhere away from his family and be done with it?*

But Demi knew what UGod would say to that.

"If I kill everyone who owes me money," Demi thought, using UGod's tone, *"then how will I ever get paid?"*

"You knew who I was when you blooded the contract," UGod said as he casually walked toward Giselle and held out his hand. "Giselle, sweetheart? Do you know who I am?"

Demi hated that tone UGod used with Giselle, above all the others. This particular one usually signaled that there would be no compromising.

"Ye…" she started but her voice faded as she glanced over at her parents.

Giselle knew exactly who UGod and the Congregation were. Carlos 'UGod' Carrion was one of the biggest crime lords in the city, and unfortunately the bastard happened to be his father.

"Yes," Giselle finally said.

Demi cringed as he watched Giselle slowly turn and begin to walk toward UGod.

"Take me…not my daughter, please!" Mrs. Johnson cried.

Demi noticed that Giselle's coward of a father lowered his head and wouldn't even look at her. Yet, her mother's sobs grew louder. There was no reason Giselle's mother needed to be present for this. "Take Mrs. Johnson to her bedroom," Demi ordered.

Giselle glanced over at Demi before turning her attention to her mother. She stopped walking but UGod waved her forward, gaining her attention again.

Without hesitation, Hines walked over and pulled Mrs. Johnson to her feet. She began to scream and fight, but Hines punched her in the face, knocking the woman out cold.

Giselle gasped and stopped in her tracks again as she watched Hines sling her mother over his shoulder and carried her toward the stairs that went to the second floor.

Hines would stay with her until they left to make certain she didn't leave the room. Demi made a mental note to have a talk with Hines later.

"You are such a beautiful young lady," UGod told Giselle as he closed the distance between them instead of waiting on her to come to him. He took her by the hand and led her over to stand in the center of the living room in front of the sofa. "Sweetheart, your father stole money from me. I won't bog you down with details except to say that he should have known better."

"Mr. Carrion, please. Just let me make a phone call. I'll have what I took here in an hour. Just let me use the phone."

"Krysta, the foot please," UGod's said. His tone was deceptively calm.

Krysta, Demi's cousin and a part of his personal crew, didn't hesitate, because just like him, she was being molded to take over the family business. She pulled her gun out and shot immediately; the silencer on her gun muffled the sound effectively, but Mr. Johnson's cries of pain seemed to shake the foundation of the house.

Giselle shrieked but quickly covered her mouth. Her entire body shook now.

There is her fear.

Demi wondered when she would start to show it, but it took her mother being punched and her father being shot in the foot.

Mr. Johnson made an effort to quiet down when he realized UGod was watching him with narrowed eyes.

Giselle's eyes were as wide as saucers now. She took three steps back in an attempt to get away from UGod.

"No, no dear, we're not done here." UGod latched his hand around her upper arm and pulled her to him.

A familiar sounding low tap caught Demi's attention. He turned to look to his left and saw Carver watching him from where he stood. Carver blinked at him, slowly. Demi looked down and realized he slid down from sitting on the counter and had moved a few steps away from it. He looked up and saw that Krysta noticed too, indicated by the unmistakable warning aflame in her eyes. Demi forced himself to step back until he was leaning on the counter.

"You see, Giselle," UGod continued as he tossed her onto an upholstered chair. "You're going to help your father. Get him an extension of sorts as well as let him know I don't play with my money. Of course, you can refuse. I'll just kill him and eat the loss." UGod shrugged as if killing a man meant nothing to him. "So, will you help your dear old dad live another day, dear?"

Lies, Demi hissed the word inside his head. He knew UGod's method of operation. He knew all too well the way the man tortured and intimidated people. He knew that no matter how much his father's victims begged or cried, when that monster decided something there was no changing his mind. He also knew that if Giselle refused UGod, her father wouldn't be the only death today. She and her mother would be killed too. UGod was famous for not giving his victims full disclosure.

Giselle silently cried. She nodded several times, as if she had to convince UGod and herself that she would do whatever it took to save her father's life.

"This is one of many lessons life will teach you, dear," UGod told Giselle. He looked to Carver. "Carver, will you handle this transaction please."

Demi watched as Giselle looked up and gasped when Carver pushed off the wall where he lazily stood.

Carver was a big dude. He played on their varsity high school team at Laurie Prep and already had professional football teams interested. The guy was a beast, and though he was handsome, Carver gave off a dangerous vibe and kinda looked it too.

Carver glanced at Demi before he placed the half-eaten apple he'd taken from the fruit basket on the table, then leisurely shrugged off his jacket.

"I'll handle it." Demi moved forward, out of the shadows of the kitchen.

He and UGod stared at each other as Demi approached. Demi knew the importance of this moment. He also knew it was vital that he didn't look away first.

UGod gave a hint of a smile before he looked away. "Carver," he said as he glanced at Mr. Johnson's bleeding foot, "Demi will handle this one. Can you get Mr. Johnson a towel please?" UGod walked away from Giselle and took a seat beside her father on the sofa, patting the stupid bastard on the leg.

UGod didn't seem to care that they were about to destroy Mr. Johnson's and his daughter's entire world. The messed-up part of it all was Demi couldn't help her get out of it. All he could do was soften the blow, sort of. And he tried so hard to keep her from this part of his world.

You can do this. This was going to happen once she came through the front door. *She might get past this, she might not, but she'll be alive.*

Giselle looked terrified when Demi reached for her hand, but she didn't refuse him. She wobbled as he pulled her to him, so he gripped her forearm to hold her steady. "Take me to your bedroom," he told her.

Acting as if they weren't acquainted was vital as well. UGod loved destroying what Demi liked, what he loved.

"Here," UGod ordered.

It was an order. As far as Demi knew, no one ever refused a direct order and lived.

There was no point in prolonging it. The act he had to commit gave him no pleasure. Demi felt like shit as he stared into the most naïve, interesting pair of brown eyes he ever had the pleasure of looking into.

Sighing, Demi nodded.

Mr. Johnson's cries grew but he didn't move or speak. The man was smart enough to know if he did the next bullet would be in his head, or even worse, the bullet would be for his wife or daughter.

Giselle looked over her shoulder at her father. Tears streamed from her beautiful eyes.

If only Mr. Johnson didn't get greedy.

If only UGod didn't have him check the books.

If only the Giselle hadn't walked through the door a few minutes after they arrived, it would have been her mother in this position and not her.

I wouldn't have felt compelled to involve myself if you'd stayed away, he thought as he grabbed hold of her hand and pulled her along. Now, she was the main attraction.

Demi stopped when her sobbing grew louder. He turned, reached for her chin, and moved her head with his fingers and thumb to face him. "Look at me, forget them," he said to her. She stared at him with those teary huge brown eyes of hers. What he saw in them as she nodded was acceptance.

Fuck, Demi thought as he pulled Giselle to him, causing her to suck in a gasp. He whispered in her ear so that only she could hear him as he walked her into the kitchen. "Don't let what happens here define who you are, Angel."

He felt her body go rigid as he placed his hands around her waist, but Demi lifted her up on the sturdy wooden dining table anyway. He had her so that her back was to everyone and they were eye to eye. Her empty kitchen was all she could see if she looked past him.

Demi heard the low sound of music then noticed the headphones around Giselle's neck. He lifted one side of the headphones and leaned into her, holding the cushioned earpiece to one of his ears and listened. Demi knew the song well.

90

"Listen to your music and keep your eyes on me, alright."
He lifted and put the headsets over her ears.
Giselle nodded again as she stared at him.

The sound of Hines stomping down the stairs seemed to wake Demi from a trance. He fastened his pants, turned away from Giselle and walked to the kitchen sink. He switched on the faucet, pumped soap onto his palms, and started to scrub. He dried his hands with a disposable paper towel as he walked past Giselle who still sat on the dining room table. He avoided looking at her as he pushed away all thoughts of what he'd just done and walked toward the front door.

He couldn't bear to look at the Angel whose wings he just ripped off. Demi also avoided looking at Mr. Johnson who sat on the sofa with his head in his hands. If he saw the man's face, that sorry-ass thieving coward's face, he might just shoot him in it.

Krysta said nothing when he motioned with a flick of his hand for her to lead the way. She opened the door before he reached it and stepped outside while holding the door for Demi and Hines, who brought up the rear.

Carver stretched his lips in a tight grimace as he opened the rear passenger side door for Demi. No matter how tough the guy looked, he had a gentle side for women and children. Demi knew his friend was affected just as much as he was by the shit that went down just now.

Demi stopped. He just remembered he wanted to talk to Hines. The fucker knew how he felt about women being brutalized unnecessarily, or even necessarily. Demi turned around and punched Hines in the nose. He heard the crunch that indicated a break, and a small sense of satisfaction seeped into the darkness that was swallowing him. It wasn't enough to wipe away what he just had to do, but he knew nothing ever would.

Hines narrowed his eyes but said nothing as he wiped at the blood that trickled from his nose.

Demi handed him the used paper towels he still held, then slid inside the car beside UGod. He didn't look over at his father, who took Carver and left the house soon after the performance began.

"Have Carver drive you to the clinic in the other car," UGod said dismissively to Hines when the man moved to get inside the vehicle.

Without a word, Hines walked to the other car, so Demi closed the door.

When Krysta climbed inside the car's front passenger seat, their driver pulled out of the parking pad on the Johnson's property.

"Mr. Johnson?" UGod asked as he flicked his cigarette out of the window then rolled it up.

Demi didn't respond. He couldn't trust what might come out of his mouth. So, he turned and looked past the seat where Krysta sat and watched the world outside through the windshield as they drove. A world he never truly felt a part of.

"Demi informed him that he had two days to settle or his wife dies," Krysta told UGod.

"Two?" UGod said, frowning.

From the way his skin crawled, Demi knew that his father was staring at him, waiting for an answer.

"Was the girl's virtue not worth a week, son?" UGod asked him, plainly.

The son of a bitch.

"I wanted to keep him motivated?" Demi responded, as if bored.

UGod patted Demi on the shoulder. "Well said. Today you've made me proud to call you son."

EIGHT

Now

DEMI

Demi took his cellphone out of his pocket as he walked into the hallway and dialed. "Yeah, Carver. Find anything you can on that license plate?" His talk with the detective told Demi that Monahan would rather see him fry than investigate the murder of Sasha and the new attempt on his life.

"On it," Carver said with a bit too much excitement.

Demi sighed as he disconnected the call. He needed to find out who was out for his blood, and he needed to find out now before Giselle and Cassiel were targeted. Looks like Carver would get what he wanted.

Easing inside just past the doorway, Demi moved to his right to let Cassiel see into the room. He didn't say anything but opted to wait for the kid's response. So, he watched Cassiel enter and walk to the center of the room and spin slowly around.

"Whose room is it?" Cassiel asked. He traced his fingers over the bedspread then the birch wood nightstand.

He doesn't like it.

Demi hoped Cassiel would like it, but then again, he didn't know anything about what a young boy would want nowadays.

"It's your room if you want it," Demi said. He slipped his free hand into his pocket and rocked back on his feet. "We can redecorate of course. Get you the things you like and change the colors."

"How long can I keep it?" Cassiel looked over at Demi as he turned and sat just on the edge of the full-size bed.

Demi's lip twitched and a partial smile played at his lips. "How long do you want it?"

Cassiel's expression became guarded as he looked away.

"What's the matter?" Demi asked. He placed Cassiel's duffel bag on the floor then walked over and sat down on the edge of the bed, but not too close to Cassiel.

"Mom says we probably can't stay long. That you might have a family and they may not be happy with us coming here," Cassiel said.

"Did you see anyone else here but us?" Demi asked.

"No." Cassiel's tone picked up and he raised his head, his face showing cautious hope.

"That's because I live alone."

Cassiel turned to look at the spacious room again. "I never had my own room. Me and mom always shared back home; and when we moved in with Walter, I had to sleep on the sofa. I always wanted my own bed." He focused on Demi again.

"The room is yours," Demi said. He didn't miss the way Cassiel flinched when he said the Walter guy's name.

"Thanks," Cassiel said as he looked away.

Demi smirked, seeing that the kid was hiding a smile. "You want to help me cook dinner?"

Cassiel's entire demeanor changed. His eyes grew brighter. "You cook?" Excitement and a bit of awe were evident in his voice.

Demi stood up just as his cell phone vibrated in his pants pocket. He pulled the device out and glanced at the text. Apparently, his associates were restless enough to contact his personal phone. They were obviously restless from not hearing from him since he lost Sasha.

Good, he thought as he slipped the cell phone back into his pocket. They needed to be on edge.

"Of course," Demi responded as he turned his attention back to Cassiel. "A man should know how to cook," he said. Demi reached out to rub Cassiel's head but stopped in midair, considering the kid may not like that kind of thing. Instead, he patted Cassiel on the shoulder, urging him forward. "I make a pretty good steak."

Cassiel and Demi walked down the hallway, passing a bathroom and the laundry room. They descended the stairs side by side, so Demi saw the grimace Cassiel had on his face.

"How about spaghetti then?" Demi asked as he led Cassiel into the gourmet kitchen.

Cassiel looked up at Demi and smiled. "With big meatballs?"

"Only if you roll them for me."

"Okay!" Cassiel swiped his hands over the marble countertop as if clearing his workspace. "I'm going to make ginormous ones!"

GISELLE

Seeing Demetrius and Cassiel in the kitchen, cooking together and laughing like they've known each other for years, was so close to how she dreamed it would be. Almost.

"I have to ask," Krysta said, sitting on the chair beside the sofa, "what's your end game here? Do you think to use Cassiel to get revenge on Demi?"

"Why…?" Giselle started then furrowed her brows. "I just want—"

"Demi to know his son," Krysta repeated what Giselle told her previously, then raised her brow. "Ok, let me lay this," Krysta used her finger to draw a circle in the air, "out for you. Demi has been through a lot and hasn't broken. I won't allow you to use that sweet boy in there to break him."

"I wouldn't ever use my son against his father."

"I hope you mean that," Krysta said, leaning in closer to her, "because I don't want to hurt you, but I will."

"Understood," Giselle said. She wanted to ask Krysta why she never liked her but asking might hint at weakness and she didn't want them thinking she was weak. *Any* of them.

Krysta peered at Giselle intently for several seconds without speaking; then she seemed to make up her mind about something and said, "Good. So, why did you wait so long to bring us Cassiel?"

"After that day," Giselle sighed, "my mother left my father and we went to Florida where my uncle lives. She talked to the administration at Laure Prep and they agreed to allow me early graduation. At that time, I was still working through my anger and humiliation of what happened the day Cass was conceived. I wanted to contact Demetrius and tell him, but I also hated what he did to me. By the time Cass was born, I was feeling less angry and started remembering how I felt about Demetrius before that day.

"But I let my mother convince me that we needed to take Cass to visit my Nana in Barbados. I hadn't gone in a while; I didn't know when I would be able to go in the future because everything changed for us financially when we left my dad." Giselle's face brightened with a smile. "I was so proud of my son when I brought him into the world, and I wanted my Nana to see him before she was too ill to appreciate her great-grandson. Only, once we got there, my mother refused to give me the money to return. She convinced anyone who could help me that I was crazy and to not aid me in any way to get back to the U.S."

Giselle remembered the hate reflected in her mother's eyes whenever the topic of Demetrius being a part of their son's life came up.

Then1992

Giselle placed the stack of small onesies inside the duffle bag beside the pile of her shirts. She stuffed in some receiving blankets next, some bibs, then baby booties. Twisting, she stretched her hand out and grabbed some cloth diapers and pins off the small shelf she used for baby stuff and squeezed them inside the bag too.

"Where do you think you're going?"

Giselle ignored her mother. She zipped up the bag then walked around the end of her bed to her bookshelf. She took her keepsake box off her 1989 and 1990 Laure Preparatory yearbooks and placed it on her bed close to where her two-month-old newborn son Cassiel slept on his belly.

She fingered through the few Polaroids she had of Demetrius before placing them in the bag. Othello, the book she kept after seeing he signed it out of the school's library before she did, was next. And finally...

"Where are they, momma? Give them to me!" she yelled.

Cassiel jerked his arm out at the sound of her yelling but she reached over and gently rubbed his back, coaxing him back to sleep.

"You must be mad if you think I'll allow you to go to that animal, Giselle Aniela Johnson," Maria hissed. "To take my grandson to those corrupt demons."

"It's his son too, momma," Giselle said. "He deserves to know he has a son."

"Only an honorable man should know of such a sweet boy. He isn't honorable. He doesn't deserve anything from you. He and his evil father took enough from us. They can't have our child too."

Giselle lifted Cassiel and placed him gently in his bassinet sitting beside her bed. She rushed past her mother and out of her bedroom.

"*My* son!" Giselle yelled as she ran down the hall. She passed her grandmother who rushed to Maria's side.

Once inside her mother's bedroom, Giselle stood in the doorway trying to decide where her mother might have hidden her passport and other important papers. She rushed forward, dodging her mother's grasp. She went to the nightstand and pulled open the drawer. She pushed items around, searching.

"I allowed you to name Cassiel after him, isn't that enough?" Maria asked.

"No!" Giselle sat on the edge of her mother's bed. She looked over at her mother and grandmother. "We are moving out today, Momma, and eventually I am taking Cass home."

They didn't understand. No one understood. After that day, after what he did, she was brokenhearted, hurt, and mortified. And when she found out that she was carrying Cassiel, she thought about ending it all. Her life and her son's. It was her mother and grandmother who convinced her that her son was a blessing regardless of the circumstances of his conception. Eventually Giselle agreed, and while she was carrying her son, when she felt him move for the first time, her first thought was how she wished she could share the moment with Demetrius.

She wanted to share her happiness with her child's father. After that, she thought long and hard about that day and what happened. She played each moment back in her head as if she was watching a movie, and she scrutinized it frame by frame. She matched it all with what Demetrius told her about his father and realized that the situation they were in couldn't have gone any other way.

Well, actually…it could have been worse.

Now

Giselle rubbed her hands together as she felt the same sting of frustration she felt when she was held a virtual captive by her mother. All the years she was stuck in Barbados, she tried to share with her son any tidbits she knew about Demetrius, but it wasn't as if she knew a lot. They technically only spent a small amount of time together.

She sighed then smoothed her hands over the blanket she had stretched out on the sofa to cover her legs. "If I wanted to return, I had to pay my way, so I got a job doing laundry and cleaning. The pampered life I lived before getting pregnant led me to foolishly believe that I could quickly make what I needed and leave. Reality was a wakeup call. When I finally managed to save enough money just to leave my grandmother's house, because caring for us both left little for saving, I discovered my mother had hidden our passports. That day I moved out and into a small room. After paying bills and caring for Cass, years passed before I got to where I could afford the cost to travel. I've been back in the U.S. for four months, here in the city for three weeks."

"Honestly," Krysta said, leaning back, "I can't say I wouldn't have pulled the same mess if I were your mother."

"She kept reminding me of how ruthless Mr. Carrion is. How he would ruin Cass once he got his hands on him."

"But you still came…" Krysta's words faded as she furrowed her brows and stared at Giselle. "Oh damn, you've never stopped loving Demi."

Giselle gasped as she looked over to the kitchen to see if Demetrius heard Krysta. His back was partially turned to her as he was showing their son something on the stove. When she looked back to Krysta, she frowned then looked down at her hands.

"Wow," Krysta said, opening her mouth in a wide O while widening her eyes. "Three months and you were hooked for life."

Giselle raised her eyes but not her head. "It was more like four months."

"Hey, don't get all sensitive. My cousin seems to have that effect on women." Krysta shook her head a few times before lifting her drink to her lips.

"Like the one who recently passed?" Giselle looked up at Krysta and immediately regretted the question.

Krysta's eyes widened briefly before she grimaced.

"I'm sorry," Giselle said. "Forget I brought it up."

"You should know that Demi loved Sasha. We all did," Krysta added, "but their relationship wasn't what you think. Sasha and Demi's relationship was strictly business, and no matter how badly she wanted to make it more, Demi never allowed it. There are lines Demi won't cross."

By the thoughtful look on her face, Giselle knew the woman wasn't done.

"One of our friends was in love with Sasha. She didn't feel the same and they never got together. Eventually, our friend realized nothing was going to happen between him and Sasha so he moved on and eventually got married." Krysta shrugged. "But that didn't matter to Demi. For him, Sasha was off limits for eternity."

"Did he want to…though?"

Krysta twisted her perfectly plum colored lips and said, "I truly don't know." She rolled her eyes up as if thinking, then shrugged again as she smiled. "If he did, he never told me. He dated other women though. He was no priest. Did you date or did you join a convent?"

Giselle frowned. "I don't think you would find my dating life all that interesting."

Krysta patted the air as she said, "Wait…don't take offense. I am truly curious."

Giselle looked at Krysta for a moment. The woman was a beauty. Had always been a beauty. Krysta didn't act like most girls and that fact, Giselle thought, turned off some of their peers in high school, both girls and guys. It appeared that Krysta didn't seem to mind though. She spent most of her time with Demetrius, Carver, and Arthur; but now, looking at her, Giselle wondered if she did mind.

"I dated but it seems I attract a certain type, and not all of them were nice." Giselle looked away from Krysta's penetrating gaze then down at her hands.

"Did some asshole put his hands on Cass?" Krysta demanded in a hushed tone.

Giselle looked up to see that Krysta's body language had changed from relaxed to ready-to-pounce. She knew Krysta liked Cass, she accepted him whole-heartedly as her cousin. Giselle was so grateful the woman took responsibility for her son just about the entire time she was laid up in the hospital. Demetrius didn't seem ready and that was alright, considering. That Krysta cared for Cass from the start was endearing.

"No! Why would you think that?"

"You looked at him after you said that some were not nice."

"No man has ever touched my son. I would never allow that." Giselle frowned, but when she realized Krysta's eyes were still on her, still seemingly searching for something, Giselle broke eye contact again.

"But they hit you?" Krysta asked.

Giselle didn't respond, hoping Krysta would drop it, but the woman wouldn't stop staring at her. "I know what you're thinking. I'm not weak. I…," Giselle started then stopped.

"My mother wasn't a weak woman, but my dad used to hit her. A lot. She always fought back. She protected me as much as she could. She even left him a few times. But he always found her, and she always went back. I think it was because even though he was a tyrant he took care of us, and deep down I think he loved us...in some sick disturbed way. And yet, he still almost killed us during one of his rages."

My god, Giselle thought as she looked at the haunted expression on Krysta's face.

Krysta finished her drink then stood. "I don't think you're weak at all. It takes strength to endure abuse," she stood, "and it takes a lot more to remove yourself from it." She offered up a weak smile.

Those were the nicest words Krysta had ever said to her. Giselle didn't know what to say or how to respond. But Krysta didn't give her a chance either.

"I'm out," Krysta said loudly for all to hear. She tilted her head in a slight nod to Giselle then made her way to the kitchen where her keys and purse sat on the long breakfast bar/counter combination.

"I thought you were staying for dinner," Demetrius said. He glanced over at Giselle, as if looking for a clue as to what happened.

Giselle knew he saw the unshed tears in his cousin's eyes because she certainly had.

"Cass made meatba—" Demetrius started to say, but the sound of the doorbell distracted him.

Krysta lifted her belongings off the counter. "Save me some. I really do have to go. I'll get the door on my way out."

# NINE

KRYSTA

Krysta rushed toward the front door. She couldn't leave fast enough. What she just revealed was why she didn't do the girlfriend thing. Sharing her shit wasn't something she wanted to do, and that's what women did. Men, they were safe. Most didn't share shit or require you to.

Well, some of them didn't.

She pulled the door open and glared at Carver.

"What's wrong?" Carver demanded as he reached out to her.

Krysta leaned back so he couldn't touch her cheek then darted around him. "Nothing," she said as she rushed toward the elevator. She stuck her hand between the closing doors. The elevator doors paused then retracted, allowing her to enter. Krysta pressed the button repeatedly for the doors to close.

As the doors were closing, Carver did the same, sliding his hand in between them. He stared at her with such intensity as he came forward that Krysta began to tremble as she retreated backward. All she saw was his eyes. Eyes that sometimes reminded her of her father's.

"Krysta?" Carver said as he moved closer. "You're shaking like a leaf."

Krysta held up her hand to keep him away as she cowered closer to the elevator wall.

Carver held his hands up and backed up a step. "I would never hurt you," he said, taking another step back.

"Krysta," Demi called to her.

Krysta looked up to see Carver holding the elevator open so that Demi could step inside. She jolted forward and wrapped her arms around Demi. She couldn't hold back the tears anymore. She couldn't hold in the pain.

"I'll take her to her place," she heard Demi say. "Can you go inside with Giselle and Cass, please."

"Yeah, sure," Carver said.

Krysta heard how defeated Carver sounded and the distress in Demi's voice. She didn't want Demi to leave his son. She didn't want to make Carver feel like he scared her. She didn't want any of this.

"It's ok. I have you," Demi said as the bell signaled the elevator doors were closing.

Krysta didn't say anything as Demi opened her apartment door with the key he had. They walked inside with him holding up most of her weight. The floor plan was almost a replica of his penthouse, only she didn't have two stories; she had one bedroom which was located down a long hallway off the kitchen, and one full bath. She also didn't have a raised floor that led to a large L-shaped balcony. Otherwise, her kitchen, living room, office, and powder room were in the exact same places as his.

"I'm sorry," Krysta said as he steadied her. He took her purse and placed it on her breakfast bar/counter. "I don't know what's—"

"Giselle told me what happened."

Krysta looked at Demi while blinking back tears.

"I didn't tell her," Krysta said as she placed her hand on Demi's chest. "I swear, I would never tell anyone about what you did."

Demi took her hand off his chest and held on to it. "This isn't about me. Krysta, maybe you need to talk about your past with someone. Maybe it would help if you did."

"No!"

"You can't keep living like you are. Not letting anyone in, not confiding in anyone, not allowing any man to get—"

Feeling betrayed, she backed away from him. "I thought I had you."

"It's not what I mean and you know it."

Krysta turned her back to Demi. The nerve… "You're one to talk. Who did you talk to, huh? Will you tell your *Angel* all your secrets? Do you think once you do, she'll look at you like she does now?" Krysta hissed.

As soon as the last word left her mouth, Krysta regretted what she said. She covered her mouth as she turned around and watched Demi lower his eyes. She saw how he exhaled, and his shoulders slumped.

"I'm so sorry, Demi," she said as she moved toward him.

"It's alright, Krysta," Demi said, backing away. "Just…just get some rest, ok."

Krysta watched as Demi turned around and walked out of her apartment. The heavy door swung closed behind him. Krysta slowly lowered her hand, still shocked that she said what she said to Demi.

Demi was the only person who knew all her dirt and darkness, yet he still loved and protected her. And…she repaid him with venom.

"Stupid, stupid, stupid," she said to herself as she turned and walked down the hallway toward her bedroom. Krysta slipped out of her shoes then pulled her shirt over her head as she walked into her bedroom, leaving them scattered on the floor behind her. She was sliding her fingers into her skirt to push it down when she heard her front door shut.

Twisting, Krysta reached down past her skirt, raised it up by the hem, slid her stainless-steel reverse serrated blade out of its leather leg strap, and placed both of her hands behind her back.

She waited.

"Krys?"

"Shit," she said, stomping forward. "You can't be here."

Carver stepped into the hallway just as she left the room and rushed toward the kitchen. They almost ran into each other.

"I wanted to check to see if you were ok," Carver said. His eyes grew wide as he moved them over her body.

"Well, as you can see, I'm fine." Krysta slid her blade back into her holster then unstrapped the holster from her upper thigh. "Turn the bottom lock on your way out." She turned her back to Carver and continued her trek to her bedroom. She turned on the lamp beside her bed then placed her holster on the nightstand as she listened for the distinct sound of her front door closing.

"Why do you treat me like this? What happened to us?" Carver asked, sounding too close.

"I'm not in the mood to talk."

"I'm not leaving until you tell me. You act as if I am your enemy. I let it slide, thinking we will be back to normal soon. But no, then you...what happened that night?"

Krysta looked over her shoulder at Carver standing in her bedroom doorway. His hair was different, faded but cut lower than usual. With him standing in front of her, Krysta couldn't help assessing his wide shoulders, well-defined muscles, and narrow waist. When she raised her gaze, meeting his hazel eyes, she felt an instant heat of embarrassment creep over her face. Yet, she couldn't look away. Krysta took a moment to look at him. Her lips twitched as she thought of how his light skin and full lips still reminded her of LL Cool J.

Except, Carver was...Carver.

Sighing, Krysta turned her attention to the nightstand and the knife. She would rather stab him in the hand and take him to the emergency room than explain herself. Feigning ignorance was the weapon she chose though.

"Refresh my memory," she asked flippantly as she opened the top drawer and put the knife and holster inside. Krysta took a hair tie off the nightstand and pulled her shoulder length bobbed hair into a high ponytail. When she didn't hear a response from Carver, she looked over at him.

Carver's brows were knitted as his eyes wondered over her body. She looked down and noticed he was tapping his fingers on his thigh.

"Why are you acting as if you've never seen a woman in a bra before?" she asked as she sat on her bed.

He scrubbed his hand over his face as he looked up to her eyes. "I've never seen *you* in a bra before."

"We used to go swimming all the time. I wore bikinis."

Carver shook his head. "So fucking not the same thing." He walked into the room and leaned back on the wall by the door. "What was that kiss about?"

"I was drunk. Just forget it."

Carver didn't say anything but the look on his face was one she'd never seen. He looked hurt as they stared at each other, her on the bed and him against the wall. Without a word, he pushed off the wall then left her bedroom. Soon after, Krysta heard her front door closing.

"Great!" she yelled. Krysta fell back on her bed and closed her eyes. Now she'd pissed off both the men in her life. One she clung to too much, and the other she was trying to desperately avoid.

"Why did you have to kiss him?" she asked herself out loud. "Why did you even go there?"

If she hadn't gone to Carver's that night, looking for him, she wouldn't have been there when Demi was attacked and Giselle needed her.

Krysta covered her closed eyes with her forearm. With her arm blocking out the light from her lamp, the scene of that night appeared in her mind. She had been restless, still reeling over the loss of Sasha. It was hard for her to make sense of things that day. Her past wouldn't stay buried in her mind, and thoughts of her future of self-imposed solitude kept depressing her. It was Demi she wanted to talk to when she showed up at Carver's that night, but her feet took her to Carver's office instead.

She entered without knocking.

He was sitting on the edge of his desk, looking every ounce of the dangerous man she knew him to be. For a moment, he looked angry as he peered at her from across the room. Instead of leaving when she saw the menace in his hazel eyes which looked green that day, she closed and locked the door behind her. He must have sensed something in her because his scowl was replaced with the familiar desire she often saw burning so brightly in his gaze when he looked at her. Desire that was impossible to misinterpret.

And, instead of running…

"You crossed the room and kissed him," she said in a mocking tone. And… "And it was incredible."

The only reason she didn't go further was the sound of one of his security alerting him that Demi was leaving. God, she wanted to go further. She had the urge to see if all his muscles were large…

"Ugh!" Krysta yelled. Realizing she wanted more from Carver was so damn infuriating.

DEMI

Using his hand to brace the edge of the bedroom door, Demi pulled it shut as softly as he could. He left his hand on the knob for a moment, thinking that maybe he should leave the door cracked for Cassiel instead of closing it all the way. Being here and having a room all to himself was still an adjustment for the kid. So, Demi turned the knob and opened the door a crack.

Demi grabbed the linen he sat on the hallway table earlier, then made his way back downstairs to the living room. When he entered, Giselle seemed to be waiting for him. She looked away as soon as he met her gaze.

"Would you like me to carry you to the room now?" Demi asked.

"No! My legs are fine," Giselle said then frowned. "Besides, I can stay here, on the couch." She reached for the blankets he held.

Demi sat the linen on the arm of the sofa. "I'm not going to argue about this. You get the room for as long as you're here." He sat on the edge of his sturdy coffee table so that he could face her. "Look," he said, "I want to let you know that you don't have to worry about money from now on. You and Cass will be taken care of."

"Demetrius, you've mistaken my intentions. I just want him to know you. No, I don't have much now but once I get situated, we will be fine."

"Cass is my son, right?"

"Of course," she said, "but—"

Demi laid his hand on her thigh. "Then I will care for his needs and yours. You are his mother and I won't see you scraping for change. You just have some decisions to make and I ask that you keep me in mind when you make them."

"Decisions?"

Demi nodded. He pulled his hand back and rested his elbows on his knees and clasped his hands in front of him as he leaned forward. "Like, where you want you and Cass to live. I'm set up here, but I won't be opposed to traveling to visit him if you want me to buy you a house out of state, closer to your relatives. I just ask that you don't move out of the country until he and I bond. You will have to get a valid license if you don't have one? You will have to choose the vehicle you want, furniture, clothing for you both. As for schools, I hope you allow my input if you stay close."

Giselle peered at him with a confused expression on her face. She felt overwhelmed by everything he said. "You would pay for all this for us?"

"You are the mother of my child, Giselle. My only child. I will do what I have to for yours and Cass' comfort."

Giselle smiled then began to chuckle. "She said you would take him from me. That you and your father would take him and never let me see him again. There were rumors that your father took—"

"Your mother?" Demi said, cutting off what he knew she was going to bring up.

Giselle nodded. Why she cast her eyes downward and began to rub her hands, he didn't know.

"I didn't leave her with a good impression of me, so I understand her fears." He reached out with his finger and raised her chin until she was looking at him.

God, she is beautiful.

"I understand your fears too. I never told you how sorry I am for doing what I…"

The words Demi wanted to say fell away as soon as he felt her hand wrap around his wrist. Demi lowered his hand, but he kept hold of hers as he stared at how big his hand was compared to hers. It was such a basic form of contact, and he was struck dumb as her warm touch offered him comfort.

"You shut me down earlier when I tried to discuss what happened, so I won't say anything other than I've dealt with it and I…" she said as her voice cracked, "we have Cass as a result. I will never regret what brought him to me."

Damn.

Becoming aware of movement in his peripheral vision caused Demi to look up and away from their clasped hands. Using her other hand, Giselle was wiping away tears that were running down her face. Demi raised his other hand and wiped away a visible tear trailing from her eye.

"I see your face whenever I close my eyes," he whispered. "I've done so much wrong, Giselle, but it's what I did to you that haunts me the most."

"I've told myself that it could have ended one of three ways that day. It could have been Carver. I think that would have broken me. And if I had refused..."

She peered at him, waiting with inquisitive eyes for his response to a question they both knew the answer to. It was a question he constantly asked himself even though he knew then, with every fiber of his being, what would have happened if she refused.

"You didn't and that's all that matters."

"Will you tell him about Cass?" Giselle asked. She quickly added, "I'm sorry, I know he is your father and—"

"Giselle," Demi interrupted, "I have to tell you something. Something I fear will determine if you want me in Cassiel's life."

TEN

DEMIGOD

Demi pulled his Escalade into the narrow dark alley, crunching over the unplowed accumulation of snow. He sat back, watching as thick snowflakes hit then melted on the windshield as Groove Theory's *Tell Me*, played softly through his speakers.

He turned the key, shutting off the ignition.

Demi rubbed his head then opened his truck door and stepped out onto the snow-covered pavement. He hiked his heavy leather coat up on his shoulders as he walked toward the side door of Cues, Ciro's billiards/bar, and pounded on the door. The front doors were locked; it was after two in the morning on a Thursday.

The slide of the peephole across its metal base sounded unusually loud to Demi as he tried to calm himself.

"It's DemiGod!" Felix yelled as his and Demi's eyes met. Felix unlocked and pulled the door open.

Demi wasn't expecting UGod to be here. But Felix never left that man's side. Knowing his father was present gave Demi pause, but he had to do this shit now or it would never stop. Letting it go another day, another second, wasn't in his DNA.

So, he stepped through the doorway and walked down the dark hall. He heard Felix lock up, but he also heard the man's footsteps going in the other direction instead of following him. The light coming from the office at the end of the hall was like a beacon. It brightened more as Demi approached, causing him to blink a few times. He suspected his senses were overloaded, a result of his resolve. Something was going to give today.

When Demi stepped into the office, he registered everyone and their positions. Ciro was sitting on a sofa with Basil, his right-hand man. They were eating out of Chinese food boxes as they watched something on the floor model television. UGod sat behind Ciro's desk. He was passing a blunt to Hines.

Everyone in the room glanced his way as he entered, then most went back to what they were doing. Only UGod and Ciro kept their eyes on him. His father and his uncle were successful because they weren't stupid. The three of them knew UGod didn't share his whereabouts with anyone but Ciro unless he needed something. Demi showing up here, at this time of morning, they knew wasn't about his father.

Ciro reached for the remote, lifted it off the coffee table, pressed the pause button before placing it back down. "We got business, Lil nigga?" Ciro looked him up and down with a twisted lip frown.

Only Ciro called him that shit, and it grated every fucking nerve in his body. Demi hated that designation. Hated it the first time he heard it.

"Yeah," Demi said. Looking at that asshole, he noticed Ciro had scratches on the side of his face and neck. It was evidence but Demi didn't need any. Seeing how the bastard left his only child and her mother was enough.

Ciro stared at him for a moment then said as he stood, "That bitch deserved it."

Demi was aware of his breathing and the way each breath left and entered his body. His fingertips tingled with anticipation. He remained calm though. This was a confrontation waiting to happen for about twelve years, and it was long overdue.

"A *man*," Demi said, emphasizing the word man, "wouldn't hit a woman, let alone mash up the mother of his child until she passes out, or his daughter for defending her mother."

"Yo, get your boy," Ciro said, glancing over his shoulder at UGod.

"Torturing bitches ain't my thing, dog. That's all you," UGod said, chuckling as if amused.

"What's wrong, *Big nigga?*" Demi said mockingly as he focused on Ciro. "You can't handle it when a man comes for you? You need your little brother to handle me? I'm going to tell you a secret." Demi shrugged off his heavy leather coat and tossed it on a folding chair that was against the wall behind him, "I learned more than you know while I was away."

Looking at UGod right now would be a sign of weakness, and Demi wasn't that weak little boy they took all those years ago. *I won't ask for permission to fuck up this asshole*, he thought as he rolled his shoulders.

Ciro smiled. He scooted around Basil's legs then walked over to stand a few feet in front of Demi. "You let this Lil nigga get on, have a piece of his own, and now look at 'em. All misguided and shit," Ciro said, chuckling. "You got him thinking he somebody. Goes off to that fancy college, make a few white friends, come back and take out a few motherfuckers and think he can run at the front of the pack with the big dogs." Ciro started barking as he raised his fists.

Basil and Hines started barking in response.

Style biting motherfuckers sounded nothing like DMX.

114

Demi rolled his shoulders again. He had a surprise for his uncle's ass, *and* the rest of them fools. The same hot blood and anger ran through him that ran through his father and uncle. What they didn't know was that Demi prepared for this day for a long-ass time. He wasn't just on some street fighting shit for extra coins. He learned to box, to take a punch, to harness his bottled hate, and to wait for the perfect moment to dish out his fury.

He raised his fists and shot UGod a quick glance and grin.

"Ciro," UGod said, standing.

But it was too late. Ciro was still laughing when he swung. His smile faltered some when his fist did nothing but cut air. Demi threw a right-handed uppercut, connecting with Ciro's chin. Then he followed it with a left hook. Ciro dropped like a dead piece of wood.

"Fuck," UGod said. "Go help him up," he said, looking at Hines.

"Oh, damn!" Basil said, getting to his feet.

Demi took a couple steps back but kept his eyes on Ciro as Hines and Basil helped his dazed ass up. Demi kept his fists up, knowing that no Carrion was going out like that. In fact, Demi was counting on it.

"Get the fuck off me," Ciro said, knocking Hines off him and pushing Basil away. He wobbled as he pulled a butterfly knife from his pocket.

"Ciro," UGod warned.

Hines and Basil backed away more.

"Just gonna teach your boy a lesson," Ciro said to UGod while blinking his swelling eye that was pinned on Demi. He led with his blade, swinging wildly at Demi.

Demi avoided each swipe.

Ciro darted forward, aiming at Demi's neck.

Demi pivoted out of the way and was able to grab Ciro's wrist, pulling Ciro around so his front was pressed to Demi's back.

Ciro used his free arm to punch at Demi's face and neck.

Demi lowered his head and pushed his hips back, but Ciro's elbow connected a couple times, grazing his shoulder and neck. No matter how much he shook the man's hand the knife wouldn't fall. After Ciro's third punch, Demi stood straight up and stepped back, jabbing his elbow into Ciro's face.

Stunned, Ciro backed up. Ciro gave little resistance when Demi took the knife from his grasp as he covered his gushing nose. "You little shit," Ciro said angrily, his voice a little muffled from the blood congesting his nose. He moved, pulling his gun out and aiming it at Demi as he held his nose with his other hand.

As soon as Demi saw Ciro was reaching behind his waist, he did the same. He ignored the barrel of the gun that was pointed at his chest and chose to look at Ciro's eyes.

"Ciro!" UGod's tone was low and threatening. "The issue is dead," he said, looking to Demi.

"The fuck it is!" Ciro yelled. "This nigga gonna die ton="

Demi cut Ciro's declaration short with a squeeze of the trigger. He didn't wait to see Ciro fall. He swung his attention and gun to UGod, who wore a look of pure open-mouthed shock on his face. Demi knew he was outnumbered. He knew that Basil had drawn his gun and was pointing it at him now.

"What the fuck did you just do?" UGod yelled as he stared down at his brother's twitching body. When he looked up and saw Demi's gun pointed at him, UGod didn't hesitate to reach for his own gun.

Demi fired. He felt the burn of a bullet entering his chest, pushing him back a step. Demi turned and fired two shots at Basil. He felt another bullet hit his side. A third grazed his left cheek. Demi dove for cover. Knocking the coffee table and the food over onto the floor, he twisted and aimed at Hines, who was rushing toward him. Demi shot between his legs as they flew up, hitting his target in the chest as he landed beside the front of the sofa.

As he looked around for UGod, Demi pushed his heels against the carpet, moving himself away from the sofa until his back hit the upholstered chair. His father was going to appear over him any second, and he knew it. Demi sat there in silence, waiting with his gun up. His pulse was racing; his eyes were burning. Where Demi sat, there wasn't any kind of barrier or cover and he'd been hit a couple times.

Fuck.

Demi spat out the blood that collected in his mouth. Live or die, he knew he killed that abusive fuck of an uncle and at least attempted to make good on the promise he made to UGod twelve years ago.

Demi promised UGod he would kill him. Well, at least he tried. He was at peace with this being his last day on earth. He honestly believed he didn't deserve another. *But,* he thought as he listened to the moaning and erratic breathing that filled the room, *I'm taking as many of these fucks as I can with me.*

Using one hand on the corner of chair to help him up while he aimed his gun in front of him, Demi got to his feet. He felt a rush of dizziness as he stepped over Hines, who looked dead. Demi kicked Hines' gun away. He made his way over to Basil, who was moaning. Demi put one in the man's head then held his gun out again as he walked toward Ciro's desk where he last saw UGod.

"What the fuck happened?"

Demi swung around to see Felix standing in the doorway. Felix dropped the bag he carried and reached for his gun, but he wasn't fast enough. Demi fired twice, hitting him in the forehead and left eye.

The husky erratic breathing amplified to a loud gurgle now. Realizing it was coming from behind him, Demi turned and continued toward the desk. He saw UGod's feet first. One was jerking inward then outward. As Demi moved slowly around the desk, more of UGod came into view. His father was flat on his back with both hands clutching his neck. Crimson blood oozed through his fingers as he tried to keep his wound covered. Wide eyes stared up at Demi with surprise.

Feeling dizzy, Demi placed his hand over his chest wound. He fought the wooziness as he raised his gun and aimed at the man who killed his mother. He put two in UGod's head. Demi sighed as he fell to the desk, using the hand that held the gun to stabilize himself. Suddenly, he felt the pain radiating throughout his body, heard the wheeze he made with every breath, and felt the strength leaving his body. Tired, Demi slid down the side of the desk and slumped to the floor.

Demi closed his eyes. To shut out the pain, he thought of what always calmed his mind when he was troubled. Demi thought of *her*. He raised his hand in front of him and imagined the way her satin curls felt between his fingers and on the back of his hand. Demi moved his hand and cupped the side of her face. He brushed his thumb over her soft cheek.

"Angel," he said, as the feel of her smooth skin felt too real.

"Demi, oh god."

"Angel," Demi said again, sounding surprised that he could hear her voice, "I've missed you so damn much." He felt her hand touching his chest… A sharp pain spiked inside his chest. "Fuck!" he cried out.

"Demi! Demi! Please, look at me."

Demi blinked a few times as he pushed away the hands touching him. He tried to focus his blurred vision on Krysta's horrified face.

"Krys…," Demi said. He paused, feeling an itch in his throat. He coughed a few times. "Get out of here."

"Who did this?" Krysta asked.

Demi watched her tear-filled eyes as she looked at him. He'd only seen his precious cousin look helpless a few times since meeting her. He hated when she did. She was his family and a female. He had to protect her from any and everything that would do her harm. But as she looked over her shoulder, at where her father's body lay, he realized her pain now was his fault.

"I'm sorry," he said, then he coughed.

Krysta turned her head back around and stared at him in disbelief. The shock on her face was too much to bear.

"I couldn't let him hurt you again."

Krysta's eyes went from sorrow to determined. She wanted revenge, he reasoned. He would accept that. She lowered her gaze.

She will probably use one of her blades.

Instead of the glint of a knife, Demi watched as Krysta raised her phone to her ear.

"Hello, I'm at 495 W. Grindstone St. There's been a robbery and shooting. Hurry please!" she yelled.

Demi felt the weight of his gun being lifted from his hands. "Krysta." he said.

"You have to stay awake, Demi. Help is coming but I have to fix this so it will look like a robbery." She kissed him on the forehead. "I think you have to keep your hand on the wound. That's what the television people do."

Demi felt his hand being moved. "Ugh…Shit," he said as he felt his hand being pressed against his chest.

"Keep your hand on it," Krysta said then chuckled.

Her laugh was dry and sounded frantic.

"If we get out of this clean," she said, "I'm going to take an emergency medical training course."

Demi watched as Krysta stood. She moved out of his line of sight, but he heard her moving around the office. As he tried to stay alert, he thought he heard her leave though the side door then come back. He didn't know how much time passed, but he had no more strength in his body to hold his wound. His arm flopped down beside his leg.

"Angel?" he questioned as he felt a pressure on his face.

"Hey," a strong voice called out. "I have one here who is barely alive."

Demi saw a bright light flash in front of his eyes before darkness took him.

Now

Demi knew he was risking more than her feelings toward him by telling Giselle the details of UGod's demise. He'd made himself the judge, jury, and executioner that night. If she wanted, Giselle could use what he told her to put him away forever. But the thought of her seeing him as an animal, despising him, fearing him, and never letting him near Cass again was much worse.

As he waited for Giselle to react, he thought about how he always found it easy to tell her the absolute truth. Demi had never lied to her, even when it was in his best interest.

"You were shot three times?"

Demi nodded. "That time," he admitted but said no more.

"Wow," Giselle said. She looked down then up at him with a frown on her face. "You could have just said your father was dead. Why did you tell me all of this? Is this some kind of test?" Giselle asked as she gazed into his eyes.

Demi shook his head then said, "No test. I want you to know what kind of man I am. I will never hurt you or Cassiel but if anyone ever tries to hurt either of you, I can't be the kind of man who waits for the law to handle it. Not ever."

Sighing, Demi added, "I can set you up, give you all you need to live well and raise Cassiel. I can do that for you, but I can't promise I will stay away. All I can promise is that I won't make your life hard. I won't interfere in your relationships, but I will want to see him."

"You're his father and I won't keep you from him."

120

He swallowed the lump of relief that was lodged in his throat. "If you welcome me into your lives, that means you and Cassiel will have to accept me for who I am. Being near me, it may come with some challenges." He looked directly at her shoulder. "But I will do everything in my power to shield you both.

"I understand," Giselle said. She shifted before she removed the throw from her legs. Getting to her feet with a grunt, Giselle took the hand Demi offered to help her get stable. "Sorry. My legs fell asleep." She wobbled a bit then settled on her feet and said, "I can handle it from here."

"I'll walk with you." He gave her no option to turn him down as he eased her along.

Demi kept hold of Giselle's hand as he walked with her up the stairs and down the hall past Cassiel's room to his. They walked in silence, him reflecting on her response and her…well, he wasn't certain what she was thinking.

He stopped short at his bedroom doorway. He didn't reach for her hand when she dropped his, but the urge was strong. Demi watched as Giselle stepped inside his bedroom. She walked to the left side of the bed, sat on the edge, then looked over at him.

"Goodnight Demetrius," she said.

Demi knew she couldn't fathom how many nights he'd dreamt of her saying those exact words while preparing to sleep in his bed. "Goodnight," he said then whispered, "Angel."

ELEVEN

DEMI

Looking over at his closed office door, Demetrius focused on the space between the bottom of the door and the floor. He saw a shadow move by. It was the fifth time in an hour he'd seen movement outside his home office door.

"When would you like me to reschedule your business meeting with Mr. Huang?" Rachal asked through the phone receiver. "He has made it clear that he is willing to extend his time in the U.S if you can get together."

"I will reach out to Mr. Huang personally," Demi said. "Have the contract for Appleby to be picked up before three, and did you send the flowers I picked out to Hendrickson's wife?"

"I included a gift card and a pink plush blanket embroidered with their surname for the newborn as well, sir."

"Good," Demi said. "Thank you, Rachal. I'm logging off early today."

"Enjoy the rest of your day, sir."

Demi disconnected the call, removed his headset, then typed a quick email to Krysta.

Krysta stayed home from work for a couple days after Giselle was released from the hospital. Mainly it was because Demi complained about his injury and how Cass couldn't rely on him or Giselle, who was injured as well. But this morning, Krysta insisted on business as usual regardless of his bullshit whining or his real reservations concerning the possible danger she faced by association. It would be business as usual for Demi too if his circumstances hadn't changed.

He wasn't hiding so much as he was spending time with Cassiel and Giselle, inside…on lockdown. It wasn't for his safety but for theirs. He was the target and though he never made a habit of using someone's loved ones against them, Demi wasn't taking chances that his enemies were as magnanimous. So, since Giselle was released from the hospital a week and a half ago, he'd been practicing some social distancing.

Demi glanced over at his door once more, noticing the shadow on the other side again. He laughed as he finished up his email to Krysta and sent it. He logged off his computer and stood. Demi extended his arms out above his head and stretched. He froze as the sharp pain reminded him that he'd been shot too, then he lowered his arms. The pain began to fade into a dull ache within seconds.

When he opened his office door, no one was there. With a knowing smile, Demi walked down his hallway and into the main living space. Cass, who sat on the sofa, looked up with anxious eyes and a smile.

Being aware of his beating heart was a constant thing these days. Demi felt each thump every time the boy smiled at him or sounded excited in his presence. He also felt it whenever Cass called him dad. He felt it each time he checked on the kid when he slept. He wasn't ashamed to admit that he often watched the boy sleep.

"You ready?" Demi asked.

Cassiel's face lit up like a spotlight. "You can play now?" he asked as he bounced up and down on the sofa.

"Yup," Demi said as he moved to the high cabinet containing his wide screen television. He opened the cabinet door, switched on the game console, and pulled out the remote controls. Cassiel was still bouncing up and down with excitement when Demi sat beside him. "Are we still exploring the asylum in disguise or are we moving to the next mission?"

"Explore!"

Demi laughed. When the game booted up, he moved the character they designed around the maze of the asylum. Listening to Cass' instructions, Demi found a new appreciation for the game. He always loved gaming but he kind of slacked off over the years, giving way to life's priorities. But since they were cooped up in the house, he decided to play a few with Cass to break up the monotony of their day.

"Should we go right or left?"

"Down there," Cass said, pointing at the television.

Demi moved their game avatar down the dark hall to the left. He was about to search a room when he saw Giselle in his peripheral vision. She was in the kitchen looking for something. "Here," Demi said as he held out the controller, "I need to talk to your mom."

The trepidation expressed on Cass' face was too cute.

"You've watched long enough. Play." Demi extended his hand out more. When Cass' wide brown eyes glanced up at him then back to the controller, Demi smiled. He knew the moment Cass decided to try it. And when Cass reached out and took the controller, Demi did a mini celebration in is head.

Finally, maybe Cassiel will take initiative and boot up the console whenever he wants to play instead of waiting for me. But he has to feel at home first.

Though, Demi enjoyed their gaming time. He absently rubbed Cass' head. Demi quickly realized his error when the kid stiffened, and was about to apologize but the smile Cass offered took him by surprise. Demi just stood there, looking down on Cass as he played the game. It wasn't until he heard a pot clang in the kitchen that he woke from the daze and shook his stupor away.

"I'll be back soon," he said.

"Ok," Cass said without looking at him.

Chuckling, Demi walked toward the kitchen.

Giselle looked over at him as he approached the long breakfast bar separating the kitchen from the living room. He saw her lips move but didn't hear what she whispered.

"Can I help?" he asked.

She wore a pair of loose-fitting jeans and an off-the-shoulder oversized see-through peach shirt. He shook his head as thoughts of running his lips over her neck and shoulder popped into his mind.

Demi had already licked, sucked, and fucked Giselle six ways from Sunday in his mind. His brain was able to conjure tantalizing episodes for him. When he was a teen, those detailed virtual fuckfests sustained him. Problem was, since he was now a man, they only made him hungry for her. In fact, he was starving.

Demi never had a problem keeping his dick under control. If he wanted a woman, sometimes his body reacted, but he wasn't some fucking schoolboy who lacked control. His dick and him had an understanding. They never embarrassed each other. He was the deal maker and his dick was the closer. They worked as a damn unit with neither of them acting a fool. But with Giselle, his dick refused to work with his mind. It acted a fool whenever she was nearby. Even when she was laid up in the damn hospital, the fucker was throbbing for attention.

And now, as he stood over Giselle, smelling the subtle fragrance she wore…his cock pulsed like a caged animal.

"I want to make you lunch," Giselle said. She moved to the island cabinets and opened a door.

Demi's raised his brow but said nothing as he leaned against the counter and watched her turn back and look up at the high cabinet above the sink. Giselle seemed annoyed. He could ask her what was wrong, risking annoying her more, or he could figure it out on his own. The only good thing about watching her move about his kitchen, subtly beating his kitchenware into submission, was that his erection ran off to hide.

"You don't have to…"

"Excuse me, Mr. Carrion. I can't seem to find your clothes to take to the cleaners?"

"*Ahh*," Demi said as he turned from Giselle, who had her back to him, to Marjorie. Marjorie was his house cleaner who came twice a week. She was a young woman who owned a cleaning service. Demi loved her work ethic and the fact that even though she ran her own company with over a dozen employees, Marjorie kept working for her original clients, who she called gold members, doing all the work herself.

"Good afternoon, Marji," Demi said as he moved to stand behind Giselle. He pressed himself up against her, feeling her soft ass against him. His cock sprang to life again and he wasn't going to blame it. Demi spoke to Marjorie as he got as close as he could to Giselle. "I've been using the bathroom in the hall. The dry-cleaning hamper will be there." Demi then lowered his head close to Giselle's cheek. He fought the urge to kiss her when he said, "I don't want you reaching up, so what can I get for you?"

GISELLE

Why she was acting the way she was, Giselle had no idea. But when she came out of the ensuite master bathroom earlier and saw Marjorie in Demetrius' walk-in closet, hanging his clothes, her hackles rose.

It wasn't like she hadn't already met the young woman. Demetrius introduced them a few days ago. There was just something that bothered Giselle today. In fact, for the past few days, she'd been in a mood. Except today, seeing the light-skinned beauty in those tight jeans and t-shirt annoyed Giselle. She knew exactly what her problem was, and it wasn't the sweet girl who was cleaning for Demetrius. The real reason for her feeling out of sorts made her embarrassed to admit. It was...

Giselle stiffened as she felt Demetrius press against her. God, he was so close that she felt his erection. *Is that for me?* How did she miss him moving up behind her? How in the world did she miss the smell of the delicious cologne he wore? God knows, the way his scent wrapped around her...

"Giselle?"

His voice... It had the ability to teasingly nibble at her self-control and sanity.

"I just need a few plates," she said. Her voice sounded unsure and shaky to her.

Giselle didn't move while Demi stayed plastered to her ass as he reached above her and pulled down three of each: plates, bowls, saucers, and glasses.

"Can I get you anything else?"

Lord...she felt hot and bothered "Uh," she said then coughed.

Giselle choked on her knee-jerk response. Demi backed away immediately, rubbing her on her back to help. She continued to cough as she backed away from the counter.

"Misses," Marjorie said, appearing in front of Giselle with what looked like a glass of water.

Giselle took the offered water, spilling some as she rushed to take a sip. When she had control over her breathing again, Giselle looked up to see everyone gathered around her. "I'm fine, she said to three concerned faces.

"You sure, momma?"

Giselle smiled. Her boy was so sweet. "I am baby," she said to Cass. "Go back and play your game."

Cass wasted no time. Giselle watched him turn and jog back over to the sofa.

"I can prepare something quick for your family today. And if you like, I can have Byron prepare full meals to bring on the days I work here. My Byron has cooked for your Mr. before, Miss Giselle."

Giselle focused on Marjorie. The young woman's brows were furrowed as her gentle looking wide eyes peered at her then at Demetrius as she nodded her head.

Your family? Did she just refer to us as a family?

So…apparently Marjorie had no designs on Demetrius.

"Byron owns one of my favorite restaurants. He's the chef too," Demetrius said, picking up on Marjorie's head-nod prompt.

"Your mister is being modest," Marjorie said as she swatted Demetrius out of the way and grabbed the glass and pulled it from Giselle's hands.

Marjorie placed the glass on the counter and took Giselle's arm, urging her out of the kitchen. Giselle widened her eyes as she looked to Demetrius. He only offered her a shrug as he turned to open the refrigerator.

"Mr. Carrion and his friend Mr. Jackson saw the potential in my Byron and me. They helped us both, partnering with us. I was able to open my cleaning service and Byron his restaurant."

Wow.

Giselle allowed the young woman to help her over to the couch, though she didn't need help. The pain from her injury was now minimal to nonexistent. She did have issues reaching, but that would subside soon too.

"Now *Marjorie* is being modest," Demetrius called out. "She and her husband are very shrewd business partners. Carver and I are nothing but silent partners." He directed his attention toward Marjorie. "You two are the masters of your success."

Husband. She's married.

"We wouldn't have had a start without you and Mr. Jackson," Marjorie said.

Now Giselle really felt like a fool. But she didn't recall seeing a ring on the young woman's finger. She looked again as Marjorie helped her sit down. Instead of a ring on her left wedding ring finger, Giselle saw an intricate tattoo that was drawn in place of a wedding band.

Odd, but nice.

"It wouldn't be any trouble," Marjorie said as she smiled down at Giselle.

"How about this," Demetrius said from the kitchen. "I will pay you for Byron to package up three meals from the restaurant for us for you to bring the two days you work here."

"I was offering it as a gift," Marjorie shrugged, "but have it your way and pay." The woman leaned down and whispered, "There is no point arguing with him, but I am sure you already know that."

"Better than most," Giselle whispered back.

"Dad," Cass called out. "Mom and Ms. Marjorie are whispering about you."

"Traitor!" Giselle said. She heard Marjorie gasp, most likely feigning offense, as she peered at Cassiel.

"Good looking out, buddy," Demi said as he pounded his chest and pointed to Cass.

"Us men have to stick together," Cass said, looking as serious as a heart attack.

Laughter burst from Marjorie's gaped mouth. Cass looked confused, seemingly trying to figure out what joke he missed.

Giselle smiled. This was nice. Only, she wasn't sure how long it was going to last.

Celestial Towers

Krysta closed her office door and locked it. She turned and was moving to walk past her secretary's desk when she realized she wasn't alone. "Evan?"

"Ma'am," Evan said as he gave her a slight nod.

She furrowed her brows as she looked at the bodyguard standing outside of her office. "Why are you here, Evan?"

"Mr. Jackson sent me," Evan said.

"Why would Carver send you here?" she asked, frowning.

"I was told if you had any questions that I should tell you to contact Mr. Carrion."

Krysta turned back, unlocked her office door, and flicked the light back on. She went to her desk, dialing Demi on her cell phone and Carver on her office line. Neither answered, but looking at her computer monitor Krysta noticed a waiting email.

She clicked the envelope and read... *If you insist on going to work, we feel that you must have protection.*

"Great," she said, "no one wants to answer."

When Krysta stepped back out into the reception area, Evan was still standing at attention.

"Ready ma'am?" he asked.

Sighing, Krysta plastered a smile on her face. There was no point in taking her irritation out on Evan. He was just doing his job. *Nope*, Krysta told herself. *I'll save it all for the boys.*

TWELVE

A week later

DEMI

The keys bounced, hitting metal against metal. The sound announced that one of the off-duty officers who handled security for The Keystone was coming. Demi glanced over his shoulder and offered officer Owen a nod.

"He's been doing this for what, like a couple weeks?" Owen asked as he approached. The officer stopped beside Demi and stared through the glass walls of the building's gym facility located on the ground floor.

"About," Demi said as he watched Cass dodge a punch then throw one. The next blow, Cass wasn't able to avoid. The solid hit connected on the side of Cass' face. Cass fell hard to the mat and Demi watched as he pushed up on one knee then stood on both feet to square off with Torrey again. *Good boy*, Demi said to himself as he felt a warm sensation of pride move through him.

"He seems to be a fast learner."

Demi turned his head and regarded Owen. When the officer reached into his pocket and pulled out a twice folded envelope, Demi reached out and took it.

"You should think about letting Torrey train Erica. He's good," Demi said as he unfolded the blank envelope and pulled out the letter.

"If it wasn't for you, Erica wouldn't be here for me to even consider self-defense training."

Demi shook his head as he looked at the man who looked closer to sixty than forty-something. Stress had a way of aging people, but lately Owen seemed to be getting back his more youthful look. "You don't have to thank me anymore, Owen. Erica is a beautiful and intelligent young woman; she didn't belong in that place. You and I both knew it, and when she finally realized that truth she asked for help."

"I will never forget what you did for us, Mr. Carrion. If you need anything else, anything…just let me know. If I am capable…"

Demi held out his hand. Owen closed his mouth but smiled as he shook Demi's hand. "This is more than enough, Owen. I respect your position in our community. Please, just keep doing your best, alright friend," Demi said as he let go of Owen's hand.

"I'll talk to Erica about those self-defense classes. Thank you," Owen said, nodding as he turned away and continued on his rounds.

Demi opened the envelope and read the first page of information he requested about Giselle's father, Alan Johnson.

The next day…

DEMI

The sound of footsteps as Dre and James Houston approached the table caught Demi's attention. He focused on Dre, the head of the Houston family, as he stopped beside the chair where he usually sat. When Dre offered Demi a nod of greeting, Demi nodded back in response. He turned his focus to James Houston, who nodded in greeting as well. Both men pulled their chairs out and sat at the round table.

None of the six men now seated at the table spoke as Torrey walked up and leaned close to Demi's side and whispered in his ear.

"Everything is in place," Torrey said before walking away, leaving the six men at the table in the restaurant alone.

"Good afternoon gentleman. I'd like to thank you for taking time out of your busy schedules to join me for this impromptu gathering," Demi said. He reached for one of the mouthwateringly scented dishes with a rice and meat mixture, and spooned a helping onto his plate. When he sat the dish back in the center, everyone moved to fill their own plates. Yet, no one moved to eat what they plated.

"You have the Stoughton family's condolences," Lionel Stoughton said, breaking the silence.

"As well as the Houston's," James added.

Demi focused on James first. James was Dre Houston's nephew. Dre raised the boy as his own after his sister, James' mother, died. He named James his successor, automatically making him a Partner. The young man was intelligent, but Demi often wondered if he had the stomach for the family business. James rarely spoke, and if he did, he didn't usually speak directly to Demi.

Demi stared at James long enough for it to become uncomfortable for the young man. James didn't cower. Instead, he looked back at Demi as he lifted his fork and took a bite of the food he placed on his plate.

Interesting, Demi thought as he raised a brow.

Carver cleared his throat. This caused Demi to slightly lower his gaze from James and tilt his head toward his friend who sat beside him on the right.

"Thank you, James…and Lionel," Demi said as he glanced at Carver then moved his eyes over the other men. "Now, the reason we are all here is—"

"We know why we're here," Dre Houston interrupted. "You want to know if we," he spread his arms out, motioning to the Stoughtons and James, "tried to kill you. But the question I have is, why is he here?" Dre pointed his flashy ring-studded finger at Carver.

"Carver being here will be explained shortly," Demi said. "I would also like to know if anyone here wants me dead enough to try and kill me."

"Do you?" Carver asked flatly as he leveled his gaze on Dre.

"Of course not," Dre said nonchalantly.

"How would we benefit from your death?" Lionel Stoughton asked, fixing his eyes on Demi. "Under your...guidance," he said carefully, "we've prospered in corporate business and our less than lawful undertakings. I can raise my head and walk with pride again."

"We all can," Dre added.

"The attempts on my life isn't the reason I've called you all together." Demi looked to each of the men then said, "First thing is, I am here to inform you that I have chosen my successor." Demi moved his gaze to each man to gauge his reaction.

Lionel's blue eyes widened only for a brief moment as his gaze moved to Carver. Oliver smirked as he also turned his narrowed eyes on Carver. Dre's brows furrowed as he sat looking at Demi with a confused look on his face. James looked to Carver, but his expression was blank.

"He isn't your blood. He can't inherit your position. That is one of the rules," Oliver said. "He shouldn't even be here, though I suppose this isn't a real meeting so..."

When Demi looked at Oliver Stoughton, the man's words faded away as he stopped talking.

The Stoughton family name was synonymous with old money. Like just about all old money families, they built their wealth in the 19th century, on the backs of slaves. Due to decades of mismanagement and family in-fighting, Lionel Stoughton was virtually broke when Demi approached him more than a decade ago with a proposition. Now, the Stoughton name was a major powerhouse and a vital player in the financial world once again. The bulk of their current gains resulted from their partnership.

Demi knew how Oliver Stoughton thought. He attended the same kinds of schools the privileged bastard attended, entertained the same kinds of people, earned and spent the same level of money. Still, Oliver was taught to believe that his skin color and name gave him some sort of edge. He thought it did even while he was at Demi's table.

It didn't.

Demi learned that it didn't matter to most that he started off as a tennis-shoe hustler. Money had a tendency of opening doors previously closed. "Who," Demi said with little influx or emotion as he gave Oliver his full attention, "made the rules?"

Now, Demi wasn't fool enough to think that he was liked or that those doors would remain open. He just needed them open long enough for him to move him and his Family in.

Oliver stiffened but didn't respond.

Demi noticed Lionel shifting in his seat. The movement was slight, as if he touched his son's leg or maybe kicked Oliver under the table. When Demi saw Carver move out of the corner of his eye, he placed his hand on his friend's shoulder to make sure he didn't react. This was the partnership. Decisions were made as a committee versus a dictatorship. Demi designed it that way so that he wouldn't make the same mistakes his father did.

"You did," Oliver finally said. He pressed his lips together then smiled. "Mr. Carrion."

Demi ignored the sarcasm of the younger Stoughton. "I started this committee because I know that no one can climb alone. We all bring different things to the table. We've helped one another in many ways, and for over a decade we have enjoyed peace and the freedom to run our own factions in this and other cities. Which brings me to the second reason I've gathered you all here today. Jackson Carver and I are longtime friends and business partners, but it is his separate business ventures that will benefit us all." Demi looked to Torrey who was making his way to the table. "I've explained how in this detailed report. I officially nominate Jackson Carver to be our Sixth."

Torrey placed a black folder in front of each man at the table. Dre was the first to pick up the folder that was in front of him and begin reading. James and Lionel followed suit. Oliver was the last, and he basically fingered through the pages.

Lionel cleared his throat and said, "You project we can increase profits by this much?"

Demi nodded. "I am aware you are under contract with another firm. That contract is up for renewal in a few months." He focused on the Houston's. "You have a liquor contract renewal coming up, right?"

Glancing around the table, Demi caught the reactions of his partners. James quirked a knowing smile. Lionel raised his brow then looked over at his son. Oliver rolled his eyes and nodded.

"You know so much about us and what we do. Yet, in ten years of being business associates," Dre said, "we still know very little about you and what all you do. You present this amazing opportunity to us," Dre looked up at Demi, "but all I see is you having an ally as a Partner."

Oliver spoke up, "It is odd. With five of us now, voting is never a tie but with…"

"This opportunity is beyond the semantics of tallying mere votes," Lionel interrupted. "Besides, we are all allies…right?"

Demi looked at James. "Would you like to chime in?"

James looked up from the open folder in front of him to Demi, then to Carver, who appeared more relaxed than Demi expected him to be right now.

"We can't expect to stay on top if we don't grow. Adding new members is pertinent to growth," James said. He lowered his head and seemingly focused back on the content in the folder.

"When do we vote?" Dre asked.

"The next scheduled meeting should be enough time," Demi said. "Next…" Demi looked over at Torrey who was standing by the door to the kitchen.

Torrey turned and went through the kitchen swinging doors. When he returned, he walked side by side with Cassiel. Torrey stopped just before reaching the table while Cassiel continued toward Demi. Looking at his son approaching in the black custom suit and red tie that matched his, Demi smiled.

"Hey Dad," Cassiel said as he came to a stop and stood between the chairs Demi and Carver sat in. "Hey Uncle Carver." He leaned forward over the edge of the table and waved to Carver.

"Lil boss man," Carver said, fist bumping Cassiel.

"This is my son and heir, Cassiel Carrion. If I should die before he is of age, Krysta will inherit my seat on his behalf until he can."

The silence in the room seemed heavy as the men around the table stared at Cassiel.

"Hello," Cassiel said, waving.

James was the first to speak. "Hello Cass…iel. Are you named after the angel?"

"Yup." Cassiel grinned with pride.

"It's nice to meet you Cassiel," Lionel said.

Dre's laughter filled the room. "You've been holding out, Demi." Dre looked at Cassiel. "Hello young man."

Cassiel smiled. "Hello, Mr. Houston."

Torrey must have prepped Cass. Demi didn't smile, but he gave Torrey a nod of approval.

"Hello," Oliver said, his expression softening for the first time since the meeting started.

Demi patted Cass on the back then motioned for him to go back with Torrey. Cassiel nodded then walked back toward Torrey. Demi focused on each man as they watched Cassiel leave. He wanted to see if he could read them. So far, he knew exactly what he knew before the gathering.

Jack shit.

Before leaving the room and going back into the kitchen, Cassiel turned back and said, "Nice meeting you all."

"Now," Carver said, pulling everyone's attention back to him, "as Demi's head of security, I have some questions."

Demi buttoned up his suit jacket as he stood. He waited as Dre walked toward him with Lionel following close behind. He held his hand out and shook each man's hand, one at a time. "Again, thank you for accommodating me," he said.

Lionel held on to Demi's hand longer. "We all are feeling your loss, Demetrius. Sasha was an amazing young woman, but nominating a sixth member and announcing your heir is important enough to call an impromptu meeting. Not to mention these attempts. They are troubling."

"Whatever Carver needs from the Houston family..." Dre said.

The offer was clear. The Houston clan wasn't old money or new money. They kind of resided in the in-between, starting their climb to fortune by providing one of the first non-payroll employee services firms owned by people of color in the late 1950s. Unlike the Stoughtons, corporate white-collar criminals who claimed clean hands by way of several generations of separation, the Houstons started with racketeering and climbed to the top with unapologetically bloody hands. They were more of a hands-on clan who worked alongside Demi's Family to maintain a unified presence, all the while making a shit ton of money that kept the peace in the streets the city's elected officials and the police took credit for.

"Thank you, Andre," Demi said. "I appreciate the offer, but I will be handling this personally."

"Respect," Dre said as he nodded. "You need anything…"

Lionel cleared his throat. "You can count on my family as well."

Demi kept the humor he felt from surfacing. The man was older than everyone in the room by at least fifteen years. He wasn't the cut-your-throat and spit down your neck type. At best, the man could hire someone, but old man Stoughton had a mind for business not blood. He allowed his family roles he shouldn't have, and that resulted in the bulk loss of a great deal of his fortune; but Lionel worked his ass off to get it all back…with the help of their committee of course. With his name, connections, and business savvy, Lionel had been indispensable to them as well.

"Thank you, Mr. Stoughton. I'll keep that in mind. How is Nelson doing?"

Lionel's lowered his head at the mention of his eldest son's name. He seemed to take a few breaths then raised his head. When his salt and pepper hair fell forward over his face, Lionel raised his hand and swatted it back.

"Nelson is strong," Lionel said. "Stronger than I ever was at his age."

"I don't know about that, Mr. Stoughton," Dre said, patting Lionel on the back. "He most likely inherited your mettle."

"He did," Demi agreed.

Stoughton nodded as he smiled at them. "I'll tell him you both send your well wishes when I see him next," he said. Lionel walked toward the front exit where Oliver waited.

Demi watched as Evan unlocked and opened the front door for the Stoughtons to leave. Demi slipped his hands inside his slacks pockets as he noticed James moving in his direction.

"Can I ask," James said, stopping in front of Demi, "is Ms. Carrion well?"

"Ms. Carrion is fine," Carver said as he walked up. His tone was low and rumbled with a clear warning that everyone huddled together had to have felt.

Demi smiled again as he regarded the younger Houston. "Krysta is taking our loss hard, but she'll be fine."

"That's our cue," Dre said, grabbing James by the shoulders and turning his nephew around. "Keep safe, Demi."

"I will," Demi said. He watched the Houstons leave the way the Stoughtons left.

Demi and Carver moved at the same time. They walked through the empty restaurant toward the kitchen. Demi pushed open one of the double doors for Carver to walk through first. As they passed through, the kitchen staff greeted them. Both Demi and Carver returned the greetings.

"What do you think?" Carver asked as they slowly walked side by side through the back hall of the restaurant.

"I didn't really sense anything more than I usually do," Demi admitted.

"Well hell," Carver said. "It could be one of them or they could be working together. Oliver is an ass but he isn't an idiot. James, the fucking twit, is smart but he's a pussy."

"James seems to be coming out of his shell. He was named as Dre's heir so Dre must believe in him."

"He's a pussy."

Demi raised his brow but said nothing to Carver about his apparent personal feelings toward James. "Lionel has Oliver in his ear since Nelson was arrested. The kid's a punk but he's a snake."

"Yeah, but the Stoughtons don't have any reason to go against you. Not like the Houstons."

Demi nodded. He spilled Houston blood the night he killed UGod and Ciro. Hines Houston was Dre's cousin. The guy wanted to make his own way and hooked up with UGod for a slice of pie instead of crumbs from their family business.

"No," Demi admitted. "But everyone's a suspect."

When Evan joined them at the back door with Helen, the manager of the restaurant, Carver pushed open the door.

"Thank you, Helen. The food was wonderful as usual," Demi said. "Add the leftovers to the shelter deliveries for tonight."

"Yes sir, Mr. Carrion."

Demi watched Helen close the back door. He, Carver, and Evan walked through the parking lot together to two waiting vehicles. Evan got into the driver's seat of his truck while Carver slid into the passenger seat. Demi moved to his waiting car. Torrey was standing by the open back passenger door. Inside, Cassiel sat with his face hidden behind a book.

"Let's go for some shaved ice," Demi said as he got inside the car.

"Can we, dad?" Cassiel asked as he lowered the book.

Demi felt his chest pulse as he smiled. He would never get tired of Cass calling him dad. "Torrey…"

"I know just the spot, Mr. Carrion," Torrey said.

GISELLE

"It was a pleasure meeting you," the Headmistress said then smiled. "Please, tell Mr. Carrion that his son is in good hands here at Ridgewood."

Giselle smiled as she shook the woman's hand. The Headmistress focused on Krysta.

"Thank you for working with us, Mrs. Talbot. My boss will be very pleased," Krysta said as she shook the Headmistress' hand.

"Anything for Mr. Carrion," the woman said. "I'll get everything situated for Cassiel for Monday. You both have a wonderful weekend."

Giselle followed Krysta out of the Headmistress' office into the main office of the school. She didn't say anything until after they were outside and approaching Krysta's car. "Why were they so accommodating?" she asked as she opened the passenger door.

Krysta got in behind the wheel. She pushed her key into the ignition then looked pointedly at Giselle and raised her brow.

Giselle sighed but pulled the seatbelt over her chest and clicked it in place.

Krysta clicked her own belt in place then backed out of the parking space. "Demi has worked very hard to become a well-respected very wealthy businessman. Most of these people know nothing of his beginnings because the streets are a world apart from the luxurious lives they live. Money, as you may remember, allows for a lot of wiggle room. These people want to be associated with him. They want to make him happy because a happy Mr. Carrion means a generous Mr. Carrion."

Giselle nodded then said in a low tone, "I barely remember how having money feels." She felt Krysta's eyes on her, so she looked over at her.

"What all happened to…" Krysta's question sort of died away as she turned her attention back to the road. "You know, I was young and stupid back then. The things I did—"

Giselle looked ahead, through the windshield. Everything about this city looked so different to her. None of the shops or storefronts looked familiar and all of them looked expensive. This didn't feel like her world anymore.

"I don't blame any of you for what happened, Krysta. So, please, just don't think about it." Giselle sighed then said, "I lived, and I did what I had to do to make sure we had food each

142

night and a place to sleep. I'm not proud of some of those things but I won't regret doing them either."

"I'd go all out for my family, so I can understand," Krysta said. She moved into the right lane and pulled to a stopped in front of a restaurant. "Let's get some lunch."

"Demetrius won't mind?"

Krysta shrugged then asked, "Why would he? By the way, Demi is the same trusting fool he has always been when it comes to you."

He trusts me?

Giselle peered at Krysta. She wondered if Demetrius did trust her. If he did, did that mean that Krysta trusted her as well? "I'm not really dressed for this," Giselle said as she watched Krysta undo her seatbelt.

"I was thinking we could do some shopping too." Krysta got out of the car before the valet could open the door for her.

When the passenger door opened, Giselle was a bit startled. She undid her seatbelt then took the offered hand and got out of the car. The young man gave her a welcoming smile before letting go of her hand.

"The usual table, Ms. Carrion?" a man asked as they entered.

"Please," Krysta said with a smile.

Giselle followed Krysta as she trailed the man as he weaved through occupied tables to one set for four people in a corner that was surrounded by a semi-circular half wall. A menu was placed in front of her but not Krysta. Before Giselle was settled, a woman appeared at their table for their drink orders.

Giselle ordered a glass of water as she looked over her menu. *No prices listed*, she thought as she placed the menu down. She felt a headache coming on. She hated having to explain she couldn't afford this.

"Did you see something you like?" Krysta asked when the waitress walked away.

Giselle looked up. Krysta was always such a beauty, with her sun kissed sand-toned skin, ever changing hairstyles, and a confidence Giselle always admired. It was odd to see her so out of sorts the past week or so.

"Honestly, I really can't afford this," Giselle said.

"Two things we need to get straight. The first," Krysta said, "if I take you someplace, it is my treat. Second, you can afford just about anything you want." Krysta went into her purse. She palmed something that she slid across the table, then lifted her hand.

Giselle looked down at the plastic card. It was shiny black and had her full name on it. She looked up.

"He told me that he didn't think you would accept it if he gave it to you." Krysta smiled. "By the way your face is scrunched up, I can only assume he was right. Why are you turning down Demi's generosity?"

Giselle didn't know how to explain it to Demetrius, but she would try to make Krysta understand. "I came to Demetrius for Cassiel's sake. I knew from the moment I found out I was carrying him, that Demetrius needed the opportunity to be in our son's life. But, I didn't and don't expect him to take care of me."

Krysta leaned forward and pushed the credit card further across the table toward Giselle. "Woman, these heifers out here in these streets don't have any reservations about spending Demi's money, and you shouldn't either. And, you have something none of them have."

"His son," Giselle said.

Krysta laughed. "No woman. Demi's attention." Krysta sat back in the chair. "He has yours too. I see how you look at my cousin."

"I don't look at him any kind of way," Giselle rushed to say.

Krysta laughed harder.

Giselle was sure she looked offended because when the waitress returned with their drinks, she appeared concerned but said nothing.

"Would you like to try one of my favorite dishes?" Krysta asked after composing herself and taking a sip of her tea.

"Sure," Giselle said, still a bit out of sorts. When the waitress left with their order, Giselle asked, "What way do I look at him?"

"Like you loooove him," Krysta sang playfully but quietly. "But you seem torn."

Concerned, not torn.

Giselle said, "I don't look at him like that at all. And…what are you, twelve?"

Krysta twisted her mouth then said, "Hey, I'm not judging and it's not like he isn't crazy about you. Lord, the man has never forgotten his Angel."

Giselle eyes widened at the name. Her heartbeat picked up. "What did you say?"

"He never forgot about his Angel." As if realizing how the information affected Giselle, Krysta smiled wickedly. "That *is* you, isn't it?"

Giselle didn't respond. Demetrius never called her that in front of anyone else. How did Krysta know the name? But Krysta did once say that Demetrius told her everything. Though, wasn't intimate stuff off the table?

"He didn't share that name with me. Demi was hurt really bad once and was confused," Krysta said as she looked down and played with her tableware, the fun side of her buried again. "He thought he was dying and when he touched my cheek, he called me Angel. He said that he missed his Angel."

Krysta looked haunted by the memory.

Giselle would bet it was Krysta's memory of what Demi divulged to her two weeks ago. Since he told her the tale, Giselle noticed Demetrius was distant and seemingly cautious around her. As if he was concerned that she was going to take Cassiel and run from him.

In an effort to distract Krysta, Giselle said, "I don't have a lot of experience with men. My last boyfriend, if you can call him that, didn't believe in monogamy and he liked to slap me every now and again. I put up with it until Cassiel started witnessing him hitting on me. One day, while he was beating me, Cass tried to confront him."

Giselle felt a hand squeezing hers. "You said your boyfriend never hit Cass?"

"He didn't. I jumped in front of Cass before he could do anything. I knew we couldn't stay with him after that. When we could, we left."

"Do me a favor," Krysta said, "Don't tell Demi about this guy. Just forget about him, alright?"

Giselle nodded. "I'd never share that with him. It's weird that I shared it with you." Giselle said, feeling silly.

"It'll be our secret."

Giselle smiled. "A secret between friends," she said, raising her water to toast.

Krysta looked confused for a moment then smiled as she lifted her glass of tea. "A secret between friends then."

They both took sips from their glasses. Their food arrived, steaming and smelling delicious. After the waitress and another woman who assisted her walked away, Krysta said as she grimaced, "As your friend, I have to tell you something. I've planned a day of shopping and pampering."

"Demetrius put you up to this, didn't he?"

"No," Krysta said, "but he wasn't opposed to it when I told him my plans."

This side of Krysta was refreshing. Back in high school, they were never friends, but now it seemed they were. Still…this whole exchange felt surreal.

Giselle asked, "Why would you do this for me?"

A hint of a smile played at Krysta's lips. "I see how great you are. When we were teens, I thought you were just another hoochie trying to get with my cousin. An attention chaser. But you've always tried to defend him, never snitched about us even though I told him he was a fool for telling you things; didn't snitch even when you should have." She frowned. "And you seemed to have raised Cass to be caring and gentle regardless of your circumstances. You are forgiving. You," Krysta said smiling, "kinda remind me of my mom. Selfless women deserve to be pampered."

Giselle placed her hand over her chest, then wiped the moisture that was collecting at the side of her eye. No one, not even her mother, ever acknowledged her efforts, not that anyone should. "Thank you, Krysta."

Krysta offered her a glossy-eyed smile. "You know, I recently lost a good friend. I think you would have liked each other. I think you came into our lives at just the right time," she said, lifting her fork with one hand and wiping under her eye with the other. "We have a long day ahead of us. Let's dig in."

Giselle couldn't wipe the smile off her face as she lifted her fork.

Hours later...

Giselle reached up and felt her hair then let her fingers slide down a thick strand that rested on her shoulder. She was over her wavy long hair and the bun she often put it in. But she wasn't quite sure she should have gotten her hair cut just past her shoulders, flat ironed, and wrapped in a sleek bob. It was vastly different from what she wore but it also made her feel a little like a new woman.

She liked it. Yet, her happiness faded when the elevator chimed, signaling they'd reached the penthouse floor.

"Stop worrying," Krysta said, handing her a few shopping bags.

"Alright," Giselle said as her stomach fluttered. She took the bags and stepped forward. When the elevator doors parted, she was surprised to see Cass waiting.

"Wow, mom," he said. "You look gooood."

Alarmed that she was going to see Demetrius before she was ready, Giselle stepped back and away from the doors then asked, "Where's your father?"

"He's in his office." Cass stepped inside the elevator. "You guys going out?"

"Why are you out here?" Giselle asked, ignoring his question.

"Cass and I have a date of our own," Krysta said as she pressed the button to hold the elevator doors open. "You got the goods?" she asked Cass.

Cass held up a few movies Giselle hadn't noticed.

"Got them. I called Uncle Carver. I didn't tell him it was your idea, like you said. He's bringing the ice cream and other treats."

"Well done!" Krysta said. She looked to Giselle. "Go on girl, you messing with our time."

For a moment, Giselle could have sworn she saw a flash of worry on Krysta's beautiful face, but she was sure she was wrong. Giselle tightened her grip on her shopping bags and moved to step out of the elevator, but Krysta placed a hand on her shoulder and leaned into her.

"Take a look at Demi's bare back," Krysta said then gave her a gentle push forward.

"Bye mom," Cass said, waving.

Giselle spun around and was about to ask what did Krysta mean, but the elevator doors closed. She shook her head, feeling the freedom of her hair flowing. "I can do this," she said as she made her way to the door.

148

Krysta told her that Demetrius was into her but most likely afraid that she wasn't feeling the same. That she had to be the aggressor, just like in high school.

"Demi couldn't make the first move back then *because* he liked you. He was afraid you'd reject him like he is now," Krysta had said. "Confident men always have a weakness and you are his."

"Well…" Giselle said as she pushed the door open.

THIRTEEN

DEMI

"Cassiel," Demi called out as he stepped out of his son's bedroom. He had a business call to handle, leaving Cass alone for a while. With the threat still out there, Carver felt he should do business from home until it was neutralized. If Cassiel and Giselle weren't here with him, he wouldn't be living so cautiously. But he enjoyed the time getting to know them.

Demi jogged down the stairs but started to slow as he set his gaze on Giselle. She glanced at him then over her shoulder at the door as she locked it. Demi swallowed as he feasted on her visage. She looked amazing. He approached her with his head tilted to the side as he focused on her bare shoulders and upper back where her hair fell.

Giselle's shoulders visibly rose then fell. Her hair looked so shiny as it moved loosely over her back and shoulders. When she spun around to face him, Demi had to fight not to grab hold of her. He had to fight so damn hard.

Her face glowed with life, her lips were plump with a light gloss, and her eyes sparkled with mischief; though they were shaded with dark liner, making her look seductive. The royal blue off-the-shoulder summer dress fit her curves nicely.

"It's not a good idea to tease me," he whispered as he looked at her mouth. He took a step toward her.

GISELLE

"I'm not teasing you." She backed flush up against the door. Unable to retreat, just like when he first approached her at the swim party at his house, Giselle felt a spike of confidence. "I'm inviting you," she said as she raised a shaky hand and placed it on his shoulder. Giselle snaked her hand up and around to rest on the nape of his neck, urging him forward, but he didn't move.

DEMI

"Where's Cass?" he asked through clenched teeth. His desire for Giselle was threatening to overwhelm his resolve.

"At Krysta's for the night."

Wait, he thought as he placed his hands on her waist, *she planned this.*

That was all Demi needed to hear. He lowered his head to taste her mouth. He groaned when they connected, remembering how good she used to taste and still did. Demi bunched the fabric of the summer dress with one fist and pulled it up, then wrapped his free arm around her waist and lifted Giselle off the floor. She locked her legs around his middle and her arms around his neck, allowing his hands the freedom to roam her body. But instead he palmed her rear end and turned and started towards the stairs. She wiggled her round ass that rested in his hands and pulled out of the kiss.

"Table," she said.

He pinned her with a scowl.

She swallowed, then added. "Making new memories."

For a moment, Demi didn't move. This woman was going to fucking break him with her strength. Fully aware of her power over him, he carried her to the sofa and grabbed the throw, then headed over and threw it on his onyx dining table before slowly lowering her on top of it. Demi slid his hands up either side of her exposed legs, caressing the fronts of her thighs as his hands pushed her dress up more. He felt her shiver as she rested back on her arms while he gripped the satiny fabric of her panties and pulled them down and off.

Demi spread her legs, got to his knees, and stared at her exposed pussy. He would wager that hers was one of the prettiest pussies he'd ever seen. The hair was trimmed and fine, the skin was smooth and dark brown, and her lips shimmered with her juices. When she closed her legs, he looked up at her, silently questioning why.

Giselle shyly looked away.

Demi gently separated her legs again. He hooked his arms under them and pulled her forward. She and the throw slid forward until her ass was at the edge of the table. His heart pounded in his chest as he licked his lips then lowered his face between her legs and dragged his tongue over her pussy.

"*Ahh, God*," she moaned as her hips jerked up off the table.

Fuck. Demi fisted his tightening balls as his dick grew impossibly hard. He spread her legs wider then opened his mouth over her pussy. He sucked in her nub and rolled his tongue over it. Releasing it with a pop, he licked her honey like a starved man who was eating for the first time.

Giselle screamed.

Her cries only spurred him on. Demi stuck his tongue into her pussy and started fucking her with his tongue as he pinched her nub. Again, Giselle's hips jerked as she tried to push his head away. He had to hold her hands as he feasted on her pussy.

Demi released her hands. He worked his pants down as she wiggled and gyrated over his tongue and face. "*Mmm*," he said, knowingly vibrating his lips over her clit. Her small hands gripped the sides of his face as she screamed her orgasm and fucked his face with jerks and grinds.

Demi squeezed her thigh while stroking his cock as he lapped up her juices. When she relaxed back, sated and relaxed, he stood and rubbed the head of his dick over her pussy, then pushed inside.

Giselle whimpered then cried out as he surged forward. Heated cushioned wet pussy squeezed his dick like a vise. "Been dreaming of this pussy," he gritted out as he closed his eyes and relished the feel of her. He lifted Giselle up from lying on the table and pulled her closer as his dick pulsed inside her. He licked his lips, tasting her cream again. The combination of her scent on his mouth and the feel of her was enough to make him a little light-headed.

"Angel," he breathed out as he stared at her.

Giselle opened her glossy eyes and stared back at him.

"I want to make love to you while looking into your eyes," he whispered.

She nodded frantically as she pulled at the hem of his shirt. Demi's movements slowed as he helped her pull off his shirt. When he looked back into her eyes, so many things hit him at once. He wanted to make promises, get promises from her, but he just moved. He slid out slowly then back in. Each movement in and out of her was an overwhelming jolt to his senses. Demi gripped the back of her neck and increased his speed.

Giselle's newly manicured nails dug into his chest. Her moans grew in pitch but shortened in span. She lifted her hand to his face and over his mouth.

Demi sucked on her finger then wiggled free to kiss her mouth as he continued, fucking her harder and faster. Her cries and his grunts mixed, warring for dominance. Demi ended the kiss as her pussy muscles flexed around his dick. Giselle was rocking her hips forward with each of his thrusts.

"That's it, fuck me. So good," he said. "My pussy so damn good."

"My dick," she declared, "is so damn good."

Demi growled as he kicked out of his jeans. He dug into her ass with his fingers as he lifted her off the table. Giselle wrapped her arms around his neck as he carried her to the sofa. He dropped her on the cushion, separating from her. Demi pulled the dress that was bunched at her waist up and over her head. He loved the way she eagerly assisted him.

Once she was free of the dress, Giselle fell back and inched her body to him with her legs open wide, offering her pussy to him. She reached for his dick. Demi pushed his hips forward, letting her guide him inside. When he entered, they both exhaled loudly.

Demi leaned over her, pushing inside deeper as he sucked one of her perfect breasts into his mouth. The pull on her breast must have excited her more because her pussy pulsed over his dick again.

"Fuck," he said as he scraped his teeth over her nipple. He placed his hand beside her head, raised up a bit, then started moving with slow strokes.

"Demi," she cried out.

"It's all yours, Angel?" he asked her as he rolled his hips to meet hers, driving deeper.

"Yes, yes. Mine," Giselle said, working his dick with him. Her pussy quaked.

"Ahhhh," she cried out.

Demi picked up speed, digging in. So close. Fuck. Fuck.

"Fuuuuuuuck," he yelled as he shot what felt like an ocean of his warm cum inside her pussy. Demi threw his head back as he pressed his pelvis to hers, rocking inside Giselle until his stream stopped.

When he was empty, Demi peered down at Giselle. He pulled his bottom lip inside his mouth and grinned. He loved the way she looked right now. His woman looked well fucked.

Giselle gave him the shy grin again then covered her face with her hands.

Demi took hold of her hands with his. "Nope," he said, smiling. "I've never seen you look more beautiful than you do right now, Angel."

Grinning, she lowered her eyes to his chest and said, "You're beautiful too."

"I'll be whatever you want me to," he said, leaning down and taking her lips. He pulled back, removing his cock from Giselle's vagina, loving the way she shivered as he did. He cupped his hand under his still hard dick to try to catch his dripping semen as he stood. He felt prideful as her eyes greedily appraised him.

She looked away when she noticed him watching her watching him. "Sorry," she said, standing.

"You've claimed it, right?" he said, pulling her to him. Demi wrapped his arm around her and kissed her on the nose.

"Yes," she said, sounding more confident.

"Then it's yours." He eased her around and slapped her on the ass. "Come on, let's move to the bedroom."

GISELLE

Demi wanted them to use the bathroom together but she didn't feel that comfortable with him yet. Peeing in front of him just felt odd. He waited outside the bathroom door, reminding her to just wipe up because he wasn't finished with her. So, she used the toilet, wiped up, and washed her hands. When she opened the door, he was waiting. When Demi walked by her, she saw a glimpse of something on his back.

"Take a look at Demi's back."

That was what Krysta said to her. So, she turned and looked at his back as he stood over the toilet. "Wow," she said as she moved toward him. She was reaching out and tracing the lines of his tattoo before she knew what she was doing.

Demi hissed as he jerked forward. "Cold hands, Angel."

She pulled her hand back. She stared at his back as he moved to the sink and washed his hands. When he looked over his shoulder at her, she pointed to his back.

He turned back to the sink, taking a washcloth from the folded pile. Demi made eye contact with her through her reflection in the bathroom mirror. "The tattoo was a way for me to keep you with me," he said, then looked down.

For the first time since she became acquainted with the confident Demetrius, he seemed self-conscious. Giselle reached out again and traced her fingers over her middle name sitting between two large angel wings. **Aniela.** This time, he didn't move.

Giselle knew why he called her angel; it was her name after all. But even though his father was Puerto Rican and African American, she never heard the man or Demetrius speak a word of Spanish. Except for translating her name.

He turned around and said, "Siempre seras mi ángel."

"What does that mean?" she asked. She never learned Spanish herself.

"You will always be my angel," he said. Demi placed a sweet kiss on her lips.

DEMI

Demi held the phone up against his ear. He took one last glance at Giselle, then he stepped into the hall and closed the bedroom door. "Coming down now," he said then closed his cell phone. Demi jogged down the stairs and headed for the door. When he pulled it open, Carver entered carrying Cass.

"I'll take him up," Demi said. He lifted Cass from Carver and turned him in his arms, laying his son's head on his chest.

"Hey, dad," Cass said, sleepily.

156

"Hi Cass." Demi looked to Carver. "Hey, stick around for a sec."

Carver nodded.

When Demi came back down, he walked into the kitchen and opened the refrigerator. He took out a bottled water then turned to face Carver. "Did Krysta tell you the plan?"

"Not yet but I'll get with her."

"I'm ready to pull this fuck into the light. I have too much to lose now."

Carver smiled. "DemiGod is back then," he said. He and Demi clasped hands and flicked their fingers when releasing like they used to when they were younger.

"That's just it," Demi said as he walked with Carver to the door, "he was never gone."

Carver smiled. "True. Night man."

Demi closed the front door. A creak behind him caused him to whip his head around and look upstairs, where he thought the sound came from. "*Hmm,*" he said suspiciously as he walked toward the stairs then climbed them two at a time. He moved down the hallway and turned his bedroom's doorknob. When he pushed the door open, Giselle was in the bed in a slightly different position than he'd left her.

He dismissed the idea that someone may have been spying on him as he walked over to the bed, placed his water on the nightstand, and slipped into the bed beside her. Giselle moaned then nestled up to him. Demi kissed her on the top of her head.

"I don't deserve you, Angel," he said to himself.

FOURTEN

DEMI

Demi unhooked his seatbelt and placed his hand on the door handle. With a slight push he opened the door. Instead of getting out of the car he looked over, trying to meet Giselle's lowered gaze. Giselle wouldn't raise her head. Though she wasn't looking at him to know that he was watching her, Demi was pretty certain she knew the driver opened the door for her.

"Is there something wrong?" Demi looked around Giselle at the large four-bedroom colonial with the for-sale sign through the opened door then back to her.

"Don't you think this is too much too soon?"

Demi sat back. "I don't," he said.

Giselle nibbled on her bottom lip and avoided eye contact with him.

"I want you and Cassiel comfortable, Giselle but if you aren't..."

"No," she rushed out as she undid her seatbelt. "It's time we get out of your space."

"That's not—"

"It's not what you meant," she said as she got out of the car. "Right."

By the time Demi got around the car, Giselle was walking toward the porch where the realtor was waiting with a smile.

Demi knew what Giselle wanted, but there was no way he could give it to her.

After waking up wrapped up in her arms in his bed the morning after making love to her throughout the night, he'd come to his senses. He was DemiGod Carrion, a murderous crime lord masquerading as a legitimate businessman. Pushing his Angel away was the only reasonable course of action.

GISELLE

Trailing her hand over the granite countertop, Giselle forced a smile as she looked up to see the realtor smiling at her. She turned away, hoping the woman wouldn't take her smile as another indication that she wanted to hear another reason why the house was perfect.

"Do you and Mrs. Carrion play golf, Mr. Carrion? Because we have a wonderful course just behind the property."

"We're not married," Demetrius said.

Giselle turned away from the two as she placed her hand over her chest. Every word spoken after his declaration faded into the background as she walked out the kitchen and down the stairs. The basement was finished with what seemed like a nice carpet, crown molding, and a built-in white wall unit with bookshelves. Giselle sighed as she walked over to the French doors and looked over the large yard.

"Do you like it?"

Giselle turned around. She bit her lip as she watched Demi walk toward her. He was dressed in a cream fitted sweater with a single black stripe running the length of the right side, and a pair of black slacks. The man was an unholy trinity to women, gorgeous with unnatural sex appeal, wealthy with a great head for business, and a dangerous aura. In addition, the way he made love was so phenomenal she knew one session would never be enough for her. How there weren't women blowing up his phone all hours of the day and night, Giselle didn't know.

Each step Demi took toward Giselle, and the way he looked her dead in her eyes, felt so intimate. It felt so nice that she smiled as he approached. He made her feel like she was the only woman in his world. That was his charm, wasn't it?

Make you feel like a queen, then...

Giselle tried to mentally shrug off her negative thoughts, but it wasn't working. "It's nice," Giselle said as she turned away from Demi.

She noticed his frown before she gave him her back. How exactly was she supposed to feel about the house other than it was nice? All she could think of was how he was pushing her away.

"But," she added, "it's too much space for just me and Cass."

"Angel," Demi said, coming over to stand beside her, "this is a beautiful house in a gated secure community close to his school. Cass will love it."

Giselle felt a pulse of pain as the crack in her heart spread. He basically just confirmed that he wasn't going to be living in the house with them—that nothing changed between them after they made love.

Fucked, she corrected in her head. She wasn't his angel. She was just an angel he fucked.

I should be grateful.

Demetrius was providing her and their son with a home, a car, and money. Cass was enrolled in a great private school. Was Demi going to come over and bless her with some dick every so often? *What did I expect?* That Demetrius Carrion was going to marry her?

"I want to keep looking," she said, looking out over the yard. She focused on the bird that landed on the deck rail.

"Alright," he said.

Giselle spun around and walked to the stairs and climbed. When she reached the top, she held her hand up before the realtor could say another word. The woman could talk to Demetrius. He was the person she focused on the entire time anyway. The woman's desperation for him and the sale could be a fragrance.

Giselle left the house and headed straight to the waiting car. The driver rushed out to open the back door. "Thank you," she said as she slid inside.

Demetrius took his time coming out. He sat beside her but didn't look at her. "Take me back to the office and Ms. Johnson home," he said to the driver.

It's six in the evening already.

Why was he going back to the office? Giselle figured what took him so long was he and the blonde exchanged personal info. Maybe the two were hooking up as early as tonight.

Giselle rolled her eyes as she turned her entire upper body to face the door and stared out of the window. Demetrius hadn't even touched her or slept in the room with her after that night. That was two weeks ago. In fact, he spent most nights out doing lord knows what. Maybe she would take Krysta up on her offer for Friday night. Maybe she did need a girl's night out.

Friday early evening
DEMI
Demi looked up as he thanked his secretary then hung up the receiver of his office phone. He stood when Krysta pushed open his office door and walked inside. Arthur "Brains" Cohen followed closely behind her.

"Demi. How are you feeling?" Cohen asked as he extended his hand.

Demi reached out and shook his friend's hand. "Feeling confused. Did we have business to discuss today?" he asked.

Arthur frowned. Demi turned to his cousin, waiting for clarification. She offered none.

"Would you like a drink?" Demi sat on a chair in the sitting area of his office.

"No thank you," Arthur said as he sat on the sofa. "I came with the information you requested." Arthur reached down and rummaged through the brief case he sat beside his foot. He pulled out a beige folder. On the tab was Cassiel's name.

"Information?" Demi again looked from Arthur to Krysta, who sat beside their friend. Demi didn't expect to see a look of shame on her face but it would have been refreshing. What he got from his cousin's expression was, **"and what"**.

"Well," Arthur said then chuckled, handing Demi the folder, "I have what Krysta requested."

Demi took the folder. He opened it and peered at the first page and read, Paternity Test Certificate. He continued reading, noting his and Cassiel's names, races, and dates of birth along with what he assumed was a reference ID number. Demi glanced at the Method, explaining how they tested, the Results, a series of boxes with numbers and letters under each of their names, then the Conclusion. He read this part silently as well.

Conclusion: Based on our analysis, it is practically proven that Mr. Demetrius Carrion is the biological father of the child Cassiel Carrion.

Demi closed his eyes and let the indisputable information sink in. He knew deep down that Cass was his but having this, even though he didn't think he needed it, was valued.

"Based on the results, Krysta requested that a trust fund be set up and changes be made to your insurance policy. The paperwork is inside," Arthur said. "Along with the private investigator's report on Giselle's mother and her time in Barbados."

Demi leaned forward, opened his eyes, and looked at his friend. He extended his hand. When Arthur grasped his hand, Demi gave it a firm squeeze. "Thank you," he said.

"Always," Arthur said, then stood. "I also included the girls' pediatrician and dentist information. I have to get going but let me know if you need anything else."

Demi stood. He walked Arthur as far as his office door.

"Oh," Arthur said as he pulled the door open, "Adrian wants you to call her to set up an introduction to the group dinner for Giselle and Cassiel."

"I will as soon as I get situated," Demi said. He and Arthur knew his response meant that he would set up something after he handled the threat.

"I'll walk you out," Krysta said.

Demi walked to the chair behind his desk and took a seat. He stared down at the papers still in his hand as he rested his elbows on his desk. He didn't know how long he sat there staring at the papers, but he realized he'd been out of it when Krysta placed her hand on his shoulder.

"You alright, Demi?"

"I can't fuck this up. I can't fuck Cass up like..."

"Like we were?" Krysta asked. She squeezed his shoulder then released him as she sat on the edge of his desk beside him. "You won't. We aren't them, Demi. You will be a great father."

"I don't want him to be anything like me, Krys. I should have never introduced him to the Associates as my heir." He looked up at his cousin and saw the frown on her face. "I'm-"

"A good man," she interrupted. "Who had to do what he had to in order to survive. Introducing Cassiel may make him a target, but it will definitely let everyone know that kid is protected by three of the deadliest people in this city. Giselle... Hell, every woman you've touched wants you any way they can have you. They see your worth even when you can't. You deserve Cass. You deserve Giselle, if she's who you want." Krysta slid off the desk then leaned down and wrapped her arms around Demi's neck.

He held his cousin to him, feeling the love she never failed to infuse in him. Before she pulled away, Demi turned his head and kissed Krysta gently on the side of hers.

"Well," Krysta said as she let go of Demi and stood, "I'll see you tonight?"

"I'll try to stay out of your way," he told Krysta as he watched her leave.

Demi would prefer to spend his night plotting his next move to unmask his pursuer, but he couldn't because Giselle and Krysta had plans to hang out tonight. He knew his distancing himself from her may result in Giselle moving on, and no matter how much he disliked the idea he refused to hold her back.

But...

Demi planned to protect Giselle, both now and after he removed himself from her and their son's lives. Well, removing himself from their lives fully was still something he wasn't totally sold on...just yet.

Weeks had passed and nothing. No further attempts on his life. It was basically business as usual for Demi. Yet, he had to assume his enemies were still plotting, and if they were ruthless, they would continue to target the people he cared about most. The problem was, Demi couldn't keep everyone safe and he couldn't continue holding Giselle and Cass hostage in his home either.

He glanced down at the papers again, focusing on the private detective's report. He skimmed the report but noticed as he came to the end that there was a two-year gap in Giselle's and Cassiel's lives before they resurfaced. It was as if the two of them dropped off the planet until they showed up in the U.S. a few months ago.

Demi unlocked the side drawer on his desk and placed the file inside. He would have to dig deeper into those missing years. Maybe that time held the reason his son was so reserved. Demi knew first-hand that your parents having little meant little to most kids. So that couldn't be the reason.

When Demi was with his mother, they had little. She struggled and made ends meet the best way she could, but Demi remembered he had tons of friends in his neighborhood whose parents were struggling too. Like him, for the most part, they were virtually oblivious to those struggles. They had fun, never realizing the state they were truly in.

Until…until he was old enough to realize he wanted the nice shoes and gear. That was when he started to hustle. Demi wondered if Cass had to do the same. He wondered how much of him was in Cassiel. How much of UGod?

"Mr. Carrion," his secretary said through the phone's intercom.

Demi reached out and pressed the button and spoke, "Yes?"

"I'm finished for the day. Is there anything else you need before I leave, sir?"

"Enjoy your weekend," he said, then raised his finger from the button.

Demi realized tonight would be a good opportunity to hang out with Cass if he wasn't going out to watch over Giselle. They'd spent a lot of time together, he, Cass, and Giselle. That is, until he made love to her. Now he avoided her, but he was determined to get as much time he could with his son. Yet, any time he was alone with Cass, Giselle usually appeared.

He realized soon enough she was shielding Cass. Demi wasn't mad at her for that. If she were smart, she would have never brought Cass into his life. She did…and it was too late now. The boy now knew him, and Demi cared for the kid. He wanted to be able to keep the vow he made, the one where he promised to never let Giselle go. He wanted to make the same vow regarding Cass as well.

Then why won't you commit?

Demi sighed. He kept asking himself the same question. He wanted Giselle. He never stopped wanting her over the years. Having her under him, hearing her breathless moans as he fucked her... Demi's cock was hard on the regular just from seeing her doing everyday damn things. Viewing that house with her a couple days ago, Demi felt being a complete family was fucking possible.

Except...it isn't.

Then1989

DEMIGOD is sixteen

"You know why I'm untouchable," UGod said as he moved up behind Demi.

Demi didn't respond. He just held the gun angled down at the man who was kneeling in front of him. He made the mistake of glancing at the woman who was kneeling beside the man, the man's girlfriend. Demi focused back on the man and tried to block out her tears and the sound of her whimpers as she stared up at him, imploring him with wide wet brown eyes.

"Why my enemies won't ever get a hand up?" UGod continued. "Because I don't have a weakness. I have nothing they can use against me. Pussy is too plentiful to give a shit about one bitch. And blood..." He glided around the woman as he looked at Demi, "can be reproduced. Zeus had bastards spread all over, ready to claim and train. When one died, he called on another. I will put a bullet in your head if you cross me just as easily as I prepare you for my throne. Catching feelings makes a motherfucker weak in this world. Remember that shit," he said then smiled.

Demi knew the shot was coming before he heard it, but he still flinched. The woman fell forward, her brain exploding through the exit wound in her forehead. Demi heard the man's screams as he bent over and tried to pull her to him. He heard the man crying out her name. Demi didn't want to pull the trigger, but he did anyway. He did it to stop the screaming. He did it because if he didn't, there would be the bodies of Jeffrey Taylor, UGod's boss and mentor, and his lovely girlfriend, Rea Collins discovered in the mansion and Demi's body in some shit alley in the city.

Though he'd shot people before, and stabbed a few, Demi had only done it in self-defense. This was different. This was an execution. An execution of someone he actually liked and learned a lot from. Mr. Taylor was a boss, but he was one of the few in UGod's circle who was actually nice to Demi.

"Take what you can carry," UGod told his crew that was scattered in the bedroom.

Demi watched everyone rush from the room. The only members of the Congregation who hung back were Carver and Krysta.

They would take nothing, he, his cousin Krys, and his right-hand man Carver. They weren't scavengers like the Congregation. They were a family.

Now

Demi rubbed his head as the memory hit him. It didn't matter if he had only one foot in the life anymore. He'd made enemies—people who held grudges because of the shit he'd done during UGod's reign and after. That was why Demi never left anyone alive who could come back later. Did he overlook someone?

Standing, Demi pulled his desk drawer open and pulled out his gun. He slipped it into his side holster then buttoned up his suit jacket. It was clear what he had to do; he knew from the beginning. He knew since the day he realized he wasn't escaping UGod. It was why he walked away from Giselle before the incident. It was the reason he hadn't touched her since they made love.

Demi had to rest his hand on his desk and breathe in and out slowly. His pulse quickened as the air he inhaled burned through his nostrils. Eventually, he ended up sitting back in his chair. The truth he'd been trying hard to delay hit him hard. He had to let them go, only…the thought of it was one of the most painful things he ever experienced in his life.

"I have to let them go," he whispered.

But…can I?

FIFTEE

<u>Friday Night</u>
The grand plan he'd come up with? Give the fuckers the target they wanted. That meant Demi needed to be out and about as often as possible. Each night, he hit different spots, making himself visible. Tonight, he was at The Nest, one of the Houstons' clubs. The spot was always jumping and though it was just as nice as Carver's, Demi preferred the latter.

As a VIP, Demi received the same amenities he got at Carver's—the roped off room, top shelf booze, beautiful women bidding for his attention. The music was loud and that usually saved Demi from hearing life stories or future aspirations from his admirers. Only, at The Nest the VIP sections were round glass-walled furnished rooms that sat on rotating platforms just a few feet above the dance floor where patrons partied around them. Music filtered through but not enough where Demi could bask in peace.

Demi looked over the dance floor not focusing on any one person. People moved with the music, some in rhythm and some way off. Looking at their smiles, he figured some were genuine and others he sensed were happy for now.

Bending his stretched-out arm, Demi put the glass he held to his lips and took a sip of the liquid inside as he continued to watch the crowd. He suspected the night would end with hot sex for some. For others, the sex may not be stellar. Whether sex was regretted, appreciated, unwanted, or nonexistent,

Friday night will eventually end for most of these people and their usual lives will continue in the morning.

"I want you to enjoy all The Nest has to offer," James Houston said.

Demi avoided the blonde with the low-cut top who kept her eyes on him since he entered the room. Most of the women didn't recognize him by looking at him but most likely they heard of him. Others who didn't know of him just thought he was some high roller they wanted to get close to, thinking their beauty and pussy were so addictive that he would wife them.

He focused on James Houston. The man looked the role of a nightclub owner as he sat on the plush leather seating across from Demi. He wore a black silk shirt with the top two buttons undone, exposing his chest hair. His attire wasn't as interesting as the invitation James offered Krysta, an all-expense paid night here. Especially knowing that Carver wouldn't like it.

Demi moved his attention from James to Carver, who was watching either James or the three stunning women sitting with James. But Demi was almost certain it was James who Carver was eyeing.

"Would you like to dance?"

Demi drew his gaze from his friend to peer at the woman now standing in front of him. The blonde who stood over him was the kind of woman who could tempt a man into forgetting the prenup he signed. Her long legs were toned, her face was a masterpiece, and her hair was short in a pixie cut. Long lashed expectant brown eyes were pinned on him.

"No," Demi said flat out. He looked past her and out onto the dance floor.

"I heard about you," the blonde said. You're that rich guy who doesn't kiss."

170

The big breasted brunette, one of the women sitting with James said, "Not even when making love?" She leaned forward, pinning Demi with her wide eyes.

Demi slowly turned from glancing at the brunette to look up again, focusing on the spark in the blonde woman's eyes.

"Ever?" the other woman beside James asked.

Still focused on the blonde, he raised his left brow. "Was that all you heard?"

A wide smile spread across her lips. She put the tip of her fingernail in her mouth and swayed from left to right before saying, "I heard that you were hung like a horse and insatiable. That most tire long before you do. That they beg you to stop after a while." She dragged her finger over her bottom lip as she lowered her gaze to his crotch. "I love a challenge. Want to dance?"

"I bet you do, and I appreciate the offer," Demi said, "but no thanks." When the shadow of the blonde moved away, Demi once again spotted his temptation.

"How about you?"

"Oh, Lucille," James said dryly to the blonde. "Carver here, isn't too social so I doubt—"

"I don't dance," Carver said.

Demi took another sip of his drink as he thought, *Poking the bear with reverse psychology won't…*

"…but you can come sit on my lap and we can talk," Carver added.

Mistake.

Demi smirked as he focused on the woman dancing beside his temptress and shook his head.

James stood. "I have business to attend. Please, enjoy your evening."

Demi nodded as James pushed the button for the room to stop spinning. He turned his focus back to the girl of his dreams.

KRYSTA

Raising her arms in the air and pumping her hands to the music, Krysta bounced up and down as she laughed at Giselle. For someone who claimed to not having partied since high school Giselle seemed to be at home on the dance floor. Men surrounded them both, waiting for the opportunity to slip pass the guys they were dancing with at the moment.

"I need a drink!" Giselle leaned into Krysta and yelled close to her ear.

Nodding, Krysta grabbed Giselle's hand then patted her handsome partner to step aside so she and Giselle could walk to the bar.

"We can get the drinks!" Giselle's dance partner for the moment yelled over the music.

Giselle began to nod, but Krysta tapped her on the shoulder and shook her head. "We get our own drinks," Krysta said to the guy and Giselle.

The guy dancing with Giselle shrugged then nodded. Krysta turned forward, noticing her partner had stepped aside. She flexed her fingers around Giselle's hand to test the grip, then led the way to the bar.

When they arrived at one of the smaller bars, this club having three—one large and two smaller—Krysta looked over her shoulder to ask her friend what she wanted. *Humph*, she thought and quirked her lip when she saw that Giselle's dance partner had followed them. She frowned when she noticed that he had hold of Giselle's other hand.

Of course, the guy was smitten. Giselle looked amazing in the body hugging off the shoulder mini dress. The heels where more conservative than Krysta would have chosen but they definitely made her friend's legs seem longer than what they were. Those hard years of living were kind to Giselle's appearance, that's for certain.

In response to Krysta's frown, Giselle spread her chestnut lined lips with her favorite glass gloss in a, "not my fault" smile. *Yeah*, Krysta thought, *this chick has no clue how to handle men*.

Krysta stepped up to the very handsome and—by the looks of his attire—wealthy man, as she gently pulled Giselle to stand behind her and said, "Me and my friend need a moment alone. She'll save you a dance."

The guy looked past Krysta with his dejected gray eyes and focused on Giselle. "Promise," he begged.

…and he *was* begging.

Krysta turned in time to catch Giselle nodding at him with an innocent smile. *Lord, Demi is going to fuck this up*. From what Giselle said, her cousin ran hot that one night and since was akin to an iceberg. The man couldn't see this woman was his future.

She ordered her drink and Giselle's iced tea, then waited at the bar; but she pinned her eyes on the VIP donut where she saw Demi and his entourage. Krysta was doing so to get Giselle to follow her gaze and see Demi. Then Giselle might want to go say hello. With Giselle up close and in his face, Demi would refuse to just watch her from afar, because that was exactly what he was doing. But what Krysta saw sent that plan up in flames.

Not entirely what I wanted her to see.

Krysta heard Giselle gasp beside her then take a step forward as she looked up at the VIP room.

"Is that Carver in that spinning room?"

The music was loud but Krysta heard each of Giselle's words as she ground her top teeth along her bottom teeth. The way the VIP room spun; it was Carver who they saw first, along with the makeup coated giraffe who was sitting on his lap.

"With the twat draped over him? Yup." Krysta heard one of the bartenders call out her drinks so she turned to take them.

When she turned to hand Giselle her drink, the woman was looking at her with a confused expression.

"Twat?"

"Never mind," Krysta said as she tilted her head back and welcomed the burn as her entire drink slid down her throat.

DEMI

"Shit," Demi whispered under his breath. He placed his drink on the side table and stood.

Carver peered around the blonde who was melted over his lap. "What's up?"

"I'll handle it," was all Demi said as he pushed the button for the room to stop its rotation. By the time the room rotated to the stairs, Carver was on his feet. Demi ignored Carver, knowing that he'd chosen the wrong words by stating he would handle it.

Demi felt a little shake as the spinning room locked into place. He pushed the glass door open and walked down the red carpeted stairs. The guard, not one of his men, lifted the thick gold cord to let him and Carver, who was on his heels, pass.

Evan, sitting at the bar, moved to stand but Demi gave him a slight shake of his head. He didn't want to take an army with him. Demi just wanted to handle this with the least resistance as possible. Plus, seeing Evan may scare off the two men who were acting as if they were here to club when in truth, they stuck out like television bad guys.

Their goal, Demi wasn't sure. The two men didn't seem too interested in him, but one was hyper focused on Giselle. She looked fucking fantastic so, were those fucks here tonight for ass. The sudden idea that she may be working with them and against his interests entered Demi's mind.

Whatever she does to me, I deserve more.

174

If Giselle was behind this, behind Sasha's murder and the attempts on his life, Demi wasn't sure how he would feel. How he would react. But he needed the truth, and if that meant waiting and seeing, he would.

As Demi made his way through the crowd, he glanced around the room. It was then that Carver sped up and pushed past him. Letting Carver lead could be a gamble, so Demi picked up his pace to catch up with Carver who was now moving even faster.

"Carver," Demi called out.

Demi reached the scene just as Carver stepped up behind Krysta, wrapped his arm around her waist, and pulled her away from James Houston. The lights above them caught a flash of silver, and Demi sighed as he watched Krysta react the way a viper would if it was surprised. She pulled a blade from somewhere on her person and had it pressed against Carver's throat before he even had a chance to put her back on her feet.

KRYSTA

Everything tilted as Krysta felt herself being lifted off her feet and away from James. She felt off center and dizzy as she was spun around, possibly due her alcohol intake. Whatever the case, Krysta managed to reach the blade she had strapped to her inner thigh and positioned it to the asshole who thought to touch her neck as she glanced to where she saw Giselle last.

When her feet hit the floor, Krysta reached for her friend with her free hand. She pulled Giselle, who looked equally stunned, behind her. Then, Krysta focused back on the asshole. Frowning, she blinked as her eyes traveled up thickly muscled arms to a toned neck. Krysta blinked again as features she knew well became clearer.

"Carver?"

As if he didn't feel the steel biting into his skin, Carver moved forward a step toward James, causing Krysta's small blade to sink into his skin.

"I told you to stay the fuck away from her!" Carver yelled.

Krysta knew she was a bit tipsy, but she was sure she didn't hear what she thought she heard. She looked to James, who sat on a bar stool with a big smile on his face.

"And why should I?" James asked.

Krysta's eyes widened as she looked from James to Demi, who looked calm as usual. She then peered around them. She counted at least five obviously armed men in close range, and three bouncers. This was the Houston's spot. Though they were business partners the situation at hand could be interpreted as Demi and Carver being trapped in a den of vipers.

And yet, neither Demi nor Carver even twitched.

She felt Carver shift right before he leaned forward toward James and at the same time, he grabbed her wrist that still held the knife at his throat. He didn't squeeze or try to disarm her. He just moved her blade away from his neck, but kept hold of her wrist.

"Because," Carver hissed, "if you don't, I'm going to cave your fucking chest in you annoying little shit."

The truth is, the Houstons and their crew are actually stuck in here with Demi and Carver.

"You really can work yourself up," James said as he smiled. He looked to Krysta and said, "Another time then."

Krysta watched as James got up and casually walked past Carver. She saw James smirk as he looked at Demi.

Another time then... And that smirk... What was that about?

It wasn't as though she had time to figure it out, because the next thing she knew, she felt a tug on the arm Carver was holding. Before Krysta could react, she was barely able to let go of Giselle's hand before she was dragged through the club toward the exit. Instinctively, she fought Carver's hold, but it was useless pitting her strength against his.

"What are you doing? Stop!" she yelled. Her demands were ignored as he continued to move them through the crowd with surprising ease. She even noticed that his grip tightened around her wrist, her knife still in her hand.

Carver walked through the exit door that a bouncer rushed to open for them. The night was warm on her exposed skin, but Krysta felt a chill run through her as the taps of her heels sounded off the pavement. Her mind was racing over what he intended to do to her. When Carver stopped on the side of the building, he spun her to face him then let go of her wrist.

"I didn't know it was you when I pulled the knife," Krysta explained as she looked into Carver's hard hazel eyes. He looked at her as if he could see right through her, then he turned his back on her, walked a few steps away, and growled loudly. Another chill ran through Krysta as she tightened her fingers over her blade. "What is wrong with you?" she asked. When he spun back, Krysta retreated, pinning her back to the brick wall.

"You," he whispered as he moved closer until they were a couple inches apart. "Why did you kiss me that day?"

Krysta's mouth fell open. Carver's transformation from angry to broken was so sudden that she almost reached up to touch his face. This man was such a force of nature.

"I…" Krysta said, "don't know." Her eyes fell to his neck where she earlier pressed her blade against his skin. "But you should forget about it. Your neck…" She slid her blade back in the holster between her thighs then reached for the small cut that bubbled with tiny droplets of blood.

Before she was able to touch him, Carver grabbed her wrist again and held it away from him. "That's just it. I can't forget it. If I'm not thinking of how soft and sweet your mouth is, I'm thinking of how succulent your pussy will be when my dick is sliding in and out of it while you ride me. I'm planning," his voice cracked as he looked away, "meals together. I want to cook for you, Krys. I'm wondering how much closet space you will take up in my bedroom. Who our kids will take after? I..."

"Carver," she said as she looked away. Her heart was going to beat out of her chest. "We're friends, right?" Her words came out slow as *everything* he said sank in. When he mentioned them fucking, she thought of one of her favorite fantasies she compiled of him over the years. It was the one of her actually riding him just like he suggested. The mention of meals together had her recalling all the times she wished she was brave enough to ask him on a date when they were growing up, and not some meal during a business meeting about the crew or some bro-like meal with Demi.

He thought of our kids?

"Aren't we?" she asked, confused about her thoughts.

He moved so close, moving her arm above her head as he pressed against her body. The flames flickering in his eyes sent a wave of trepidation along with a spark of lightning throughout her, only to settle in her throbbing pussy.

"I don't want to be your friend, Krys." He placed a soft kiss on her bottom lip as he used his other hand to caress her jaw and chin. "I want to be your man."

SIXTEEN

DEMI

Giselle seemed worried and possibly a little uncomfortable. Demi watched as she switched from meeting his gaze, over to the exit where Carver took Krysta, and then back to the man she basically spent the entire night dancing with. It might help when she did look over at Demi that he wasn't staring directly at her. But he asked himself, where he would be today if he didn't make folk a little uncomfortable?

When he saw Giselle lean into the man who'd been sticking to her like glue the entire night then pat his arm, Demi tilted his head in contemplation. Giselle said something to the man before walking over toward Demi. He rose from the bar stool. Instead of looking at Giselle as she made her way over to him, Demi focused his gaze on the man. There was no smile on Demi's, no questioning gesture, no interest at all. What Demi was conveying with his body language was a clear threat.

By the way the man's eyes widened, the threat was clearly received.

Demi looked down at Giselle when she stopped in front of him. She looked up at him with her lips parted but didn't say anything as she crossed her arm over her chest and rubbed her hand over her bare arm. Her nervousness gave Demi time to look her over for the hundredth time that evening. Her dress fit perfectly, displaying her body in such a way that even a pious man would question his intentions.

"Could you…"

Demi's touch, a finger under her chin to raise her gaze, halted Giselle's words. He wanted to look into her eyes when she spoke to him. Giselle swallowed when he raised his brow. She licked her luscious lips before pressing them together, giving him an instant hard-on.

"Could you take me home, please?" she asked.

Demi caressed her chin with his thumb as he stared into her beautiful brown eyes. Without a word, he dropped his hand to her bare arm and trailed it downward, loving the subtle tremors he provoked, until he felt the twitch of her fingers. He threaded his fingers through hers. For a brief moment, Demi thought she would pull her hand from his by the way she looked down at their clasped hands. He took in a short breath as she raised her head. She didn't look at him, but her fingers tightened around his.

Exhaling, Demi realized in that moment he wanted more than anything that Giselle wouldn't reject him. He knew he was fucking lost, because his whole stealth mode shit was blown with just a squeeze of her hand. He pushed aside thoughts of Giselle's possible involvement in attempts on his life.

Demi looked at Evan and made the hand signal they used for Carver. Evan leaned into a microphone he wore on his lapel then gave Demi a nod before standing and leading the way. The crowd parted for Evan, and therefore for Demi and Giselle. When they got to the exit, Demi let go of Giselle's hand and took off his suit jacket and wrapped it around her shoulders.

Outside, Evan pointed to the side wall of the club. "They are on the side of the building, sir," he advised Demi.

Demi motioned for Giselle to wait with Evan. He wasn't sure what he would see. He wasn't worried about Carver but he was concerned how Krysta would react to his friend's caveman antics.

What he found was the two of them locked in what looked like a scorching kiss. For a moment, Demi rejoiced as he watched the fruits of his labor ripen but then…

Krysta pushed Carver away.

CARVER

The feel of Krysta's lips parting and her tongue wrestling with his was fucking heaven. He gave her waist a squeeze as he pulled her body into his. His cock throbbed but this time it ached with anticipation, and not like a desperate asshole admirer from afar.

Carver was alright with her knowing how turned on she made him. He pressed against her mouth, making the kiss wilder, harder. He knew she wasn't one of those fragile types. Krysta was a wild, passionate, no half-stepping boss. They were both alphas and he was ok with that. She was proving him right by the way she dug her nails into his chest.

Fuck a wildcat. Krysta is a lioness.

"Mph," Krysta moaned. "Stompmm," she mumbled.

Krysta bit into his bottom lip, causing Carver to pull back as she pushed him. "What the…" *Fuck,* faded as he peered at the woman in front of him. He moved to cup her face but Krysta cowered, shrinking back and away as far as she could into the brick wall.

But it was the tears running from her eyes that made him freeze in the spot he was in. He stumbled back and away from Krysta. The look on her beautiful face sent a debilitating ache through him. A sound from his right caused Carver to turn his head to see Demi standing there.

Carver raised his hands in the air as he continued to back away, not certain what he was trying to express. At a loss, he spun around and started to walk toward Demi. "I won't touch her again," he said over his shoulder as he passed by.

GISELLE

The high-pitched whistle of the kettle pulled Giselle from her thoughts. Demetrius' actions were such a contradiction compared to his words. It was so confusing that she didn't know how to act around him. Sighing, she pushed off the counter she was leaning on and turned to the stove. Only, she saw Demetrius turning off the stove burner and grabbing the kettle.

She watched, mesmerized, as he poured the steaming water in the waiting cup, returned the kettle to the burner, and stirred two teaspoons of sugar and a drop of honey into the cup. When he turned with the mug in his large hand, she saw the hanging tea label and thin string.

Giselle smiled. "You take good care of her, don't you?" Giselle asked.

"We try to take good care of each other," Demetrius said then grimaced. "I also think we enable each other." He walked out of the kitchen and down the hallway.

Giselle stayed put. She was worried about Krysta, but she knew that Demetrius was the one who Krysta most likely wanted comfort from. Though she counted Krysta as a friend, she didn't want to pry during such a personal time.

The scene during the drive home was surreal. Giselle could still hear the way Krysta sobbed in her arms as they huddled together in the back seat. Somewhat uncomfortable, Giselle did the only thing she could think of. She placed her hand on Krysta's back and rubbed the small circles she imagined in her head.

It was what she did whenever Cass was overwhelmed. Her son never protested it, so Giselle gave him a backrub whenever he was upset. Only, she also kissed Cass' head, and told him everything would be fine. Did that work with adults? Lord knows no one ever told *her* that everything was going to be fine.

Giselle leaned back against the counter. They were having such a great time too. Tonight, men flocked to her—men of various ages and ethnicities. They all wanted to spend time with her. *Based on my appearance.* Giselle grimaced at the thought. She was mature enough to know what kind of time most of those men were interested in. But attention was attention, and one very handsome man seemed to genuinely be interested in her enough to maybe want to get to know her.

What was his name again? Giselle looked up to the ceiling as she tapped her chin with her finger.

"Horace," she whispered to herself.

"Is that the name of one of your admirers from tonight?"

Giselle stood up straight and peered over at Demetrius as he came to stand in front of her. She wondered if he went to the barber daily to keep his shape up so tight. His brows were slightly furrowed as he looked down at her. His eyes were hooded, with those flecks of amber seemingly ablaze. The man's thick smooth lips were wet as if he just ran his tongue over them.

Wake up!

Giselle didn't know how long she'd been staring up at Demetrius. All she could manage was nod in answer to his question.

Demetrius slid his hands inside his slacks pockets. "Are you interested in this…Horace?"

"He was very nice," Giselle said as she continued to stare up at Demetrius.

Demetrius looked up as if he was thinking over her response before he smiled at her.

That was all it took; a simple smile and Giselle felt her stomach drop. She swallowed and he tilted his head as if he knew how he affected her.

"Well," Demetrius said, backing away, "I think I've done all I can do for tonight."

"I think I'm going to stay for a while," she said.

"Good," Demetrius smiled again, "give me a ring when you're ready to come home, I'll come down and get you."

"Alright," she said.

"Oh, and Angel," Demetrius said as he leaned into Giselle, brushing his lips against her ear, "I'm nicer."

A shiver ran through Giselle's entire body that was so intense she had to close her eyes. When she opened them, Demetrius was leaving through the front door. She heard the click of the bolt lock as he turned it from the outside. Only when she knew he was gone, did she exhale.

"You didn't have to stay."

Giselle looked over at Krysta. Her friend was leaning on the wall with most of her body hidden. Part of her beautiful champagne-colored pajama set was visible, but Krysta's red puffy eyes grabbed Giselle's attention.

"How do you know I'm not here because I need your advice?" Giselle asked as she walked over to Krysta.

Krysta's bottom lip trembled then she lowered her head. "I'm so messed up, Giselle."

"Oh, Krysta," Giselle said as she moved around the wall and wrapped her arms around her friend. "Come on, let's get you to bed."

Giselle held on to Krysta but let her lead the way. She'd only been in the apartment a couple times, and each time she waited by the door. Even from her usual waiting spot by the door, Giselle could tell Krysta's condo was beautifully decorated in a modern style. It was similar to Demetrius', except it was smaller and there was just a single floor. Giselle could have seen herself in the same setting if things had happened differently for her.

Shaking the thought out of her mind, Giselle held on to Krysta while she sat down on the bed. Giselle was loosening her hold when Krysta scooted over and gave her hand a pull so that Giselle had to lay with her. So, Giselle joined her friend on the bed. They stretched out facing each other for several quiet minutes. Giselle watched Krysta's tears slide from her closed eyes as her own slowly opened and closed. She slowly started drifting off...

"I wasn't always like this."

Giselle was jolted to awareness by the sound of Krysta's softly spoken words. She even managed to open her tired eyes before Krysta opened hers. At least she hoped she did.

"I was somewhat normal." Krysta blinked. "As normal as a girl could be with a minor drug lord father who wanted her to be a boy. I think Ciro wanting a boy was the driving force behind his dislike of Demi. Or it could have been he didn't like competing with Demi for Uncle Carlos' attention. They were really close you know, my uncle and my father," she said.

"I didn't," Giselle said.

"Yeah," Krysta whispered. "My uncle Carlos and my father were close, but I think my father wanted to be the HNIC."

"HNIC?"

Krysta's lips quirked into a slight smile. "Head Nigga in Charge."

"Oh, I knew that." *No, I didn't.* Giselle inwardly cringed.

Krysta's smile spread. Seeing her smiling, Giselle smiled as well. But Krysta's smile fell away, and her eyes filled with tears again.

"I think that was why he treated us the way he did. He had to have total control. My mom used to walk on pins and needles, scared he would backhand her for any small issue. If breakfast wasn't ready when he sat down, slap. If she didn't dress me the way he liked, in sneakers and baggy clothes, slap.

If the water in the shower wasn't hot enough, slap. I am ashamed to admit that, after seeing it so much, several times a day, I got used to it. It was life and I thought it was normal.

"But when he signed me up for unisex basketball and football and we met the Carvers... You see, Carver's father was in the life too. Only, Mr. Carver was nothing like my father and uncle. He was more of a white-collar drug dealer with a low-key and charismatic nature. Still, he and my father hit it off. I used to love going to their house, pretending I was interested in being just one of the boys. It was nice that their sons, Jackson and Jamal, didn't mind me hanging out with them."

Giselle realized with a start she didn't even know Jackson Carver had a brother. There was so much she didn't know about Demetrius or the others.

"I saw Carver's parents kiss, and the way Mr. Carver always seemed to like touching his wife. Being around them made me see that my family wasn't normal. Yet, I still didn't try to protect my mother. I told myself a slap here and there wasn't too bad, and my father never hit me. He would yell at me, but he didn't hit me. It wasn't until Demi came to my house unannounced for the first time that I realized how bad my mom had it.

"You see, no matter how close we were, Demi rarely came to my house. He hated my father just as much as my father hated him. For appearances sake, my dad more or less kept his hands off the visible parts of my mom. I was sort of embarrassed about her, so I rarely had friends over and the rest of our family usually steered clear. Funny huh," she said with a halfhearted chuckle, "I was embarrassed about her letting him beat her."

"You were young, Krysta. You didn't know any better."

"So was Demi." Krysta sighed. "My cousin wanted to see me before he left for college. See, he got a full ride and got to go off into the world. I, on the other hand, didn't take my education too seriously. I did what got me by even though Demi tried to tell me to do better. Well, he was in a hurry and wanted to see me. So, he dropped by. I didn't make it to the door in time to stop my mother from opening it...

Fresh tears fell from Krysta's eyes, following the path of the dried streaks from earlier then soaking into the pillow where her head rested.

SEVENTEEN

Then1992/October

Krysta was just now seeing the numbers, 07734, on her pager. *Shit*, she thought as she pulled her black tank top over her head. She wasn't sure when Demi sent the message "hello" but the chime of her doorbell sent a wave of anxiety through her entire body.

"I got it, mom!" she yelled. Krysta went to smooth her hand through her hair when she realized it was still wrapped in a volcano under her silk scarf. Krysta pulled off the scarf as she ran out of her bedroom. She tossed the scarf at her bedroom door as she ran down the stairs.

Krysta came to a sudden stop halfway down the stairs, halting her hand that she was using to finger comb her hair. Her mother, Tammy, held the door slightly ajar. It was open enough for Krysta to see the big smile on Demi's face falter slightly as his gaze swept over her mother then past her mother to see her on the stairs.

"Demetrius," Tammy said, smiling. "I'm sorry I missed your graduation party."

Shit, shit, shit! Krysta started to slowly descend the stairs. She watched as Demi's lips spread into a hesitant yet genuine smile.

"No worries, Auntie Tammy," Demi said before leaning down and kissing her mother on the cheek. "You can send me some goodies to make up for it, if you like."

"Hey," Krysta said as she pulled the door back and away from her mother's grasp. She slipped in front of her mother and placed her hand on Demi's chest. Krysta applied pressure, moving Demi back.

"Put on a jacket, KC," Tammy said.

"Mom," Krysta whined. She heard the concern in her mother's tone, but Krysta just wanted this encounter over with. She continued to push at Demi, urging him with both hands to turn around, but he planted his feet and crossed his arms. Krysta rolled her eyes before turning around. She didn't hear the screen door open as she marched to the hall closet and grabbed her Rebook windbreaker, so she knew Demi was still standing in the doorway. Krysta pulled the windbreaker over her head then stomped back toward him.

Tammy only smiled when Krysta passed her.

"Happy," she hissed at Demi but the word was meant for her mother.

What the hell does she have to smile about?

Krysta pulled the front door closed behind her then elbowed Demi as they moved down the porch stairs and on to small section of the paved walk.

"I thought we were going to meet up later at the diner?"

The path from the porch turned left, leading to another section of stairs and the detached garage. Krysta noticed Carver leaning on Demi's truck with his legs crossed, looking all edible. She wasn't sure when she started to crush on Carver; it was subtle and sudden. When they were younger, he was her homeboy, but him being so close, so nice, and dressing so fresh, she started to see him differently. Not to mention he was flipping gorgeous.

Krysta hid her smile with an unnecessary rub of her nose. She fought the urge to move that same hand over her hair to make sure it was in place, but she used it to wave at Carver.

Instead of waving back, Carver stared with narrowed eyes at the windbreaker she wore.

"Change of plans," Demi said as they descended the last set of stairs. He turned to her, grabbing her shoulders. "But first, what the fuck happened to your mother's face?"

Krysta would normally shrug, because what happened to her mother was the same shit different day. She went to great lengths to keep some folks from knowing the embarrassment her mother was and what went on in her house. Demi was one of those folks. Krysta discouraged her mother from participating in school stuff, and she didn't have friends over much and never when the bruises were visible. Above all, she stressed to everyone that she didn't like people just showing up at her house.

As Krysta looked into her cousin's eyes, she prepared herself for his disgust. Only, what she saw wasn't pity. He was pissed. She'd seen Demi angry, but the way he looked now suggested he was livid.

She thought about lying to him but that idea faded quickly. Everyone knew Demi had mommy issues. He seemed to gravitate to everyone's mothers. When they hung out at Carver's or Brains' houses, Demi always found a reason to spend time with their moms, be it helping with the dishes or with the younger kids, or just talking over lemonade. At first, they all thought he was just a horny teen hound dog who had a thing for older women, but it soon became apparent he just genuinely enjoyed spending time with them.

Now, Krysta felt a stinging behind her eyes. She felt guilty about keeping her mother so guarded from him. *But mom is such an embarrassment.* Demi wouldn't like her mother if he knew how stupid she was.

"She spilled beer on his shoe," she said, deciding to be honest. When Demi's brows furrowed in confusion, she looked down.

"And he hit her because of that?"

"My mom's a klutz, Demi. She fucks up a lot. Ciro—"

Demi gave her a gentle shake, which caused Krysta to look him in the eyes again. "And that means it's ok to beat on her, because she makes mistakes?"

"I didn't say that!" Krysta yelled as she wiggled out of his hold.

"Did you know about this?" Demi turned his angry gaze on Carver.

Remaining relaxed, Carver said, "Naw, man. I mean, I saw a bruise or two on her arm last winter, but she told my mom she slipped on ice or something. We don't see Ms. Tammy much."

Krysta felt Carver's eyes on her back. *Great. Now he knows too.*

"What!" she yelled as she turned to face Carver. She didn't need their judgement.

Carver pushed off the car and stood straight. "Does he do that shit to you too?"

"No," she said, turning to Demi then back to Carver. She got the feeling they didn't believe her. "No."

Carver raised his brows then tilted his head.

Krysta's gaze followed the direction Carver was motioning. *Shit, double shit.*

Parking on the street was Ciro, her father. He never hung around the house during the day. Why the hell was he here now? Knowing Demi and how angry he was, Krysta started grabbing for him but her cousin was quick, turning and shaking her off with little effort.

"Carver," she said, spinning to look at her friend, "stop him."

"When Demi gets like this," Carver said, grabbing her arm, "it's best to just think of places to bury the bodies." He turned his head and spit on the grass as he eyed her father.

Krysta jerked and tried to pull away but Carver pulled her to him, her back to his chest. Normally, being pressed against

Carver would be considered a win, but right now she wanted nothing more than to stop Demi. Her father was a hateful bastard and a killer. "You're not going to stop him?"

"This ass whooping was a long time coming, Krys," Carver said close to her ear.

Krysta stopped struggling as much as she watched Demi cross the yard toward her father.

"You keep rubbing against me like that, you're going to wake the dragon."

Krysta stilled. "Are you fucking serious right now?" she asked looking over her shoulder at Carver.

He bit down on his bottom lip, holding back a grin. "Hey, I'm just trying to be a gentleman and warn you."

Krysta shook her head and turned her attention to one of her worst nightmares come true. Demi was standing face to face with her father. His hands were in his pockets, which was worrisome. After she got to know him, she realized it was a gesture or tick that he did when he was fuming. Demi's back was to her but Krysta would bet money his face was a mask of calm and false peace. Another of his tells—his tone was so low she couldn't tell what he was saying, or if he was saying anything at all; but she knew from her father's nodding that Demi was talking.

Ciro, on the other hand, looked angry. He kept shifting from one foot to the other as he shook his head. When he started talking, or rather yelling, he was quite animated and anyone within a mile radius knew what he was saying. He yelled threats and even flicked Demi on the chest.

Demi looked down, probably at the spot Ciro touched.

"Oh shit." Krysta never prayed but she found herself praying now.

"He won't hurt him with you here. He respects and loves you too much," Carver said.

Krysta frowned. She leaned away from Carver so she could look at him over her shoulder. "I don't think Ciro loves anyone. And as for him respecting—"

"I meant Demi," Carver interrupted. "If you think your pops can go toe to toe with Demi," he shrugged, "you're crazy. You don't know Demi like I do. You don't know how feral he is. He keeps that part of himself from you because he loves you. You are all he has left since…" Carver stopped then added, "So…he cares what you think of him."

Krysta was both surprised and shocked. Carver thought Demi could take her father? *Damn.* As that sank in, the other words Carver said seemed to suddenly reached her brain.

What? Krysta felt her face tingling the same way her feet tingled when they fell asleep. She never thought about how Demi really had no one but her. She looked over at Carver, focusing on his profile.

…and Carver.

They both had Carver.

When Krysta turned back, Demi was turning his back on Ciro. She felt Carver release her as she continued to watch Demi as he came closer. On his face was a look of concentration.

"New plan," Demi said. "You're coming with us." He moved to open the passenger door.

Krysta looked across the lawn, seeing Ciro walking toward the house. He didn't even seem to notice she was standing there as he looked back and cut deep slashes into Demi's back with his eyes. She had come to accept her father ignoring her. Ever since she sprouted tits, he treated her…well, he barely treated her at all.

"You mean the new-new plan," Carver said.

"I can't go with you." Krysta looked at Demi.

"It's only an eight-hour drive," Carver said. "Now I won't have to sit eight hours with him alone."

"You're going too?" Krysta asked Carver.

Demi took hold of her arm and urged her forward. "That was the new plan," Demi said as he ushered her into the front passenger seat. "Carver is going to hang for a bit. Now you can too and keep him company when I'm not around."

"Wait," Krysta said as she tried to move around Demi. "I don't have any clothes, my toothbrush, girl stuff."

"We'll go shopping," Carver said. "Get you what you need and a new jacket too. So, you can take that shit you're wearing off."

"Give it a break, Carver," Demi said. "Come on, Krys. It'll be fun."

With all thoughts of her mother and father gone, Krysta sighed, feigning irritation. She hated to admit it, but she didn't want Demi to go away to college. She felt like he was leaving her behind. Plus, the grip Carver had unknowingly built around her heart was tightening. She took every opportunity she got to be around him without it being obvious.

"Fine," she agreed, "but my company won't be cheap."

Demi laughed. "Has it ever been?" He closed the front passenger door once she was inside.

Krysta watched him as he walked around the front of his truck.

"Yet, you're wearing that cheap ass jacket Isiah gave you," Carver said.

She looked over her shoulder to stare at Carver. "What is your problem with Isiah?"

Carver stared into her eyes for a few heartbeats. His hard expression softened, and for a brief moment she saw doubt in his eyes.

"Nothing," Carver finally said.

"Whatever," Krysta said as she rolled her eyes and faced forward. She was disappointed he wouldn't say what was on his mind, but she was more disappointed in herself. Krysta said whatever she wanted to everyone. She was aggressive and sure of herself, but with Carver she felt like a demur lady in distress.

The truck rocked as Demi climbed into the driver's seat. He inserted his key and started the truck. "Anyone up for breakfast first?"

"Hells yeah," Carver called out from the back seat.

"I could eat," Krysta said, feeling a bit defeated.

Now

GISELLE

"I found out later that Demi told my father he was a coward that day, and that if he ever touched me that he would kill him." Krysta wiped a tear from her eyes. "Ciro didn't take Demi seriously. The first time he hit me was the first time I tried to get in between him and my mother. I was tired of it. That was Ciro's last time hitting me...or anyone else."

Giselle leaned forward and placed her hand on Krysta's. They sat face to face with their legs crossed on the bed, but Giselle was staring down at their connected hands. "I'm glad Demetrius was there for you."

"I thought I was smart. But," Krysta said, shaking her head, "I was just like my mother."

Krysta looked up and what Giselle saw, so much pain, it ripped her open.

"I started dating him a few years ago. A guy who knew me and my family. Ray was always so sweet, quiet, and handsome, but unassuming. I imagine they all are in the beginning. I fell for the lie that he showed me. I let him in my heart. But he knew my weaknesses and after a while, he used them against me. At first, because I fought back, I didn't think it was abuse." Krysta sniffed. "He knew that I wouldn't tell Demi. That I was too proud to admit that I was just like my mother."

Giselle swallowed the lump that collected in her throat. She knew all about being on the receiving end of a jerk who wanted to feel big by making a woman feel small. "How did you get away from him?"

Krysta sighed. She wiped at her cheek with the palm of her hand. "After about six months of living with him, I came home and Ray was gone. He left a note. Can you believe that…a damn Dear Krysta note? He said that he had an opportunity on the west coast that he couldn't pass up. After reading his letter, I ran to our bedroom to check the closet, then the bathroom. Everything he owned was gone. But I didn't feel happy. I felt numb, tired, and ashamed. I stayed in his apartment until the lease was up. Since then, I've avoided having any serious relationships with men."

Giselle nodded but knew better than most that you can't focus on what went wrong in your life. She felt a connection between Krysta and Carver. A strong one.

"But you like Carver," she rubbed her thumb over Krysta's hand.

Instead of a verbal response, Krysta just stared at her with red eyes.

"You can't blame Carver or any other man for what that asshole did to you. Carver—"

"Scares me," Krysta interrupted.

Giselle sucked in her unspoken words and just stared at Krysta. As far as she knew, Carver wasn't abusive in any way. Was she that pathetic when it came to seeing the signs or was she blinded by her trust in Demi so she ignored any warning signs Carver let slip?

"He's never hurt me," Krysta said in a rush.

Thank God. "Then how does he scare you?"

Krysta exhaled. "He is a big man who is quick to anger. What if—"

196

"Wait," Giselle said holding up her hand. "Has he ever hit a woman he's dated?"

"Well…not that I know of."

Frowning, Giselle lifted Krysta's hand up between them. "I think you need to talk to someone. A professional." She saw Krysta's eyes widen. "I know some people in our community frown when it comes to outside help. People of color are strong and proud, but we can also be affected by trauma. I will admit that I didn't get professional help. Maybe I should have…should. I'm so confused right now. I didn't have anyone or anything but my thoughts after what happened with Demetrius. Then I got myself into a horrible situation with another man. Now, I am so confused about what is going on between me and your cousin. What I do know is that I don't fear him or for my safety when I'm with him. I never have. Not once." Giselle felt the truth of her words wash over her. "What I fear is the distance he is putting between us." She sighed as she focused on their clutched hands. Giselle whispered, "I am scared my heart won't recover if I lose him again."

"He loves you, Giselle. Demi has always loved you."

I want to believe that. Giselle shook her head. "We are talking about you. We weren't close back then. I often wished we were, but you were…"

"Rough around the edges," Krysta said, raising her brow and her shoulders.

"Eh," Giselle said, shrugging.

They both laughed. As they did, Giselle felt something click in place. Maybe it was the connection she never felt with her friends in school. She'd always sensed something was missing between her and her group of friends but was never able to put her finger on it. Yet, things just clicked between her and Krysta. Giselle felt it.

As she composed herself, Giselle asked, "Will you consider talking to a professional about your fears?"

Krysta looked at her, seeming to lose all the humor that reflected in her eyes just seconds ago. For a moment, Giselle feared that the "something" that clicked was about to unclick. Then Krysta smiled. "I'll think on it."

EIGHTEEN

GISELLE

As she pulled Krysta's front door open, Giselle wondered what happened to Ms. Tammy, Krysta's mother and Demetrius' aunt. Was Ms. Tammy happy now? Was she even alive? Giselle wanted to ask Krysta, but the question seemed so out of place as their conversation went on.

Giselle looked down at the doorknob as she turned the bottom lock and stepped over the threshold.

When she looked up… "Demetrius?"

Demetrius pushed off the wall just as the heavy door closed behind Giselle, pushing her forward. She stumbled a couple of steps into the hallway but kept her eyes on Demetrius as he pressed the up button on the elevator panel. He was still dressed in what he wore to the club, a pristine black button up shirt with the sleeves rolled up a quarter of the way and black slacks with a blood orange tie. His clothing and shoes always looked brand new to her. He always looked debonair and put together, yet she always had the instant urge to dirty him up…by sitting on his face.

Lowering her head to hide the warmth creeping up her neck and face, she asked, "You stayed out here the entire time?" Giselle didn't try to hide the wonder in her voice.

Demetrius didn't answer.

A shadow of movement caught her eye. What she saw was his extended arm and hand held out for her. Without a thought,

Giselle walked forward and placed her hand in his. The elevator chimed then opened. Neither spoke as they entered hand and hand. They didn't speak as they rode the elevator or when they got off on the penthouse floor. But they did keep hold of each other's hand.

As they walked toward Demetrius' front door, Giselle let her fingers relax, ready to let his hand go, but Demetrius tightened his hold. Automatically, she tightened hers. She said nothing while she watched him open the door, when he locked it behind them, or when he led her upstairs to his bedroom.

"I sent the sitter home a while ago. I'm going to look in on Cass," Demetrius said as he finally let go of her hand.

Okay. Giselle raised her hand up and held it against her chest. Her mind was racing with questions. Demetrius was so confusing to her.

Is he coming back to the room? Does he want me to wait for him? Giselle rubbed her hands together as she looked inside the bedroom. *Did something happen? Was this about Horace giving her attention? Is Demetrius jealous?*

As if she moved on autopilot, Giselle found herself sitting on the end edge of Demetrius' bed. She slept in this room since he brought her home, but tonight she felt more out of place than she had on that first night.

Not knowing what to do with her hands, Giselle smoothed them over the blanket beside her thigh then placed them in her lap and started rubbing them together. She straightened her back with a start and turned her eyes on the bedroom doorway when she heard his footsteps.

Why am I so nervous? Giselle looked down at her hands again.

"You looked like you were having fun tonight."

Giselle's movements were slow as she nodded her head, but her heart was fluttering like a hummingbird's wings. She focused on Demetrius, taking in how good he looked as he relaxed against the wall inside the bedroom. He wasn't looking at her, he had his head lowered and was looking down.

Was that a question?

Her response replayed in her mind a couple of times, but Giselle couldn't form the actual words. She did have fun, and she felt the night ended too early; but she was half worried about Krysta and half excited about the way they connected earlier. And now she was alone with Demetrius, and his attention was focused on her.

It wasn't as if he ignored her these past few weeks, but he hadn't done anything that could be mistaken as interest, either sexual or relationship wise. Their relationship seemed one of consequence and mutual respect, like co-parents with their kid's best interest at heart. If it wasn't for the way he treated Cass and how close the two had gotten, Giselle would have found another place to live shortly after they arrived here.

It was only sex, Giselle reminded herself for the hundredth time since that night they were together. *Just sex.*

"Is something wrong?" he asked.

Giselle focused and, realized she was staring down at Demetrius' shoes. When she looked up and saw him standing directly in front of her with his head leaned to the side with his questioning gaze on her, Giselle opened her mouth to speak. But again, her voice faltered.

Feeling overheated, Giselle ran her tongue over her dry lips as she looked up at him from where she sat on the bed. Demetrius' brows furrowed as he watched her. He took a step back then slipped his hands in his pockets.

His response was so…unexpected.

Frowning herself, Giselle remembered that he often put his hands in his pocket when he was trying to remain calm. The question was, what was he worked up about?

Giselle sighed. Instead of a fluttering heart from her infatuation (because if she was being honest with herself, that was exactly what she was…infatuated with Demetrius) she was feeling the heat of anger crawling up her spine. Trying to figure him out was too damn hard. Not knowing what they were to each other was the single most frustrating thing in her life right now. When she put it all in perspective, she realized she'd been experiencing this uncertainty since she was seventeen years old. She wanted to scream curses, hit something, hit him.

"What are we to each other?" Giselle whispered. She placed her hands on either side of her legs, curled her fingers on the edge of the bed, and pressed down with her palms as she raised her shoulders and peered at him. "Aside from being Cassiel's parents, are we associates? Are we friends? Because, honestly, I don't know what we are."

DEMI

Demetrius had to force himself to stay planted behind the spot he chose to represent the imaginary barrier between him and Giselle. Still conflicted about what he had to do, he knew if he got another taste of her, he would keep her without careful consideration to her or his business.

And that was what he was trying to do. To carefully consider the life she would have with him if he told her how he really felt about her. And yet, a question instead of an answer popped inside his head, and it was playful and seductive.

"What do you want us to be?" Demetrius asked. He knew he should be shutting the conversation down, but he was hopeless.

He watched as Giselle raised her hands and covered her face as she inhaled. He could see she was frustrated. Hell, he was too. He wanted her to know the danger she was in. She and Cass shouldn't even be in his home right now, but he was selfish.

Giselle uncovered her face. Her brows were raised as if she was questioning someone, her eyes wide and seemingly sad.

"This is my fault," she said then laughed. "You haven't changed. You're still playing the games you played when we were teens. Give me an inch and my mind will make it a yard, all the while," she smirked as she looked at him, "you feel nothing."

Is that what she thinks?

Demi clenched his jaw but decided to remain silent as he watched and listened to Giselle unburden herself.

"I don't know what I thought would happen. I guess I hoped…that you missed me, maybe even wanted me. That Cass could make you see that I'm worthy." She shook her head and chuckled again before lowering her head. A single tear ran down her cheek. "Will I ever be good enough for you?" she asked as she looked back up at him.

That one tear tore through Demi like a jagged double edge blade as Giselle's haunting laugh replayed in his mind. He lowered his head as he tried to focus on his thoughts and not the pain he obviously caused Giselle.

"I should have never stayed here."

"I'm the villain in this story, Angel," he said with his head still lowered. "I am the hunter and you've always been the prey. Me the murderer and you, the victim. You are an Angel and I…" He raised his head and looked at Giselle. He watched as tears rained from her eyes, her body shook, and she sucked in air, hiccupping with each breath. "Every day, I remind myself what I did to you. Every day I struggle to keep my hands off you. Every damn day, since I first saw you, I told myself that I can't have you. Because," he said through clenched teeth as he placed a hand on his chest, "I do want you." Demi turned his back to her. He took a step away but stopped and turned his head so that she could see his profile. "You were right. You never should have stayed here. I'll make other arrangements for you and Cass tomorrow."

Demi sucked in a breath as he used every step he took, heavy and deliberate, to put distance between them. He tried to block out Giselle's sobs by focusing on his thoughts.

She's better off without you.

GISELLE

Giselle peered down at the nightie Krysta encouraged her to buy. It was white and made of thin lace. Krysta told her it was innocent and pure. That was how Krysta said Demetrius thought of her…innocent and pure. Lifting the delicate material out of the drawer, she quickly pulled it over her head and threaded her arms through it before she lost her nerve.

Her hands shook as she smoothed the sides over her still damp hips where the material settled just below her round bottom. Giselle walked out of the bedroom barefoot. She took hold of the banister as she descended the stairs one at a time. The hardwood floors were chilly but that didn't bother her.

"I do want you."

That was what Demetrius said. His words were so startling, and she was so upset that she didn't respond at the time. Well, it wasn't as if he'd given her much time to, either. And when he added that she should never have stayed with him…

Her eyes burned just thinking of it.

Giselle gripped the doorknob to Demetrius' home office. Her palm felt clammy as she turned the knob until it stopped and leaned forward to push open the door. Her gaze fell on Demetrius's outlined form, made visible in the dark room due to the faint light streaming through the huge window. He was already pushed up on his elbow on the pull-out sofa bed and looking in the direction she stood. If she could see any more than his outline, she was sure she would see that his eyes were focused on her as she closed the door behind her and turned the lock on the knob.

She wanted to see him but was too afraid to turn on the lights. What if he wasn't happy that she followed him? What if her coming to him was a mistake?

"Understand that if you do this..." he said then paused.

Giselle tried to breathe normally but her chest rose and fell rapidly as she strained to hear the words he was going to say next. The door was the only reason she was still standing. She would not let him dissuade her though, no matter what he said.

"If you give yourself to me tonight, Giselle," he paused again then said, "I will never let you go. You will be mine."

Don't run to him. Be cool, Giselle told herself as she pushed off the door and began to walk toward Demetrius. Each step she took was on shaky legs. Giselle was grateful they were hidden by darkness because Demetrius seeing how happy she was right now would be too embarrassing.

Before she reached the bed, Demetrius extended his hand out to her. Giselle's lips spread wide, stretching so that her teeth were on full display. Her heart was beating so hard she was sure he could hear and possibly see it. Again, the dark was a comfort.

As Giselle straddled Demetrius, he relaxed back on his pillow. Her nightie rode high up on her thighs, allowing him to rest his warm palms on either side of them.

She gasped, her pussy clenching with desire at the feel of his thickness. What Giselle didn't know before, that she did now, was that Demetrius was naked beneath her. They hadn't so much as touched each other in an intimate way since what she called her Kinky Kitchen experience. So, having his hands on her bare skin and feeling his cock engorged, throbbing, and nestled under her quim had her so wired she could barely think straight.

"Are you mine, Angel?"

My God yes! Giselle's stomach dropped as his sultry deep voice heated every nerve in her body. She nodded but when she felt his finger gently caress her chin then lips, she whispered, "Since our first kiss."

Demetrius' cock pulsed beneath her as if her words moved him. He traced his finger from her lips and palmed the side of her face. His hand tangled in her hair, loosening the volcano wrap as he gripped the back of her neck and pulled her face down toward his. The lace nightie that pressed against her breasts irritated her skin, but all her discomfort faded into the background when their lips touched and he pushed his tongue into her mouth then sucked on hers. All she could think of was having him inside her. Her body had the same thought because Giselle found herself grinding her uncovered pussy over his meaty cock.

He closed his fingers, fisting her hair. The gentle tug was enough to break their kiss. Demetrius' eyes seemed to glow in the low light as he looked up at her. "And the business I'm in—"

"Is dangerous," Giselle said, cutting him off, and hoping she banished any objections from his head, "but, I want to be by your side."

She wanted to get back to the reason she came to him. Her whole body and mind ached for him. She slid her hand down to the point where their lower bodies were joined and gently, but firmly, slid her hand around as much of his cock as she could. The feel of his cock had her sighing, and at the same time Demetrius sucked in air. His cock was so hard, so thick, that she had to close her eyes as she shamelessly shivered with anticipation.

In many ways, Giselle wished she didn't feel the way she did about Demetrius. She wished she could walk away from him and just love him from afar. She knew that her priority should be the safety of her son, and being with Demetrius was placing him in the spotlight and it could be a dangerous spotlight. But Giselle also knew that she never felt so clear minded, so safe, so complete as she did when Demetrius was focused on her.

I'm only human. When she looked into his fierce eyes, Giselle was worried that she'd said the wrong thing. Her concern lasted just a second before Demetrius was easing her head down again. This kiss was full-on heat and need. He took her mouth and licked, bit, and sucked like she was the last viable nourishment on the planet.

Giselle couldn't wait a moment longer. She grudgingly pulled back, missing Demetrius' kiss immediately, and rose above him, rocking forward as she pushed her ass up in the air. Her intent was to guide his cock inside her. But before she could, Demetrius wrapped one of his arms around her waist and moved her up more so that her chin was hovering over his forehead as he closed his fist around her hand and moved his cock over the juicy flesh of her pussy. She bit her lip and moaned with every slick pass of his round head over her pussy, her nub pulsing in ecstasy. After a couple passes, Demetrius lined the head up to her opening, and began slowly and deliciously easing into her.

Whimpering sounds escaped Giselle's mouth and over her quivering lips; and they increased as he pushed inch after mind-blowing inch inside of her. It was like this the two times he touched her before. *Is it always going to be like this?* She cried out into his neck as she settled onto him, taking all of him inside her. Her overly sensitive pussy quaked repeatedly as she came over his cock.

"I'm never letting you go," Demetrius said, holding the sides of her face in his hands.

Giselle nodded frantically as she began to ride him. He felt so good, filling her so completely, she barely had to move much but it also felt so good she couldn't concentrate on a rhythm through the mini orgasms that relentlessly rippled through her without letting up.

After stalling a few times, Demetrius grabbed her waist and locked her in place with his cock buried inside her. He moved her with him, and the next thing she knew she was on her back with one leg up over his shoulder and the other resting on his hip. Demetrius looked down at her, his eyes hooded and his jaw tight, appearing sexy and dangerous. He quirked a smile, looking more seductive than a man should be allowed.

He's going to rip me apart.

A quiver of fear swept over Giselle; she placed her palms on his chest and prepared to hold him back a bit. But, he didn't move.

"Marry me."

"Whaa…?" Giselle blinked a few times as she looked up at him. She felt her entire body go rigid as her mind tried to make sense of what he said. She knew the words, but her mind couldn't define them.

"Marry me," he asked again.

Huh

When she still didn't respond, his lips spread wider, showing his pearly white perfect teeth in the low moonlight. Giselle was still in her stupor, trying to digest what he said, wondering if she heard him right. But then passion took over her again.

Oh my God I can't think about that! He can't expect me to have a conversation now.

Demetrius was moving in and out of her, creating such an amazing friction. With just a few strokes and mini orgasms, she was on the verge of cumming harder than she ever had.

"Marry me," he said again and again between moaning his pleasure. Demetrius let her leg down off his shoulder after a while and lowered himself over her. He kissed her seductively as he continued to pose his question. With every pump he asked her the same question. The more he worked and the closer he got to completion, the more his tone grew demanding; and the more he grunted he missed syllables of the phrase as he spoke with the side of his face against hers and his mouth beside her ear.

Giselle felt the beautiful reality of being in his arms. The orgasm hit her like a speeding freight train. Giselle's limbs locked, her toes spread, she buried her face in Demetrius' chest and she screamed. He continued to pump as he came inside her, causing her orgasm to drag out to the point of her seeing specks of light behind her lids. She felt like laughing and crying at the same time, the intensity of her emotions wringing tears from her eyes.

Several deep breaths later, Giselle raised her head that was nestled into the crook of Demetrius' neck; she held him tight to her. When she came down from the clouds and was able to recall that she was in Demetrius' office, he was up on one elbow staring down at her.

"Marry me?" Demetrius asked as he wiped her tears away with his thumb.

She nodded repeatedly as she tried to see his face past her tears.

"I hope these are happy tears, Angel," Demetrius said, looking uneasy. He continued to wipe away her tears.

Giselle laughed. "The happiest," she managed to say right before he kissed her.

"Good."

Her smile faltered a bit as she felt him hardening inside her.

NINETEEN

GISELLE

As the elevator came to a stop and locked on Krysta's floor, Giselle heard a pleasant chime. She stepped out into the hallway when the metal doors parted. Giselle wasn't sure if her presence was wanted or needed as she hesitantly walked down the hall toward Krysta's place.

We're friends.

Those were the words Giselle kept telling herself throughout the morning, but the words still didn't ring true in her ears or in her mind. Did it even matter? They didn't have to be friends for Giselle to be concerned about her. That was also running through her mind.

Besides, Krysta wasn't answering her text messages or her phone the few times Giselle called. She wanted to share her good news—that they were going to officially be family soon. But Krysta seemed to have dropped off the face of the planet. Not only was Krysta ignoring her, she was ignoring Demetrius as well. He told Giselle that he tried to reach Krysta too.

According to Demetrius, Krysta often shut him out when she was in a mood; that she would most likely show up at work on Monday as if nothing strange happened. Yet, even

Demetrius sounded concerned when he called from the office and asked Giselle if she talked to Krysta yet.

Giselle shook off the uncomfortable sensation streaking up her arm as she raised her fist and knocked on the door. She waited for a few seconds before knocking again, this time with more force. Giselle leaned closer to the door then placed the side of her face on it to listen.

"Ms. Johnson?"

Giselle jumped away from the door and whipped around. With her hands clasped and pressed against her chest, she tried to control her rapid heartbeat.

"Sorry I startled you. Mr. Carrion asked me to offer you my assistance."

Giselle looked at the young man for a moment. He looked no more than eighteen years old. She remembered seeing him around the building over the past few weeks. He didn't wear a uniform like the rest of the staff; he was always dressed in a dark suit. Demetrius and Krysta seemed to like him.

"Can you let me inside?" she asked him. She knew it was a stretch. He would probably recite some legal jargon as to why he couldn't let her in Krysta's condo, but when he moved forward, she sighed in relief.

"Of course," he said.

She stepped back to give him space. Giselle wasn't able to see what he was doing, with his body covering his actions but soon enough he was pushing the front door open. "Thank you…" *What was his name again?*

"Jason, ma'am," he said, smiling, "and it is my pleasure to be of service."

Giselle's lips spread into a half smile as she nodded then walked past him to go inside Krysta's place. She took a few steps forward, but when she didn't hear the door close behind her, she looked over her shoulder at Jason. He stood with his body pressed up against the open door, looking at her.

"I am to stay with you until Mr. Carrion arrives."

He must have seen the confused look on her face.

He added, "Mr. Carrion's orders, ma'am."

She nodded again, feeling a little more worried than she was before. She turned and called out Krysta's name as she approached the hall where the bedrooms were located. It was clear shortly after she entered that Krysta wasn't inside. But Giselle took her time looking through each room.

"Krys?"

Carver's voice boomed throughout the condo, alerting Giselle and most likely the residents on that floor that he was there. His heavy footfalls told her he was coming, but Giselle was still startled when his large frame filled the bathroom doorway. The look on his face touched Giselle's heart; for the first time since knowing Demetrius' friend, Giselle felt the need to hold him. He looked so…broken.

"She's not here," Giselle said. She fought the motherly urge to offer comfort to the sad and desperate, and resisted touching him.

Giselle looked at Jason who stood just to the right of the front door. He was standing there for over ten minutes now. What if his boss was looking for him or he had some building duties to take care of?

She looked over at Carver who was walking from the hall that led to Demetrius' office. His head was lowered but she could see the tension on his face. She watched him as he walked between the furniture and took a seat on one of the chairs. With him seated, she turned her attention back to Jason.

"Jason, you can get back to your duties. Carver's here now."

"I'm fine ma'am," Jason said. He remained as stiff as a soldier with his gaze forward.

"He was given a direct order." Carver was seated on the chair with his body leaned forward and his elbows resting on his leg. His head was low and his eyes hidden as he rubbed a hand over his short hair. "He won't move from your side until he is told to."

"This building provides this kind of security to its residents?" Giselle asked. She knew the price tag for living here was borderline extreme, but the lavish amenities seemed to justify the cost. But add in the security and the fee seemed a steal.

"The owner of the building only provides this kind of security for their VIPs," Carver said low and under his breath.

"Who…" Giselle started to ask, but the front door opened and Demetrius walked in.

He glanced at her, offering a smile that faded when he turned to face Jason. "Contact one of our guys at the precinct, and tell them to issue a BOLO for Krysta's car. Evan is checking some of her usual hangouts so you are point here. I don't want Krysta to know we've been looking for her when she pops up, so be subtle and use that pretty boy charm with her neighbors and the unassociated staff when you talk to them."

"Yes sir," Jason said. He looked to Giselle and nodded. "Ma'am." Then he looked at Carver. "Sir."

"I want to know everything, even if it sounds insignificant," Carver said to Jason.

Jason nodded then left the apartment.

"Anything on the building's surveillance?" Demetrius asked as he shook off his suit jacket and threw it over the back of the sofa. He walked over and sat down beside Giselle.

Demetrius surprised Giselle when he snaked his arms behind her neck, cupped the side of her head, then pulled her into him and placed a chaste kiss to her forehead. His lips were warm on her skin and she missed them immediately when he leaned back. Giselle even shivered as his breath swept over her skin.

This man.

She felt her face flush as she remembered that they weren't alone. Public displays of affection weren't really Demetrius' thing. Giselle looked with wide eyes at Carver to see if he saw their exchange; but the man sat on the edge of the chair with a haunted expression on his face, looking at his hands and the cell phone they held.

"I've asked for everything since Friday night. Albert will call me when it's on its way. I also asked him to hack into the phone company to get her records," Carver said. "I don't want to wait."

They know people who can do that? Giselle suddenly felt she was imposing; that she was witnessing something she shouldn't. She shifted her position, preparing to stand, but Demetrius tightened his hold on her neck.

"You know people who can do that?" Giselle asked, skeptically.

"When you find that you need various skills to succeed, you do your best to master them, or at best the basics," Demetrius said. He raised his arm from behind her neck, placed his hand in her lap, and linked his fingers through hers. "If you have the money, you buy, partner, or invest in the companies that excel in these skills or services so that you will always have them at your disposal."

"Do you own this building, Demetrius?" Giselle asked, voicing her suspicions.

"This building and more," Demetrius said.

His words were as plain and subtle as if he was reading a shopping list, as if this building wasn't spectacular.

DEMI

"What did you two discuss on the side of the club Friday night?" Demi asked Carver. He didn't want to pry but he needed to know if his cousin's running off was consistent with her normal behavior or if her and Carver's conversation was the catalyst for something more.

Carver raised his gaze, looking like hell froze over. His eyes were red, he was unshaven, and he looked as though he was wearing something he picked up from the laundry bin. The man looked as if he hadn't slept in days—two days to be exact, and that made Demi more curious than ever about what was said.

"In so many words, I told her I loved her." Carver rubbed his head. "Fuck!" he yelled as stood and started pacing behind the chair.

Demi winced as he watched his friend unravel. He wanted to say something to help. "Why would you do that?" he asked.

"I don't fucking know. I just…I'm tired of waiting for her to catch a clue. Then James wouldn't back off." Carver walked back to the chair and plopped down. He moved his hand over his face, rubbing it repeatedly over his forehead and eyes.

"Has she disappeared before?"

Demi turned his head to face Giselle and watched as her brows pinched together as if she was trying to figure something out. He planned to ask her what she and Krysta spoke of as well. Giselle was the last person to see his cousin before she disappeared.

"She's been known to go off the grid from time to time," Demi admitted.

"But she never dips without giving Demi a heads up," Carver said standing.

It was rare to see Carver visibly rattled. The man was no nonsense, but he rarely stressed the big or small stuff. He was usually smiling but was more the "fuck 'em—they don't matter or kill 'em then adjust"—type of guy. But Krysta was the man's kryptonite. From the day Demi met Carver, he knew that the guy was head over heels for his cousin even if Carver didn't. It took some time for the guy to figure it out. For Carver and Krysta both to figure it out.

"I wouldn't be too worried," Demi said as he pinned Carver with a look of disappointment. He assumed his cousin would have handled Carver's confession better. "But aside from what happened Friday with you two, I don't like the timing." Demi gave the back of Giselle's hand one last rub before sliding his from under hers and standing. "With the attacks on my life and her overseeing a few major projects at work it seems unlikely she would run off. I have an uneasy feeling."

"I fucked up," Carver said. He threw himself back on the chair, allowing his head to rest on the edge of the headrest and look up at the ceiling.

"You might have scared her, but you didn't fuck up," Demi said as he started down the hallway toward his office. He needed a minute alone, some time to breathe. The air in the living room seemed thick, stifling.

Just stepping inside his office made him feel infinitely better. Demi locked his office door and made his way to the sliding door that led to the balcony patio.

Outside, Demi folded his arms over his chest and looked out over the city. The sounds of mid-day in the city comforted him, but it wasn't because he was partial to city living. In truth, Demi was tired of the rat race and bored with the nightlife and the attention it brought. Lately, all he could think of was a less complicated life, a life in one of the houses he'd seen with Giselle and Cass, throwing cookouts with Krysta and Carver by his side.

Could he have it all?

Even at a time like this, he thought as he dropped his arms, leaned forward, and gripped the glass and metal railing. "Always the selfish bastard," he whispered. "Always thinking of yourself and what you want."

But thinking of himself, fighting for what he wanted, it was how shit got done. He needed to be what he was. Trying to keep that part of him tethered was going to get the people he loved killed. Demi raised his head to the sky.

Fuck!

FUUUUCKKKKK!!!!!.

He prayed Krysta was safe because if her disappearance was connected to the shit that was following him...if anyone harmed Krysta, he was going to turn this city into a morgue.

Days later

Giselle glanced over her shoulder and moved her gaze over the man who was following her since she stopped in front of a shop window to admire a purse. She continued along the moderately busy sidewalk for a half block then walked up to another store front window and tapped her chin as if she was really interested in the shoes on display.

Who is he?

Giselle made her way over to the shop's door, pulled it open, then stepped inside.

He could be one of Demetrius' men.

Except, he didn't look like someone she met before.

Inside the shoe store, Giselle walked over to the display in the window and lifted one of the shoes in her hand. She tried to look inconspicuous as she watched for the man to pass.

"Welcome to Pumps, my name is Tara. Would you like to try those heels on?"

Spinning as she jumped with fright, Giselle fumbled with the shoe, but she didn't drop it with the shop woman's hand out to help. "Sorry," she said as she handed over the shoe.

"No," the woman said. "I shouldn't have scared you."

Giselle managed a smile as she moved her fingers through her hair. While sliding her hand down the side of her neck, she glanced out of the window at the passing people.

"Is everything alright, Miss? Is someone bothering you?"

Giselle turned her head and looked to the woman. She was young but had expressive eyes. The eyes of someone who knew fear.

The young woman glanced over her shoulder at another woman who was watching them from behind the counter. "We can help," she said then looked back at Giselle.

The woman behind the counter nodded.

Giselle touched the young woman's hand. "Thank you but I think I may have just freaked myself out. But," she smiled, "while I'm here, I may as well try these on." She tapped her finger on the shoe the young woman now held.

Walking the few blocks back to the car was unnerving even with the sun shining above. Giselle felt so uneasy that she didn't even continue to her scheduled job interview just a block further down from the shoe shop.

Giselle opened the back-passenger door of the car she was using and tossed the shopping bag inside before pushing the door closed. After settling into the driver's seat, she sat her purse on her lap, reached inside of it and pulled out the small cellular phone Demetrius gave her. Her finger hovered over the first digit of Demetrius' contact number when her cell rang, startling her.

Letting out a small yip, Giselle jostled the phone in her hands. She caught it by slamming it against her chest with her hand. When she raised it to see who was calling, she didn't recognize the number.

"Hello?"

"Giselle," a male said, "this is Horace. We met last weekend at The Nest."

"Horace, how did you get this number?" Giselle asked.

"Listen," he said, "I was wondering—"

"Uh," Giselle interrupted, "I've started dating someone since that night."

Horace hummed. "Really?" he paused, "well, we can still be friends."

"Friends?" Giselle asked. She didn't have many friends, with her mother lording over her life and raising Cass. "I don't think—"

"Do you have so many that you don't need one more?" he asked.

"No! Not really," Giselle rushed out. His laughter brought on a slight smile from her.

"Good," he said. "What are you doing now? Let's meet for lunch."

"Lunch?"

He laughed again. "Yes," Horace said. "Have you eaten?"

"Well," she exhaled, "no. But I have a lot on my mind and—"

Horace interrupted again. "All the more reason to meet up in a crowded public place. Who better to talk to or just to distract you than a friend?"

Giselle furrowed her brows as she stared at her steering wheel.

"Come on…It's just lunch. I can be at Sophie's at Wabash Mall in fifteen."

Wow, he's close. She was about ten minutes away. "Fifteen minutes…alright." Giselle agreed.

Giselle drove around the parking structure until she came to the third story lot. She slowly passed each occupied parking space, looking for an empty one. Passing a few rows without success, Giselle gasped with excitement and put on her blinker to claim the spot where she saw a vehicle backing out. When the vehicle was clear, she pulled into the parking space then looked at her watch. It was a few minutes after the agreed-upon time.

The now familiar sound of a low beep notified Giselle she had a message. She reached over and stuck her hand inside her purse and felt around until she found the small cell phone. She flipped it open and saw the envelope on the display screen.

Horace: Where did you park?

Giselle peered out of the windshield at the location post then typed: Third floor, C lot.

As she pushed open the door and got out of the car, she noted how dark it was in the parking garage. Giselle grimaced, wondering if her bags were alright in the back seat, but she figured with the low lighting they would be hard to spot. The image of someone breaking the window of a car that didn't belong to her, because she carelessly left bags in view, was enough of an incentive for her to open the back door and grab the shopping bags.

Giselle saw a couple of men walking in her direction as she walked around to the trunk of the car. Once she opened the trunk, she placed the bags neatly inside and closed it. She turned around and was about to walk toward the mall entrance when she realized the men she glimpsed earlier were a few feet from her. If she started forward now, they would cross paths and possibly collide. So, she smiled at the approaching men and waited for them to pass.

But when the two men, one tall with a Caesar haircut and the other bald and stout, stopped in front of her, Giselle frowned then asked, "Can I help you?"

"Give me your keys," the stout man demanded.

"Excuse me?" Giselle asked as she frowned.

"The keys to your car," he repeated, "…give them to me."

Instinctively, Giselle took a step back and shifted to hide her purse with her hip and at the same time extended her arm and held up her hand. "It's not my car."

"Don't make this hard Miss," the tall one said as he reached for her purse.

"Hey!" someone yelled.

Relief spread through her as she glanced away from the men to see Horace walking toward them. She looked back at the two men standing in front of her, hoping they would run off when they saw her friend. But what happened next wasn't how she thought it would play out. Instead of running off, one of the men, the short one, pulled out a gun and aimed it at Horace.

When the shot rang out, a piercing ringing sounded in Giselle's head. She squeezed her eyes closed and jumped, backing into the car as she bent over and covered her head with her hands. Someone was tugging on her arm that the purse was hooked on. Thinking fast, Giselle pushed at her attacker, dropped the purse, and made a run for the breezeway that connected to the mall.

But she didn't get far.

She was stopped short, losing a shoe as one of the men wrapped an arm around her waist from behind. She screamed, "Take the car! The keys are in my purse! Let me go!" She wiggled and struggled to get free. At one point, her eyes connected with Horace, who lay face down a few feet from where she last saw him standing.

For a moment, the sight of Horace shocked her into submission. All her fight faded as she stared at his still form and the blood that was leaking from beneath him. But when the man carrying her adjusted his grip on her, Giselle renewed her struggling and screaming.

"We have Cassiel."

Giselle stilled. The tall man who held her gave her a shake before he placed her on her feet on the ground. Breathing hard, she turned and focused on his beady little eyes.

"Show her," the short one said as he pulled her keys from her purse.

The tall man extended his arm and held out a photo in front of her face. Giselle covered her mouth as she stared at the image of Cass tied to a chair with a gag over his mouth.

"If you want to see him again," the short one said, "you will stop fighting and get in the car."

Giselle narrowed her eyes at the man as she grabbed the photo. On closer inspection, she noted the look in her son's eyes. Without another thought, she opened the back door of the car that was already unlocked and got inside.

"Did you take care of the guy tailing her?"

"Yup."

"Then tie her up."

Giselle closed her eyes, silently praying her son was unharmed.

DEMI

The light indicating his secretary was trying to reach him was flashing again. "Yes, Franklin the gains are noteworthy, but I am interested in the impact our presence has had in the neighborhood. Get me that information. Also, I'd like to know what we can do to improve that area. Speak to the people who live there, not any of the city's representatives."

A notification tone sounded so Demi absently picked up his cell phone that was resting on his desk. He unlocked the phone and pressed the envelope that signaled he had a new message.

Krysta: Needed a few days. Sorry I didn't tell you before. Will contact you soon.

As Demi forwarded the message to Carver, he looked up when he heard the sound of his office door being pushed open. The look on his secretary's face was one of urgency and concern.

"Franklin," Demi said as he watched Rachal rush over to his desk, "something came up. I'll contact you soon." He didn't wait for a response before hanging up the office phone.

"Sir," Rachal said as she reached over his desk and lifted the phone receiver and held it out to him. She tapped the button for line two. "There's been an incident at Cassiel's school."

Demi sat forward, took the receiver from her, and placed it to his ear. "Hello."

"Mr. Carrion," the caller said, "we have a problem."

As Demi listened, he raised his cell phone and used his left hand to hold it steady; then he moved his thumb to click on a contact and text one word, CRIMSON.

Demi lowered his head in a slight nod at the police officer who passed in front of him, then he focused his gaze back on Detective Monahan. The detective stood beside another officer and the school's security guard across the room. The foot traffic and noise level inside the administration office of the school was loud and growing louder.

Turning his attention away from Det. Monahan, Demi angled his head, focusing on the conversation the school's security guard and a police officer were having. It was damn near impossible to hear all of what they were saying clearly, though some words reached him. So, reading their lips was all he could do. By the way the guard was sweating, his wild-eyed gaze, and his stuttering through his interview, it was clear the middle-aged man was nervous. Demi reasoned his discomfort could be due to a few reasons:

His failure to protect a student could be eating him up.

The possibility of being fired may be worrying him.

Maybe he was nervous because he was in on it.

The school guard turned his head and made eye contact with Demi. The man sucked in a breath then immediately looked away. Then, it was because who's child it was.

"…if I were you," Monahan started but stopped.

The detective most likely paused what he intended to say due to Demi exaggerated sigh. Demi rubbed his brow in an attempt to calm himself as he focused his gaze on Monahan, who was now in front of him, effectively blocking the officer and the school's security guard from his view. Demi licked his lips and smirked with a chuckle that told most who knew him that he was annoyed.

"You just don't know," Demi said, "do you?"

"Know what, Mr. Carrion?" Monahan asked.

Demi shook his head. In doing so, he noticed the security officer nodding before turning and walking away from the officer questioning him. That Demi was once again having to deal with Monahan was testing his patience. He had no time to play cat and mouse with this man.

"I was saying that if I were you, I'd leave this to the professionals." Monahan glanced over his shoulder.

Demi noticed Monahan eyeing Carver who just stood from where he sat across the room and walked over to the door.

"We don't need your troop here mucking up our investigation. Unless," Monahan said, turning back to glare at Demi, "you want to get something off your chests."

"You're right." Demi stood. He looked to Evan who was standing over by the receptionist desk. "The professionals need to handle this."

Evan met up with Demi at the door, opening it for him. As they stepped out into the quiet hallway, Evan spoke low but loud enough for Demi to hear, as his thumbs swept deftly over his cell. "There is a witness who called in the abduction. A kid named David Fallston. Still no word from Andrew, the man we have on the misses."

Demi tightened the grip he had on the phone he held in his hands for the past forty minutes. He felt Evan's eyes on him but said nothing as they walked down the hallway. He'd been waiting to hear from Giselle or the people who had Cassiel.

Evan's phone rang.

"Yes, get there first and keep everyone else out," Evan said to the person on the other end. He hung up the phone. "One of our insiders has access to the kid and is waiting for you."

Demi nodded as Evan pushed open one of the double exit doors. Outside was the scene of a mass exodus in front of the school. Cars filled the drop off loop. Parents and caretakers were being assisted by officers and staff as some demanded their children's release. Others were crowded around the yellow police tape that sectioned off the crime scene.

"Have you contacted Pedro's family?" Demi asked as he looked over at the blood stain beyond the yellow tape.

"Michael transported Pedro's father and brother to the hospital. He's still in surgery," Evan said. "Carver wants us to meet him over in the staff parking lot. It's this way."

Demi and Evan changed direction. As he walked, Demi pressed the call button on his cell. "Call me. It's about Cass." The message he left Giselle now was different from the prior ones. He didn't want to tell her any information over the phone to scare her, but now...

Now, he just wanted to hear her fucking voice, and if that meant revealing their son was in danger to get her to respond to his calls, he would...had. Though, he had a feeling she wasn't going to call. He just didn't want to admit that his woman and his son were both out of his reach.

Whoever is behind this is living their final hours.

GISELLE

As soon as she became aware, Giselle yelled, "Cassiel!" Blinking in the darkness, she pushed up on her elbows and listened to the sounds around her. There was no response to her call for her son, but there was an array of sounds to make out.

At some point during transport, Giselle woke and discovered she was blindfolded, bound, and gagged. Her hands were now free. Giselle pulled the blindfold off her face, letting the cloth rest around her neck. She moved her gaze around the room she was in. It was dark but there was light coming from the open bathroom behind her.

"A motel?" Giselle frowned. She'd been in enough to recognize the setting.

Giselle pushed up and off the bed. She absently glanced down at the rope that hung from her left wrist as she rushed over to the door. Taking hold of the knob, Giselle applied pressure to turn it. There was no give, so she pulled at it using all her strength.

The window.

She moved to it and pushed the curtains back. Her shoulders slumped when she saw the metal shutters that covered every inch of the window. She turned and ran to the bathroom.

Met with the same metal shutters on the high small window over the toilet, Giselle slammed her fist on the wall. "Cass!" she screamed, "are you here?"

Hearing no response, Giselle walked back into the room. Her finger grazed the edge of the bed as she sat back down. Tilting her head, Giselle glanced over at the side table. There was no phone. Just a bed, a long six drawer dresser, a small refrigerator, and two side tables.

At least it wasn't filthy.

Giselle squealed at the sound of someone pounding on the motel door.

"We're leaving in ten. Use the bathroom because we ain't stopping." A voice called through the door.

TWEN

About 5pm

Demi followed Mr. Fallston out onto his front porch and shook his hand. "Thank you, Mr. Fallston for allowing me to talk with your son," he said.

"I'm sorry David wasn't able to give the police much to go on," Maury Fallston told him.

"If he remembers anything else," Carver reached into his pocket and handed the man a card, "call us."

Mr. Fallston nodded.

Demi extended his hand to the police officer who waited on the walk. "I appreciate your help, Owen." Demi said.

"Anything to help, Mr. Carrion," the officer said.

Carver walked up with a pensive look on his face. "No call yet?"

Shaking his head, Demi pulled his phone from his pocket. He had it set on vibrate and ring. It hadn't escaped him that no ransom demand had been made. Demi dialed as he made his way to the car. "Torrey," he said, "send cars for the Partners. Tell them this isn't a request." He hung up and was already at the car drafting a message when Carver caught up to him. He typed the last word into the text message then hit the send button. "I've called a meeting," Demi said over the roof of the car as he pulled the door open. He sat down in the seat and started the engine.

"I'm going with you," Carver said, sitting in the passenger seat.

Demi nodded then looked at the side mirror while he pulled out onto the street and headed for the restaurant. With all the information he'd gathered amounting to jack shit, he was at a loss. He was no closer to finding his son or determining Giselle's whereabouts. Holding on to his sanity was just about all he could do.

They drove in silence for over twenty minutes. Just as Demi pulled his vehicle into the parking lot of the restaurant, Carver's phone rang. Carver answered then pointed to the phone as he began talking. Demi nodded, understanding that his friend would come inside when he was done with his call.

Demi was closing the door to his vehicle when he saw Evan walking toward the restaurant's back door. When Demi walked over, Evan was waiting and pulled the door open for him. Inside, Torrey waited. He stepped in pace beside Demi as Evan trailed behind them.

"Dre Houston is on his way. James and the Stoughtons are inside, waiting," Torrey said.

Demi quickly moved through the kitchen and headed for the dining room table they used for their meetings. Demi eyed each man as he approached, wondering if any of them was involved. He was looking for a tell.

James stood a few feet from the table. His cell phone was pinned to his ear and his mouth was moving. He offered Demi a nod but turned his back and kept talking on the phone. James seemed relaxed but busy.

Lionel Stoughton was already seated at the table. He looked flustered and annoyed. Oliver was also seated at the table. His legs were stretched out and his head was relaxed back as if he was sleeping.

"Demetrius," Lionel Stoughton said as he stood, "what is the meaning of this? I am a very busy man. You can't just make demands—"

"Sit down," Demi said. His tone held none of the politeness it usually did.

Lionel slowly sat down as he stared, looking gob-smacked with his mouth open, at Demi. Oliver opened his eyes wide and sat up. He looked at his father for a second then turned to glare at Demi.

"Keep me notified. I will call you back," James said to his caller before walking over to the table. He stared at Demi as he took his seat.

"I'm not going to repeat myself so we will wait for Dre," Demi announced as he looked to each of the three men seated. He sat down and focused his gaze on the table in front of him.

Oliver cleared his throat as if he was about to speak but Dre entered the room, loudly expressing his irritation with one of Demi's men who followed. Oliver, along with the other men at the table focused on Dre.

Except for Demi. After seeing his men cleared out of the room, he closed his eyes and tried to breathe.

As Dre got closer to the table, he addressed Demi. "I was in a very important meeting. This shit better be—"

"Sit down," Demi hissed. He had his hands fisted in front of him and could feel his anger about to explode.

"I don't know who the hell you think I—"

"We're well aware of who the hell you are," Carver said as he placed his hand on Demi's shoulder. "And, I'm certain you all know who I am. So, I need you all to shut the fuck up and listen because the man you know isn't the man sitting here," he squeezed Demi's shoulder, "right now. DemiGod's wife is missing and his son has been kidnapped. We want to know if any of you are involved."

There was some chatter amongst them while they looked at each other in confusion, and it was insignificant and unhelpful. Demi opened his eyes and looked at the Partners.

Each man brought something to the table that made the other's businesses run smoother. Not to mention, peace between the people who ran the city was always lucrative. That someone here possibly wanted to end that peace was foolish…in more ways than one.

Demi saw indignation from Oliver and Lionel. He saw disgust from Dre. But it was James whose eyes showed what Demi thought was sympathy.

"Do you know anything about this, James?" Demi asked.

James shook his head and said, "Only that he was taken. I told my guys to put their ears to the ground and bring me whatever they find."

"Look," Dre said as he leaned forward. He was a hand talker, so he moved his hands as he spoke. "Whatever you got yourself into, it has nothing to do with us. We have a business arrangement and nothing more. If it isn't business related, we aren't getting involved." Dre then looked at Carver with disgust. "And he shouldn't even be in here. He isn't a Partner…yet."

Demi pushed his chair away from the table, scraping it across the floor, and stood. "Each of you may think you know me pretty well. What you need to understand is, you don't," he said, looking to each of the men around the table. "I started this partnership because I know that to climb you need to build relationships and network. But I've grown so much since then. Let me show you how much." Demi looked over his shoulder at Carver. "Shut it down." He then looked back to the men at the table.

"What does he mean, shut it down?" Lionel asked.

Oliver shrugged, looking confused. "I haven't a clue."

Dre frowned. "What the hell are you talking about, kid?" he asked as he began swatting James' hand away. Dre seemed to want Demi to explain and he resented James' attempts to calm him down.

"Until now, you've only heard stories of who I am. For your sakes," Demi said, "I better not find any evidence that any of you are behind this or the attempts on my life."

"Let go, James!" Dre yelled before focusing back on Demi. "We are equals in this. No one outranks the other. You can't just threaten us."

Carver's voice was clear as he spoke into his phone. "Close up shop," he said. "Everywhere."

Demi glared at Dre. He spread his lips into what he knew was a smile that was more sinister than sweet. He turned away, leaving everyone at the table in an uproar. Demi reached into his pocket, pulled out his phone, and pressed the number three button until the call connected "Shut all business down."

As he and his men made their way through the restaurant, Demi told himself that he made the right decision. He never planned to show the Partners his reach. Yet, he wanted them, his men, and the entire city, to know that as long as his family was out there without him, no one was going to rest easy.

"They've found something," Carver said as they reached the back door of the restaurant.

Demi spread his fingers out to release the tension in his arms then closed them at his sides. He patted his leg with his closed fist. His feelings, the helplessness that filled him with every unanswered ring of her cell phone, coupled with not knowing where his family was, filled Demi with an uncertainty that he promised himself he would never experience again.

"Tell me where," Demi said. He walked through the door being held open for them then got inside his car. Demi took in a deep breath then exhaled.

"I can drive," Carver offered as he gazed at him from the open passenger door.

"I've got it," Demi said, though he wasn't certain if he had it or not; all his senses were numbed and his emotions were heightened. All he knew was that feeling the steering wheel in his hands right now grounded him. He needed to drive.

Demi stood in the shadows of the parking garage looking at the scene from a distance. He couldn't take his eyes off the body that lay covered on the ground. It was Carver lifting the police tape for the female officer to duck under that got his attention.

"This is Lisa," Carver said when they were close. "She arrived on the scene first and questioned some witnesses."

The woman, an officer, appeared nervous as she looked at Demi, but she spoke with a steady tone. "A witness stated two men, one short and bald and the other taller with short gelled hair, was reported hassling a woman when the victim approached. They shot the victim and it seems they showed the woman something that immediately calmed her, but the witness wasn't close enough to see what it was. After they showed her this item, the woman got into the car willingly."

"What kind of car?" Carver asked.

"A black sedan, new." She shifted from one foot to the other as she looked over her shoulder at her fellow officers who were working the scene then back to Demi. "Um, the body is ID'd as Horace Dillinger. Thirty-two years old, from the west side, some petty thefts and drugs convictions when he was younger but nothing in the last five or so years that he's been arrested for. He's been clean."

"Known accomplices?" Demi asked.

The officer nodded as she pulled out her pad. "Looks like his brother has been in Gilford Correctional for the past two years."

That was the same information Demi received Saturday morning after having the man checked out.

"Thanks, sweetheart," Carver said as he handed her his card. "Give me a few days on that matter we discussed."

She nodded then whispered, "Thank you."

Demi and Carver walked toward the car. Carver pulled something from his pocket and held it out.

Demi took it, knowing immediately it was Giselle's cell phone. He held it up and looked at the last number dialed. It was his number. He then looked to the last number that called. That call was from Horace and it didn't last long.

"Police reported a body was found in the shopping district about ten minutes from here. Basic descript sounds like Andrew," Carver said as they walked.

"Have Evan confirm."

"He's already in route." Carver placed his hand on Demi's shoulder. "I can go," he said. "Jails don't bother me."

Demi looked over at his friend who walked beside him. "I'll handle it."

About 9:00 pm

The sun was setting. Demi stared from his seat on the hood of his car, at the orange glow of the sun as it hovered in the pale bluish gray sky. He looked down and rubbed his hands over his head, going over all that he knew.

- Cass was taken from the school around two pm; his security injured.
- Giselle was taken about an hour and a half later; her security killed.
- Horace Dillinger, who she met at the club, was dead.
- No contact from the kidnappers.

Sighing, Demi eased his hand into his pocket, pulled his phone out, pushed the answer button, and placed it to his ear. "Yea," he said.

"Sir," Torrey said through the line, "All business is closed. We've sent out the code red and the word is getting out. All of the businesses you are affiliated with have been informed. Most have closed down business for today and await word on when to reopen. People loyal to you have either left work or called out. Reports say that all business for the Stoughtons and the Houstons have been greatly affected. A lot of places throughout the city are basically closing, closed, or lacking enough support to stay open. I've informed everyone that first responders and hospital staff are exempt, as you've requested."

"Thank you, Torrey. If you hear anything…"

"Of course," Torrey said. "Where are you? I can—"

"I'll check in later," Demi interrupted.

"Yes, sir."

Demi ended the call, slid his phone into his pocket, then looked up. Sounds coming from the door close to where he was parked had Demi pushing off his car hood and standing. Three men appeared, two of them were prison officers. The other was an inmate. Demi pinned his eyes on the man he'd come to see.

"Didn't know you had this much pull," the inmate said as he shuffled forward. He looked up into the sky, took a deep breath, then smiled before fixing his eyes back on Demi.

"There's a lot you don't know about me, Nelson."

When Demi looked at them, both of the officers backed away and walked off to the side, leaving Nelson Stoughton and Demi standing alone together. Nelson frowned as he watched the officers settle beside the wall, out of earshot.

Nelson nodded as he smiled and looked back to Demi. "I heard you swore to never set foot inside a jail. Thought it was just some badass musings," he said as he moved his gaze around the employee parking lot of the jail. "I see you've managed to keep true to that."

Being in the jail parking lot was still uncomfortably close for Demi. "Horace Dillinger," he said as he stepped closer.

"Well," Nelson said as he lifted his cuffed hands up and scratched his lower ear. "Horace is a friend of mine. I asked him to do me a favor."

234

"Why?" Demi narrowed his eyes.

Nelson frowned as he looked at Demi. "Whatever you're thinking, it's wrong."

Demi nodded as he pushed his hands into his pocket and sucked his teeth. "Dillinger is dead and someone has my wife and son. Tell me what you know. Is Oliver involved?" In Demi's mind, Lionel, Nelson's father and head of the Stoughton clan, wasn't capable of pulling this off. Nelson was too smart but yet he was stupid enough to try to protect his brother Oliver, even though Oliver had him set up and was the reason he was in prison.

"Damn," Nelson said, looking away then back to Demi. Shaking his head, he said, "Look," leaning forward, "Oliver is a complete ass, but I don't think he would hurt your family. I don't know what his end game is for me, but he isn't a killer. I—"

"My wife and son!" Demi yelled.

Nelson sucked in a breath while taking a step back. The sound of his shackles clanging seemed louder than what they were.

Demi also noted that one of the officers jumped forward, but the other officer placed his hand on the man's shoulder and shook his head when the officer looked back at him.

"Oliver isn't a killer. His fight is with me. Horace was to be keeping an eye on Krysta. If he got mixed up with your woman, it's unrelated."

Krysta?

Demi took in a deep breath. He closed his eyes, remembering Nelson and Krysta had a very short fling a few years back. Demi exhaled as he reigned in his anger. As he did, he spread open his fisted hands that were still in his pockets. "Tell me if you know something," Demi said, putting his mask of calm back in place, "...anything."

Nelson seemed to nod absently then, looking Demi straight in the eyes, he said, "Look, Oliver is an idiot. Yes, I asked Horace to watch Krysta because of what happened to

Sasha. I wanted," he looked down, "to keep an eye on her. But I know nothing about your family. Hell, there isn't even a buzz about it in here yet." He raised his shackled hands and pointed to the prison.

A haze of red seemed to cloud Demi's eyes as he turned and stepped away from Nelson. He didn't pay attention to his surrounding as he walked back to his vehicle. It wasn't until his phone rang that he even realized that he was inside of it. Demi heard the phone ring again as he worked it from his pocket.

"DemiGod?"

Blinking a few times, Demi swallowed before saying, "Yes?"

"Look," Carver said then sighed. "Seems we may have to consider she maybe—"

"She isn't." He refused to believe Giselle was behind this and was about to say as much when his other line beeped, alerting him to another call. "I have to go."

"Wait! Look, there has been activity at her old house. We have to—"

Demi didn't even announce that he was clicking off. He placed the cellphone on the dashboard and started his car at the same time his phone rang again. Demi picked the phone up but didn't recognize the number. "Hello."

"Demetrius..."

"Giselle? Angel, where are you?"

"Clairmont Avenue," she said in a low tone. "Come alone."

The call disconnected.

TWENTY-ONE

Then1983

When he heard voices downstairs, Demi kicked his sheet away. He rolled over then slowly pushed off the bed and stared at the flickering black and white static image that came on the television after the station shut down for the night. The cassette tape his homeboy J-boy made was playing on low. Afrika Bambaataa's *Planet Rock* just ended then dead air before *White Lines* by Grandmaster Flash and the Furious Five started up five seconds into the song.

Shaking his head at his friend's shit effort at making a mixtape, Demi swung his legs off the bed and rubbed his head as he glanced at the big black flip clock on his dresser. It read just after three in the morning, but that couldn't be right. His mom had to work in few hours and she never stayed up late or woke this early.

Except, the voices rising from downstairs told him that she was up.

Demi placed his bare feet on the wood floor but quickly raised them and hissed. *That's damn cold.* Fully awake now, he used his toes to lift his socks from the floor and pulled them on one by one. He pulled on his sweatpants, the shirt that he took off and tossed across the bottom of his bed last night, before walking over to the window and pushing the curtain aside.

Remnants from the snowfall a few weeks ago was still piled up at the bases of the street lights. The glow from one of the lights bounced off a shiny black Maxima, grabbing his attention. Demi narrowed his eyes. He saw the same car pulling off from in front of his house last week. He couldn't make out who was driving it and when he asked his mother, who was standing in the doorway watching it ride away, she wouldn't tell him.

Demi looked over his shoulder. The voices from downstairs were growing louder. He let the curtain slide free of his fingers as he stepped away from the window and moved toward his bedroom door. The floorboards creaked with every step he took.

Now2:00 am

Demi gripped his steering wheel harder the closer he got to his old neighborhood and the only place he ever felt was truly home. As he slowly turned onto the narrow street that was Clairmont Ave, he took in the state of his old hood.

Rowhomes on both sides of the street looked occupied but stood in disrepair. Some looked abandoned, and one corner unit was missing a section of the roof and a good chunk of its side wall. There was trash littering the gutters and sidewalks. It was two in the morning, but a few blocks over people were still out and active. Demi suspected this block wasn't the bustling mecca he remembered so fondly even in the daylight.

Continuing down the street past the house he once lived in, Demi stopped at the intersection. He turned right then made another right into the alley that was behind his old house. He drove past his house then onto the side street and parked.

It's quiet.

Demi got out of the car. He also noted that the vehicle Giselle was taken in wasn't out front or back. The only evidence he had that she could be here was her call. Demi pulled his hood over his head as he walked away from the car. After he got the call from Giselle, he traded his suit, tie, and luxury car, for jeans, a hoodie, and a non-descript car he kept at the old apartment he still leased.

As he slowly moved toward 315 Clairmont Avenue, Demi remembered the house being much bigger. Looking at it now, as he climbed the cracked marble steps, it seemed small in comparison to what he'd built up in his mind. He could admit that UGod's vision for him surpassed what he may have become if he'd grown up here. Still, this was home, the only place where he felt truly safe until…

Until UGod came and fucked it all up.

He still had no clue who was behind this. But whoever it was knew more about him than he liked. Demi lowered his gaze to the doorknob but realized the door was ajar. Using the tip of his booted foot, Demi eased the cracked door open. He stood in the doorway for a moment, listening to himself breathe as he stared into the living room.

Demi frowned.

Someone was seriously fucking with him. He peered over at what was visible from his vantage point, trying to make sense of what he was seeing. Even in the darkened room, Demi noted the furniture, the curtains, the decorations, all resembling the original items from his youth. He felt angry, empty, and conflicted. And, he wasn't afraid to admit, he was fucking freaked.

If he hadn't witnessed UGod's and Ciro's coffins being lowered into the ground himself, he would think they were behind this. But certainly, it was someone who knew about his past. Wanting to get to the bottom of it more than ever, Demi moved inside. He absently kicked the door closed with the heel of his boot like he used to as a child.

As the surprise of seeing the setup of the home he hadn't seen in eighteen years sank in, the sounds of humming and clanging coming from somewhere further inside reached Demi. With a scowl still on his face, he moved through the living room, past the stairs that sat in front of the dining room, and headed toward the kitchen where a light was on. As he slowly moved closer, the humming and other noises grew louder.

Just before he reached the arc that separated the dining room and kitchen, some of the items inside the room became visible to him. Demi saw a chair under the kitchen table, a row of cabinets and shelving, and he saw a pool of dried blood on the floor.

Demi immediately looked away from the blood as he moved under the arc and entered the kitchen. He unexpectedly locked eyes with Cass. His son said nothing as he sat on a metal and red vinyl chair at a small white and metal table located in the center of the room. Cass did slightly shake his head as he moved his eyes to the left.

"I know you have a gun. Put it on the floor and kick it away."

Demi took two steps back as he gawked past the gun that was pointed at him and focused on the person holding it. Even through the passing years, even though his memory of her had all but faded, there was no mistaking who he was looking at standing on the other side of the open refrigerator door.

"Mom," Demi whispered as he took a step forward.

"Daddy!"

Demi grabbed his arm as his wide eyes fell on his mother. The sound of a gun going off wasn't new to him. The burn of hot steel searing through his flesh wasn't either. The sound of Cass screaming for him and sobbing was.

"I was aiming for your heart, you piece of shit. Toss the gun and stand in that corner." She used the gun to motion to the table from a stooping position, still using the refrigerator door as a shield.

"Shh," Demi said to Cass as he applied pressure to his wound. "Calm down son," he said, keeping his eyes on his mother. Her hair was longer, she was much thinner than he remembered, and she had a tightly puckered scar that started from just above her right eyebrow and jaggedly traveled up her forehead and disappeared into her hair.

"Don't talk to him. Not a word!" Madeline Gaines yelled. "Gun then corner!"

Demi let go of his arm and slowly moved his hand into his hoodie pocket and pulled out his gun. He tossed it on the floor in her direction then backed into the corner where the pool of blood was drying.

"Don't cry, sweetie," she said. "I won't let him take you from me again, Demetrius."

Demi looked at his mother then to his son who was sitting back down in the chair, wiping at his eyes and seemingly trying to calm himself.

"Please," Cass said with a shaky voice, "don't hurt him anymore. Please."

Madeline moved from behind her refrigerator door shield and walked over to Cass as she kept the gun on Demi. "My sweet boy," she said as she bent and kissed the side of Cass' head. As she spoke, she cut her eyes at Demi. "He will be nothing like you, Carlos. You tried to kill me. You took my son. Had your whore raising him as if she is his mother."

"She's my babysitter. I swear," Cass rushed out, "Please let her go home,"

Giselle?

It was then that Demi looked down at his feet resting in the sticky blood. Was this Giselle's blood? "Is this her blood?" Demi demanded.

"No," Cass said. He began stroking Maddie's arm when she looked at Demi.

"Why are you talking to him, Demetrius? He was never good to you. When I told him that I was pregnant with you, he said get rid of it. When you were born, he came to the hospital with diapers. He named you and stayed at my place with us for about a month. Never once in that time did he touch you.

"And one day, he left, leaving us two thousand dollars and a note on a napkin that said he wasn't coming back and to tell you he died. The money, he said, was for my trouble." She pinned Demi with her lips curled in a growl and her nose crinkled. "For my trouble!" she yelled.

Taken aback by both her words and her hateful gaze, Demi tilted his head as he opened then closed his mouth. He wanted to deny that he was UGod. He wanted to curse the blood running through his veins. He thought of all the years of pain he endured. The beatdowns, being talked to like he was a pet instead of that asshole's kid. The feeling of being on guard every single day…all the ways he suffered.

It infuriated Demi that despite what he endured under UGod's thumb, how much it hurt to hear how much his existence was despised, he never realized just how much his mother suffered. Her expression of her pain was like a dark sludge, thick and tainted with sin, smothering out the only goodness he knew as a child. Demi groaned, feeling as if her pain had hands and was choking him.

Still, Demi couldn't say that UGod ruined his life like the asshole ruined his mother's. With the shit Demi was into then, at that age, he could admit he could have died on this street. Still, given the choice, he would have never left his mother's loving arms. With her love, he may have changed. But UGod tried to kill her, instead he wounded and disfigured her. Now she was messed up in the head too. That broke Demi's heart.

"You can't hurt my dad," Cass said in a gentle tone, as if cooing her while still softly crying.

Hearing Cass' pleas, having him involved in this mess, his mess, was unbearable.

Maddie's arm had drooped a bit, possibly from the weight of the gun, but now she extended her arm again. "But he doesn't love you, Demetrius. He never loved you."

Demi raised his hand, causing Maddie to straighten and focus solely on him. He pushed his hoodie off his head to show his full face. He tried to maintain a relaxed expression. "Mom," he said calmly. "Look at me." He held his hand to his chest. "I am Demetrius, your son." He pointed to Cass. "That is my son, your grandson Cassiel, and you're scaring him." He held his bloody hand flat and facing down in the air. "Put the gun down."

"No, no!" she screamed. "You're a liar. Always a liar. I've watched you, followed you. Saw you acting like a big shot. But I never saw my son. I thought…" She shook her head as if clearing the thought. "That girl, she shouldn't have died but the lord will forgive me once I rid the world of your evil. It should've been you. We tried again, but there were too many people at the club that night. Then," she looked down and smiled at Cass, "I saw my baby."

"You were responsible for the car bomb that killed Sasha?" Demi asked as he lowered his hands to his sides. He looked into her eyes, hoping to see…a hint of rationality as he tried to breathe through the pain of the truth.

"I didn't mean for her to—"

"Stop," Demi said calmly as he clutched his chest with his bloody palm.

"Dad, please," Cass begged as he sobbed.

"Leave the room, Cass." Demi ordered.

Maddie reached for Cass but he was able to duck away. Demi didn't spare his son a look to see if he left. He knew Cass would do what he said. When he saw his mother's gaze following Cass, he said as he started forward. "You are scaring my son."

"He's my son. Mine!" she screamed as she raised the gun and fired once. "I should have never set eyes on you. You were my greatest sin. Now you want my son. He's mine. MINE!" Maddie narrowed her eyes. "I will never rest until you're dead," she hissed, before pulling the trigger again.

He didn't so much as flinch when the bullets hit the wall behind him. "I'm sorry I was a little shit when I was a kid and gave you such a hard time," Demi said as tears welled in his eyes. "I'm sorry your life wasn't full and happy." Demi knew the closer he got, the more accurate she would be.

She shot again. Again, she hit him but only grazed the side of his cheek.

"I'm sorry he did this to you, mom." Demi rushed forward. Her eyes widened as he grabbed hold of her hand and pushed it up and away from his head as the gun went off again. "You," he said as he forced the hand that held the gun down while looking into her eyes, "don't know how much I missed being with you. How I missed the soft timber of your voice. Your comforting scent."

Maddie fought to maintain control of the gun but she was no match for Demi's strength.

As he stared into her eyes, he didn't see recognition or even fear. What he saw was unadulterated hate. It was a hate that he knew well. It was the same hate he harbored for the man she wanted dead. He knew that kind of hate never died. It festered until it was satisfied.

A single tear dropped from his eye. "You told me to never stop fighting to survive. That I deserved everything."

"You deserve death, you murderer," she growled, trying to get control of the gun.

"Maybe I do," Demi said.

Demi shuttered and squeezed his eyes closed as the sound of point-blank gunfire ricocheted through his body. Droplets of blood sprayed over his face and body. He stood there, holding his mother's limp body up and pressed to him.

GISELLE

It had been a few minutes since she'd heard the last gunshot, but Giselle still refused to let go of Cass. She tightly held him, her hands over his ears as they huddled together in the corner of the room. When she felt Cass stir, she released his ears and allowed him to move back enough for them to look at each other. Seeing his beautiful face again, she pulled him to her and kissed him repeatedly,

"Dad," Cass said as he pushed away from her and stood.

Giselle grabbed his wrist before he was able to turn and run off. "Wait," she said, whispering. "Let me go first. You stay behind me. Run outside if you get the chance."

"Alright," Cass told her as he helped her to her feet.

Ignoring the pain that radiated from her wrists and ankles, Giselle moved in front of Cassiel and made her way out of the low-lit room. The floorboards creaked and bowed a little in spots but kept stable. Once at the stairs, she pinned herself to the wall as she descended one step after the other.

At the bottom, Giselle looked to her right, toward the kitchen. The light was on but…

"Mom," Cassiel said, his voice cracking.

Giselle turned to look at her son then looked in the direction he was staring. To her right, down the hall and past the living room, she could see the front door was open. In the bright moonlight, a figure sat on the marbled stairs, stooped over.

"Demetrius," Giselle said as she grabbed Cassiel's hand and rushed toward the front door. Her socked feet slid a few times over the wood flooring as she jogged, but she kept her balance. "Demetrius," she whispered as she stopped in the doorway.

He didn't look up. He just kept his head down with his hands over it.

"Mom," Cassiel said while tugging on her shirt sleeve.

Giselle passed through the doorway but had to work her way down from the top step because the width of Demetrius' frame made it impossible for her to move around him. Once her feet touched down on the pavement, she moved in front of him.

Demetrius moved so fast when he saw her that Giselle yelped. She didn't even get to see his face before he pulled her down to him and buried his face in her neck. His body gently trembled as soft sounds of his crying tore at her heart. Never had he shown this kind of vulnerability to her. All she could do was cry with him as her heart ached for the man she loved.

TWENTY-TWO

The afternoon after the shooting

DEMI

"Mr. Carrion," the nurse said as she stepped into the room. She glanced at the bed. When she spoke, she spoke in a whisper. "We need you to stay in your room during afternoon rounds."

Demi shook his head as he looked down at Giselle and Cassiel. "Just put me in here with them," he said, also whispering.

"We aren't one of the fancy hospital's you're used to, Mr. Carrion. This is all we can offer as accommodation for your family while you're here, and most do not get even this," she said, wrapping her hand around his IV pole. She took two steps away from the wall Demi was leaning on then looked over her shoulder and raised her brow at him in challenge.

Demi kept his eyes on Giselle and Cassiel, who lay together on the hospital bed. He frowned at the middle-aged nurse when he turned and focused on her. "I just want to watch them for a minute more," he said.

"If you don't take care of yourself, how will you care for them?" she asked as she narrowed her eyes at him. Whatever she saw in his face softened her expression. "Fine. But just for a minute."

Demi offered her a bow of his head and said, "Thank you."

"Whatever," she said, smiling as she released the IV pole, walked to the door, and pulled it open.

As the nurse moved to leave, something in front of her on the other side of the door caught Demi's attention. Looking up, Demi saw two detectives standing outside the room. He took hold of his IV pole and followed the nurse out into the hall where he regarded the men.

"Mr. Carrion?" one of the detectives asked as he held up his badge. "I'm detective Shultz and this is detective Gullet. We have some questions."

"If you're up to it," Gullet added.

Demi nodded before leading the two men down the hall and out through the security door to the nearest sitting area. He went to an area that was off in the corner, positioned his IV pole out of the way, then sat down in one of the chairs. Shultz sat down in a chair beside him while Gullet chose one across from them.

The two men looked like complete opposites. Aside from Shultz being white and Gullet visibly of Asian descent and possibly something more Demi couldn't say, Shultz was younger and seemed more reserved. Meanwhile Gullet was older and appeared to be a bit looser, if looser had a look. Both wore suits but Gullet didn't have on a tie.

"We have your initial statement taken on the scene, but we just have a few more questions." Shultz flipped open a pad and read from it. "Your fiancé made the call to you alerting you where she was. Why didn't you alert detective..." he looked at his pad, "Monahan or BCPD of what was going on before driving four plus hours and engaging yourself?"

"I was told not to. I didn't know who had them and I didn't want to take chances."

"The decedent, Ms. Madeline Gaines. She's your mother, correct?"

"Yes," Demi said, trying to talk around the lump in his throat.

Shultz pulled a couple pages of his pad over the one he was on then looked up at Demi. "She was shot in that same kitchen in the spring of 1983. It was reported by her neighbors she had a son who also disappeared that same night. That case went unsolved," he said.

"Your son," Gullet interjected, "told my officer that Ms. Gaines kept referring to him as Demetrius and claimed he was her son. That his father, Carlos Carrion aka UGod, shot her in the head and kidnapped him and that she planned to kill him…you. Carlos Carrion your father?"

Demi lowered his head. "Biologically."

"Did you witness the shooting when you were a child?" Shultz asked.

Sighing, Demi thought back to that day. "I heard it. When I ran into the kitchen, UGod's brother grabbed me. I could only see her hand and some blood. He thought he killed her. I thought he did too when no one came for me."

"Why didn't you tell someone?" Schultz asked, with a frown.

Demi chuckled as he looked at Det. Schultz. "The kid I was then, would never snitch no matter what. For me, taking that man's abuse, knowing what he did to my mother, it only fueled my drive to be nothing like him."

Gullet pinned Demi with a sympathetic grimace. "It's hard for some to understand how things work for those raised in certain circumstances."

Demi got the feeling Gullet had his own horror stories. He looked back at Shultz. "Does your pad say what happened to her, after?"

Shultz looked to Gullet.

Gullet shrugged as he said, "Regardless of his beginnings, Mr. Carrion fought the obstacles in his way and became a law-abiding citizen and hugely successful businessman. Initial evidence supports exactly what the witnesses stated so I see no reason to withhold your findings about Ms. Gaines. And, he is her closest living relative."

Shultz nodded. "Your mother survived the gunshot but was in a coma for about five years. With extensive physical therapy she was able to recover some but mentally, as you know, she didn't fare well. She was placed in a transition home and treated in an outpatient facility for post-traumatic stress disorder among other things. Ms. Gaines did well with her treatment but was involved in an incident in 1993 when she attacked a man at a park, claiming he stole her son. She got off with a warning, mostly because the father chose not to press charges. She lived basically a quiet life until she dropped off of the grid about eight months ago, which was reported by her psychologist."

"The men who kidnapped your son and fiancé were Winston Beck and Arnold Pegg. Winston, a patient at the same outpatient clinic where your mother received treatment, was being treated for a drug addiction. Arnold Pegg was his friend and junkie buddy. Cynthia Pegg, Arnold's sister, told us he was hired by some lady to kill her ex-boyfriend, Carlos..." Gullet motioned to him with a flip of his hand, "...you for five grand. During one of those attempts, Sasha Fuchs seemed to have gotten caught in the crossfire.

"Their plans changed when Ms. Gaines was informed you had a little boy with you. From your son's statement, your mother promised them the ransom you'd deliver when you came thinking you would get your son; but when they delivered your son to her with a bruise across his cheek, she decided to poison them. She shot Winston. He must not have cared for meatloaf. Their bodies were discovered in the basement."

Gullet sighed as he stood. He motioned for Shultz to stand. "Well, Mr. Carrion, I am sorry this all happened to you. I firmly believe you had no choice when you tried to wrestle the gun from her. It is unfortunate…the results. I hope experiencing every milestone of your son's life, alive, well, and being there to offer him love and support, will be some kind of comfort for you." Gullet extended his hand.

Demi stood and shook the man's hand. "Thank you."

"Hmm," Gullet said then walked away.

"Thank you for your time, Mr. Carrion. Seems we have all we need," Shultz said before awkwardly extending his hand.

"If you need anything more," Demi said, "please don't hesitate to contact me."

A month later...

The music pulsed through her body as she made her way down the long hallway. The last time Krysta was here, the night Demi and Giselle were shot, she did something on a whim. She kissed Carver. As she stepped up to his office and placed her on the door, Krysta thought of how big of a mistake that was.

Closing her eyes, Krysta sighed. *You can do this.* No matter how mad Carver gets, she needed to deal with the mess she started. She was on a mission to clear the air between them.

Krysta gave the door a knock.

"Come in."

His voice sent a chill through her causing her entire body to shake. "You can do this," she said quietly.

Pushing open the door, Krysta saw Carver sitting behind his desk. His attention was on a computer monitor and not her. This gave her the opportunity to look him over.

Carver had always been gorgeous. She couldn't help being extremely attracted to him. He was her very first crush, but it was his family's connection to hers that convinced her that they were better as friends. Even to the point of ignoring how he felt about her.

Krysta caught him checking her out too many times to count. He gave her the most adorable and meaningful birthday and Christmas gifts, never forgetting once in all the years they've known each other. Carver also kept his relationships from her, never parading anyone he dated in front of her, even back when they were in high school.

But his no-nonsense brutal nature, his muscled form, and his quick yet deceptive temper scared the hell out of her. He also didn't fit her idea of her perfect guy, which was the brainy, thin, and innocent-looking type. Yet Ray was all of that and ended up being exactly what she'd been running away from.

"What is—" Carver moved his gaze from the monitor and focused on her. He was up on his feet and moving toward her in a blink of an eye.

Krysta stepped backward into the door, closing it.

Carver stopped a few feet away and raised his hands, and he took a couple steps back. "I won't come any closer. Just don't leave, Krys."

Her chest ached. As Krysta looked into Carver's panicked and fearful eyes, she teared up. She did this to him. She made Carver afraid to be himself.

"Krys," Carver said, his voice cracking, "Please, whatever I did to hurt you, I'm so sorry. Know that I would cut off my hands before ever using them to touch you in anger. I'm not Ray."

Krysta gasped loudly as she placed her hand over her mouth. His words opened a floodgate of emotions. Tears streamed from her eyes. She always wondered if Demi and Carver had something to do with Ray's leaving, but when she asked Demi, he seemed confused and began to question her about it. Krysta was able to end the conversation without giving away her situation with Ray. She never thought to question Carver, assuming he wouldn't make a move without Demi.

He saved me.

She closed her eyes and sobbed. Warmth surrounded Krysta as strong arms embraced her. Her hands were locked between her and Carver, allowing her to feel his chest. His rich, sexy, masculine scent always had a way of making her drop her guard. It was one of the reasons why, whenever they were together, she kept him from touching her. Now, she needed his touch so much.

"Thank you," she whispered.

Carver's entire body seemed to relax around her. "I didn't kill him," he said as he rested the side of his face on her head, "but I fucking wanted to. If I thought for a second that you would have forgiven me, I would have buried that bastard."

Krysta laughed. She pulled her hands from between them and wrapped them around his waist. Being with him like this felt so damn good that she snuggled in closer. Krysta inhaled, feeling safe, feeling home. It was just as her therapist said.

"I love you," she said, squeezing him.

Carver placed his hands on her shoulders and held her away from him. His eyes were narrowed as he stared down at her. "Krys…baby, don't…" he shook his head as his ran his tongue over his lips, "please don't play with me."

"I love you, Jackson Carver," Krysta said, again.

"Woman," Carver said, just before he took her head in his hands and kissed her.

Like she expected, his kiss was gentle, all consuming, and expressive of the love she desired. It sparked a new fire and mission in her. The fire rose as she wrapped her arms around his neck and was raging by the time he pulled back and out of the kiss.

"Carver," she said, licking her lips as she looked into his dreamy light brownish-green eyes. "I uh," she looked down, feeling her face burning, "been dying to feel you—"

He silenced her with a kiss then stepped back. "Don't say some freaky shit Krys or I swear to God, I will take you right here and now."

Krysta bit her lip as she raised her brow. With a wicked grin, she reached behind her and used her finger to search for the doorknob. When she found it, she turned the lock.

"So, you like dirty talk?" she asked, with an even wider wicked grin.

The next day
DEMIGOD

Demi flicked the turn signal down as he stopped his car at the traffic light. The red glow of the light sparked his memory of standing over his mother's lifeless body. The metallic scent of blood filled his nostrils, causing them to flare. He blinked a few times, focusing back on the road as he proceeded to make a right turn.

Demi drove past the front of the building to the rear, where he pulled his truck into the empty parking lot beside a dirty white four-door sedan. He turned his truck off, removed the key from the ignition, pushed open the door, and got out. He looked up at the dark sky, feeling a peace only the countryside can offer. It was a sky unhindered by city buildings and smog, yet he saw no stars.

"You're like one of those stars, Demetrius. Bright and perfect. You remember that, son," his mother said, smiling.

He experienced her talking to him in memories more frequently since the events of the previous month. Things he thought he completely forgotten started coming back at random moments throughout each day. Sometimes, he needed a minute to collect himself.

Like two days after that night while he was washing his hands in the bathroom, his mind conjured an image of his mother smiling at him. The thought had him in a bad way. Demi had to sit on the ledge of the tub and breathe through the pain. He knew his mother wasn't the person her circumstances made her. She was the woman who loved him first, she was his first love.

Demi crossed the parking lot. He grazed his gloved fingers over the waist-high brick wall as he walked around it and descended the stairs. He knocked on the back door, glancing to his left then his right. He'd been here a few times over the years, and yet this place still gave him the creeps.

A devil with the creeps. He chuckled.

There were some clicking sounds then the door was pulled open.

"What's up, DemiGod," Carver said, giving him dap.

Demi clasped hands with his partner and leaned into a hug. "You know that DemiGod shit is set aside when the suit is on, right?"

"No doubt," Carver said, smiling as he moved aside. "No doubt."

Demi walked inside the room. As usual, the place appeared sterile and cold.

"Hey," Carver said as he closed and locked the door, "I wanted to say thanks for giving me and Krysta your blessing. She found it a huge comfort."

"I'm always rooting for her happiness," Demi said. "And yours."

Demi meant it too. To him, Carver never hid his interest in Krysta. Though, Carver never really threw his feelings out to the world either. Demi felt that was Carver's mistake, not being clear with how he felt from the start. What's obvious for some isn't always clear for others. It was why he asked James to give Krysta a bit of attention. Demi knew it would annoy Carver and push him to play his hand.

Yet, Demi had no idea Nelson Stoughton still had designs on his cousin.

That shit may become a problem.

Carver patted Demi on the shoulder as he passed. "Thanks, man."

"How's business?" Demi asked as he followed Carver down a long hallway.

Carver shrugged. "Consistent. People die regularly so I'll always have business," he said. "Had to remodel a bit. Got a new furnace." Carver stopped and opened the door for Demi. "He's in here."

Walking through the door, Demi focused on the rectangular wooden box that was on the floor. As if on cue with their entrance, the box began to jerk and muffled noises could be heard coming from it. Demi moved over to the coffin-shaped box, bent on his haunches, lifted the lid, then moved it aside enough to fully expose the man inside.

Demi watched the man's eyes widen then his brows furrow as he began struggling anew while trying to talk through his gag. Reaching inside, Demi lowered the gag and asked, "Last words?"

After clearing his throat, Monahan yelled, "Are you both insane? I am an officer of the law!"

"Yeah, that means jack shit to us," Carver said, standing over the box.

Demi raised a brow as he looked down at the detective. "If you were just a thorn in my side, you wouldn't be here. But," he grimaced, "being an ass isn't your only offense, is it?"

Monahan gasped. "Wha…what are you talking about? You're the criminals. Not me. Let me out of here!" he demanded.

"Cadet Ally Danvers, Cadet Denise Bishop," Carver spoke the names, casually. "Carolyn March, who worked as a department secretary for only three weeks before you assaulted her."

Demi watched Monahan closely as understanding then fear reflected in his blue eyes. "You managed to scare them into keeping their assaults a secret. Even scared a couple into leaving the police department, but you made a grave error when you chose Officer Lisa Witcombe. When you raped and tried to silence her, she realized you acted with such ease that it couldn't have been your first time. She dug a little and what she found were other women who you've assaulted and silenced."

"You see," Carver added, "Lisa isn't the weak little girl you thought she was. She's a bulldog. Lisa managed to convince them to allow her to video record them telling their stories."

Demi watched each of their statements where they recalled the encounters with Monahan. Lisa even provided a recording of Monahan threatening her to keep quiet.

"Then," Monahan spoke up as his eyes frantically darted from Carver to Demi, "I should be arrested and charged. I should have my day in court."

"There was an offer on the table that Lisa relayed to the women, to go about this the legal route, with all legal fees paid for by an anonymous Good Samaritan. But it seems you managed to diminish their trust in the justice system." Demi gave Monahan a satisfied grin. "Each of them refused to go the legal route, and it's all thanks to you." Demi sighed as he stood.

"Wait!" Monahan yelled as Carver began to slide the lid back in place. "You can't do this to me!" He paused and asked, "Why do you care what happens to those broads? You're no saint yourself."

Demi held his hand up. Carver stopped moving the lid, allowing them to see Monahan's eyes and him to see theirs.

"Do I need a reason?" Demi asked. When Monahan frowned, Demi smirked. "There was one thing I was expecting, what most people in your situation start crying out,"

Demi said while staring at the detective. "Yet you didn't deny the accusations."

"Would you believe me?" Monahan asked, his face a mask of fear and anger.

"No," Demi said, waving Carver on.

"Nooooo!" Monahan yelled. "Let me out. We can work together. Be a team, us three." Monahan's movements jerked and rocked the coffin. "I have connections. I can keep the cops off your back. I can help you."

The desperation in Monahan's voice didn't move Demi at all. Demi smiled as he and Carver lifted the jerking coffin up onto the rolling slide table.

"Now why would I need any of that? I am a respectable legitimate businessman. Besides," Demi said, chuckling, "rapists are beneath us."

Carver pressed a button. The coffin began rolling forward as the furnace door opened. The rocking and the bumping noises coming from the coffin became more frantic. Demi instantly felt the heat from the flames, so he backed up.

"Why didn't you use the cardboard boxes? This wood seems too good for him."

Carver shrugged. "I haven't been in here in months. Abel moved shit around after the remodel. I couldn't find the cardboard ones."

"Ahh," Demi said.

Monahan's words turned to screams as the coffin met with flames.

"You used his cuffs," Demi said, "will those burn?"

Once the coffin was all the way in, the furnace doors closed. The screaming stopped soon after.

"Eh, when I run the magnet over the ashes, I'll recycle them, any fillings, or pins. What do you want done with the crushed bones?" Carver asked as he led the way to the door they'd entered. "I can give you a deal on urns."

"The dump is fitting," Demi said as he walked through the doorway. "You destroyed all the evidence Lisa handed over?"

Carver nodded as they walked toward the back door. "I did. There is nothing linking him to them or them to us."

"Well," Demi said, opening the door to get outside. He breathed in the fresh night air then looked back at Carver. "I'm headed home. Feel like a run in the morning?"

"Naw," Carver said. "This is gonna take about five hours. I'm sleeping in. May come down and have lunch with Giselle and Cass, though."

Demi waved then climbed the steps. As he walked toward his truck, he thought of how he couldn't wait to get home.

Demi locked the front door then turned and walked into the living room. He stopped at the edge of the sofa and lifted the television remote, but he stared at the screen as the news caught his attention.

"…a month later and no one has any answers as to why the city came to a sudden standstill. Why did businesses shut down and an overwhelming number of workers, city employees included, close up shop, leave work, or call off before their shifts began?" the news anchor reported. "Though many have tried to get to the bottom of it, countless individuals and business owners have refused to be interviewed for this story. One wonders if this was a social media stunt or a call to action from some type of political group, but no one is claiming responsibility."

"We were informed the financial loss has the city comptroller looking into matters, even as things seem to have gone back to business as usual," the co-anchor added. "In other news…"

Demetrius pressed the button on the remote, turning the volume down on the television. He looked down at Cassiel who had his head resting on the arm of the sofa and his feet under Giselle's thighs at the other end. Her head was resting on her arms that were folded on the other arm of the sofa.

Demi smiled.

My son.

He placed the remote on the coffee table in front of him. Demi knew Cassiel was mentally strong and carried a lot of traits that made him a Carrion through and through. The difference was Demi was going to show and give his son the love he was denied by UGod. With his tutelage, Cassiel will inherit an empire and run it like a well-oiled machine.

Before Giselle and Cassiel came into his life, Demi loathed being in between two worlds. He wanted to shed his criminal background and be just a legitimate businessman. Now, he embraced being a hybrid.

"You're back," Giselle said, groggy from sleep.

Demi looked over at her. She stretched her arms out above her head as she sat up. His smile widened. They waited for him to return. Demi had to place his hand over his chest as his heart pulsed. The fullness, the love he felt for them right then almost forced him to his knees.

"Did you take care of what you needed to?" She asked as she untangled herself from Cass and got to her feet. Giselle walked the length of the sofa and stopped in front of him.

Demi looked down. He still wasn't sure if he deserved their love. With each of the lives he took over the years, he made excuses as to why. He'd felt that each was necessary to take to reach his goal. What he didn't understand then was he had nothing to fight for. Nothing. Yet, every sacrifice he made, every life he took, all he worked so damn hard to accomplish, it all secured his spot in Hell for sure. But it also, in a way, prepared him for…them.

It all meant nothing without them.

"I did, Angel." He bent and placed a chaste kiss on her forehead.

Giselle bit her lip and looked down, as if she was nervous and blushing.

Demi watched as a slight shiver worked its way through her. "Go on up," he said. "I'll carry Cass up and put him in bed."

Giselle backed up to give him room as he moved to pick up their son.

"Wake him up. He's too big to carry," she said as she turned and headed for the stairs.

"Woman," Demi said in a playful tone as he lifted Cassiel up off the sofa, "I will carry my boy until I can't."

"It's *your* back," she teased, as she peered at him from over her shoulder.

"That you will be massaging," he said with a grin and a wink.

She gave him that shy grin he loved so much then turned and jogged for the stairs.

No. Demi wasn't sure he deserved their love. He knew he was the Devil—the Devil they made him, and he now fully embraced the role. It made things interesting. Made him stronger, smarter, and more deadly because he now had more to lose and more to protect. He proudly owned the title of DemiGod the Devil. With no regrets.

THE END

Please consider leaving a review!
Read on for excerpts…

ABOUT THE AUTHOR

Shea is a woman in love with the idea of love so it's no wonder she writes Romance Novels. The East Coast native is a romantic to her core and reads and watches anything with a love story. She especially likes binging on Romance TV around Christmas time.

She enjoys meeting people and chatting, collecting Barbie dolls, toys, anime, and is addicted to The Sims games. Shea also loves music and has mentioned that she writes better when she has movie scores playing as white noise in the background.

This new and exciting author writes Adult Romance in the sub-genres of Contemporary, New Adult, Paranormal, Sci-Fi, and Erotica. Come…Taste A Sample.

Head on over to my website www.Sheaswainwrites.com for
Upcoming Releases,
Character Dream-casting

IF YOU LIKED THIS BOOK SIGN UP FOR MY NEWSLETTER
THANK YOU

Heaven on Hell Island

If Bleu St. James relied on her first impression of Chris, she might have let him drown. But there is something about him that inexplicably draws her in. Maybe it was something she saw when she stared at his calm face as the plane they were on fell from the sky. Now stranded on a mysterious deserted island, Bleu must not only contend with the elements, she must depend on a survivalist who also happens to be a hate-filled extremist.

Chris Stokes can't keep his eyes off the well-dressed woman, even though he was taught that her kind is beneath him. Her very presence makes him feel inadequate in every way. Yet, Bleu saved his life and he owed her. That means doing his damnedest to keep her alive. Only, Chris can't deny how alluring Bleu is or how badly he wants her to see *him*, and not the man he no longer wants to be.

This book contains some views and language that may be uncomfortable for some. This story is about change, growth, and is for adults 18 years and older. Readers discretion advise.

Excerpt Below

Chapter 1

Dulles Intl. Airport
International flight 4816
Departure Gate 23

April 8th

Her

BLEU LIFTED HER dark sunglasses above her eyes and glared at the two men who sat in the seats facing hers. A gentleman who looked to be of Middle Eastern descent just hurried away after a brief discussion with them. Now they were discussing the "problems" in the United States, rather loudly. Of course, the problems were due to everything and everyone else.

She didn't spare them much more than a glance and was about to focus on the magazine she just bought from the newsstand when one of them spoke to her.

"What the fuck are you looking at, Dark Meat?" It was the one whose head was completely shaved except for a long flop of blond hair that covered one of his eyes.

Bleu smirked as she raised her perfectly arched brow at him. They stared at each other for several seconds before she got bored, lowered her glasses, then stood.

She heard Flop-Over say something about hoity-toity dark meat to his friend, a guy who clearly loved tattoos. Their laughter followed her as she found another seat closer to the boarding gate.

As she took a seat that faced away from them, she thought, *Now I won't be able to see or hear the conversation of Neanderthals.*

Him

"What the fuck are you looking at, Dark Meat?" Thomas asked the black woman sitting across from them.

Chris watched her with curiosity, wondering what her response would be. Why he gave a fuck, he wasn't sure. Yeah, for a darky, the chick was hot. He'd seen a good number of black women he could admit were good looking but he never felt an inkling of interest in them.

But her…

Her skin was smooth and reminded him of warmed walnuts. Her hair was sleek and black, cut short all around but it was long enough in the front that she had to sweep it to the side. Her clothing, a very white shirt, and khaki long shorts, looked brand new. He was certain her sparkling stud earrings were real diamonds. Even her sunglasses looked like they cost more than his monthly rent. Her scent–*the Gods probably didn't smell half as good*–was intoxicating.

She probably has a "Sugar Daddy".

When she raised her brow at Thomas, briefly allowing Chris to see her dark seductive eyes, then smirked, Chris couldn't help but laugh to himself. Thomas and the chick competed in a stare off for several seconds before she lowered her glasses and stood.

Chris watched her walk…no, stroll away.

Some of them darkies pull you in, Chris. It's how they were made. To tempt the better races.

Chris closed his eyes in an attempt to purge his father's words from his head.

"Hoity dark meat needs to be put in her place," Thomas sneered as she walked away. "Don't know if I want to choke her with my hands or my cock."

"Sara will cut your shit right off," Chris responded. He intentionally sounded bored with the whole situation, as if he had little interest in *Her*.

Thomas laughed.

Chris absently joined in but he continued to watch *her*.

Her

Bleu glared at the *Fasten Seatbelt* sign that flashed above her head as the plane shook violently, jostling the passengers from side to side. Several overhead compartments burst open, spilling luggage onto the passengers. She leaned her head out into the aisle and saw two flight attendants who were strapped into their seats. Bleu wasn't comforted by the looks they gave each other before undoing their seat belts and rushing to assist a couple who were bombarded with the luggage.

The sheer panic expressed on their faces shocked Bleu into a silent prayer. She almost felt guilty for not going to church in over five years but that feeling passed with the next series of brutal shaking and shifting of the airplane.

When the aircraft suddenly dipped, Bleu saw one of the attendants grab a passenger for support. The other attendant flew up, crashed into the ceiling of the plane, then fell to the floor. Until now, the passengers seemed to make an effort to remain calm, just as the attendants requested. But now, screams and gasps filled the cabin. No one was buying that this was just turbulence anymore.

"Carla," the attendant's voice bellowed above the screaming.

But Carla, the other attendant, didn't answer. She looked unconscious.

Bleu closed her eyes. Her fingers ached from the death grip she had on the armrest of her seat. Her rigid posture was the only tell that she was scared to death. Her breathing was steady, and if she had a mirror she would see that her face reflected a calm she didn't feel. She trained her entire life to put her best face forward, to never let anyone know what she felt or thought.

What was she thinking right now?

She was thinking that she and every passenger on this plane was going to die. It was that simple. Bleu had flown a million times before so she knew that this was different. The other passengers knew it too.

Oddly, she had the silliest thought. *You don't know any of these people you're about to die with.*

With her stoic mask on, Bleu couldn't help her perusal of the frightened faces of her fellow passengers. They were all strangers. Bleu shut out the calls for help and the shouts to God as she looked over her shoulder to her left, at the pair from earlier who sat in seats across the aisle, one row behind hers.

Why she looked at the two men, she didn't know. Both had an air of danger about them but with Bleu's sheltered upbringing, even the postman seemed a bit nefarious. She grasped on to the fact that these men weren't *complete* strangers like the others aboard the flight. Maybe that was why she chose to seek them out.

Bleu recalled the brief, albeit annoying encounter she had with them right before boarding the airplane.

Now I'm going to die with these Neanderthals, she thought.

"*Dying is dying,*" Nana's disembodied voice whispered to her. "*It makes no never mind who you travel to the pearly gates with. Just be happy you made it.*"

Nana, Bleu thought with a sigh as the noise around her increased to deafening levels.

The sounds of screams, hushed prayers, and useless instructions filled the airplane cabin. The freak storm came about so suddenly, Bleu figured that there was nothing anyone could do. Their collective prayers were enough to raise the roof but sadly they weren't capable of saving them as lightning struck the back end with an ear-piercing boom.

Bleu covered her ears as she squeezed her eyes shut. The loud explosion overshadowed all other sounds around her. She managed to hold her scream in but her breathing picked up and her heart raced.

LOVE and INFECTION

A Para-Sci Romance

Should half-dead look so good?
When your best friend is infected with some kind of rage
zombie virus, do you…

A. Run for your life?
B. Put a bullet in his brain?
C. Trust that he won't hurt you?

When Jasmyn Saunders sees Akin Pratt moves at a predatory
speed and use his superhuman strength, she knows she
should be afraid of him. But Jasmyn refuses to be scared of
the man she loves, even if he technically isn't a man at all
anymore. Keeping her feelings in check is vital to their
survival in more ways than one. Just a kiss from Akin may
infect her, but it feels like the world is ending, and she wants
to tell him how she really feels—before he is too far gone to
care.

Akin is losing his humanity with each passing minute. One
thing still familiar to him is his desire for Jasmyn, which is as
strong as his newfound abilities. Yet, more than ever he is

determined to keep her at arm's length. The infected are constantly attacking, mercenaries are out to kill them all, and the anger he's kept locked away his entire life is harder to tether. But he refuses to give in completely to the infection raging inside him until Jasmyn is safe even if that means sacrificing himself.

Excerpt Below

LOVE and INFECTION

Akin

Gymnasium
present time

"We need to kill him while he's out of it."

Vance. That sounds like Vance. I should rip his damn head off, Akin thought.

"He told me his parents work at the GenTech. He gets bit then injects something into his arm. I'd rather wait to see if he changes into one of them."

That's…Corey.

"Then let's search him," Vance suggested, "after you shoot him."

"If you want to go inside that cage and search his pockets, help yourself. But I'm not shooting that man until I see that he's a zombie."

Zombie? Cage?

"Wait…are we qualified to really say that's what they are?" another person said, "I mean, we really don't know. Right?"

"I know that I saw a lady's throat ripped out by one of those things. I watched her die. And I watched her jump up, scream, then try to attack the closest person next to her," Corey said. "She totally avoided everyone like her. If that doesn't qualify as a zombie, I don't know what does."

Akin lay still as everything that happened came rushing back to him. Except some things seemed unclear, murky. The clearest thought, the one that kept overshadowing the rest of the things going through his mind was…

Jasmyn is okay. The only thing that matters is Jasmyn.

"It's been two hours. He should have changed by now."

That sounds like Mr. Perry...maybe. Where are the others?

"What are you, a damn expert? We don't know what this is or how it works," Vance yelled.

"Exactly. So, you're not an expert either, Vance."

Jasmyn.

Her voice wrapped around Akin like a warm soft sweater.

The funny thing was, even with his eyes closed, Akin knew she was in the room before she even opened her mouth. Somehow, he also knew she was physically fine, aside from the scent of... The scent of blood was in the room.

Akin opened his eyes. He sat up then got to his feet and glared around the cage he was in. He focused on a lumpy pile of blue gym mats a few feet away. He saw an unmoving arm sticking out from beneath those gym mats. Frowning, he realized he was standing on something cushiony. Looking down, Akin saw that he was standing on top of a red gym mat. Did they lay me here with him? At least he could take comfort in the fact that he wasn't under the mat.

"Fuck!" Vance yelled out.

Akin swung his gaze over to Vance who was squatting beside Corey, a few feet away. Vance stood up straight and raised the bat he held, ready to strike.

Akin blinked, tried to focus, then blinked again. Something is off with my eyes, he thought. He blinked both a few more times then closed and opened one eye at a time. He realized that he couldn't see any colors out of his right eye; everything was all black and white when he closed his left eye.

"Akin!"

Jasmyn.

Akin turned his head in the direction of her voice. He focused on Jasmyn. As he sensed, she seemed mostly unharmed, but her heart was racing. She looked confused, worried.

"Oh God, Akin," Jasmyn said as she covered her mouth. Her eyes started to shimmer with tears as her body shook.

Akin moved to the gate which had a padlock on the other side of it. They locked me in. Why? He looked up, seeing that the equipment cage didn't reach the ceiling. He could climb up and over but it would take time and he wanted out, now. Akin grabbed hold of the locked gate.

"He's…calm, see," Jasmyn said, looking around at the others.

Calm? Not on my best day, Akin thought. He lowered his gaze as he watched Jasmyn move toward the cage door. Toward him.

Vance stepped in front of Jasmyn and pushed her away from the cage. As she fell to the floor, Akin grabbed the frame of the cage door and pushed. He narrowed his eyes, glaring at Vance as he pushed again. Akin felt the gate give a bit.

"Shit," Corey said as he stood.

"Shoot him!" Vance yelled as he backed away from Jasmyn.

"No!" Jasmyn screamed as she scrambled over to the gate on her hands and knees. She stood with her back to Akin and spread her arms opens as she stood in front of the gate, becoming a barrier between him and them.

"You need to get out of the way," Corey ordered.

Akin glanced at Corey who held the gun to his side. Was he going to aim it at Jasmyn's?

"I'm not going to let you kill him," Jasmyn said, glancing over her shoulder at Akin with determination in her voice.

Akin broke the hook on the lock with his third push. He stepped out of the equipment cage and moved up behind Jasmyn. Myn, he thought as he lowered his head, taking in her sweet scent. The need to touch her was so strong that Akin's fingers tingled but he resisted the urge to do so. He sighed as a whiff of her scent hit him. Unable to resist any longer, Akin felt her shiver as his lips lightly brushed over the sensitive skin of her neck and inhaled deeper.

Why did I just smell her?

Though, her scent was like a calming balm washing over him.

Akin realized Jasmyn was stiff as a board and she smelled…scared? He looked up, focusing on the gun that was pointed at them. He wrapped his arm around Jasmyn's waist, turned her around to face him, then lifted her up off her feet, and spun them both so that his body was her shield and his back was to the gun.

"Akin?" Jasmyn said as she looked over his shoulder at the others.

She trembled against him as her palms rested against his chest. He sensed that she was afraid but he wasn't sure if it was for him or because of him. He was about to ask when the air around him…sort of shifted. Akin tilted his head and looked to his left just in time to see Vance swinging the baseball bat at his head.

Akin lifted his chin as he narrowed his eyes and raised his hand. He caught the baseball bat and squeezed the barrel with one hand. The wood splintered under the pressure then cracked.

Vance gaped at the jagged half he still held, then looked at the half Akin held.

Akin raised his hand and stared at the splintered bat for a few seconds, thinking of ramming it through Vance's chest, but he looked back at Jasmyn, who he still held with his other arm. She looked pale and afraid.

Of me.

He immediately released her and backed away as he let his part of the baseball bat fall from his hand to the floor.

"Akin," she pleaded, stepping toward him with imploring wide eyes.

"Don't." Akin held up his hands to stop her from advancing. He couldn't risk her being near him. Not when he was stronger and his thoughts darker than they'd ever been. His voice didn't even sound the same to him. "Don't…come any closer," Akin said as he backed up until he felt the wall behind him. He slid down the wall until he was seated on the hard floor. He needed time to think about what was happening to him.

THEDEVILTHEYMADEME